To Charlie

M000306736

BLACK JACK

By Jean Holloway

Hope you like this more,

J 2010

Published by PHE Ink
P. O. Box 940217
Houston, TX 77094

PHE Ink and the portrayal of the quill feather are
trademarks of PHE Ink.

The cataloging-in-publication data is on file with the Library
of Congress.

Library of Congress Control Number: 2009929625

ISBN: 978-0-9824475-0-5

Printed in the United States of America

June 2009

Genre: Fiction/Thriller

Dedication

I dedicate this book to my husband of thirty-seven years. Frederick, I love you so much it is hard to put into words. I was lost until you came into my life and could have never done any of this without you.

You are always there for me as my strength and my rock. I love you more than I ever thought possible and I am so blessed to have you by my side. You *ARE* my Marcus.

Acknowledgment

Thank You, God for giving me this blessing and allowing me to see this day.

Well, who would have thought that some twenty-seven years later I would write the sequel to *Ace of Hearts?* I hope that Shevaughn and I have both matured!

And thank you, Dana Pittman of Nia Promotions for your friendship, support and encouragement. The cover is better than I imagined. I am eternally grateful to PHE Ink, my new publisher. Ladies, I will be your guinea pig anytime!

Special thanks go to Shonna Peters and Sarah Yarborough for taking the time to read, edit and give me constructive criticism. You helped me make *Black Jack* all I wanted it to be.

I cannot forget my family and new fans. You encouraged me to continue writing. Here it is… hope it is worth the wait.

Prologue

Helene put the menu down, took off her glasses and pinched the top of her nose, massaging the corners of her eyes. Concentrating on the menu's small print made them so tired. She looked up, blinked hard and, in doing so, brought his handsome face back into focus. *Maybe I should have left that second glass of champagne alone.* However, it's not every day a lady got to share a bottle of Krug Grand Cuvée'77 in Napier's, the most exclusive French restaurant in the Portsborough area.

Tonight's definitely a cause for celebration. She still couldn't believe she'd been dating this young man for the past three months. *Young man, humph, never thought I'd be referring to a man in his fifties as young, although it's all quite relative, isn't it?* Although proud of her sixty-eight years on earth, right now she wished she could turn back the hands of time.

The last few months were like a romantic dream.

What about the money?

The thought flickered like the restaurant sconces' candlelight against the wall. Damn, why did her mind always go back to that? It spoiled one of life's best moments by nagging at her.

About a month ago, he'd asked her for a considerable loan, one hundred and ten thousand dollars to be exact. Although it took over half of the remainder of her fortune and her mind told her it really wasn't the smart thing to do, her body quickly overruled the objection. She knew, in time, it would be well worth it. Besides, he looked so distraught while he explained his temporary dire financial predicament and petulantly requested her help, how could she have said no while looking at that persuasive face? It would only be for a short time and he promised to repay her, with interest, as soon as his stocks rose as predicted. She would have it back before Thanksgiving, the beginning of December at the latest. What the hell, she'd never gambled before and gambling for love made it worth the risk.

When Helene's husband, Frank Elliott, died almost four years ago, he left her a surprise in the form of an insurance policy that netted her a comfortable three hundred and seventy thousand dollars. After she sold their little Mom and Pop store and paid off their mortgage, she no longer needed to worry about money. Bored, she began filling her time by going to auction houses. She never bid on anything, although it meant less time spent in her empty home. Besides, one day she would come across that ultimate treasure.

Then, in late May, on an ordinary day, at yet another ordinary auction, she spotted him. He walked right down her aisle. As he approached, she quickly grabbed her jacket and purse from the padded, folding chair next to her and nodded for him to sit.

My God, he's beautiful, in a sexy, animal kind of way. Her first thought surprised her as he sat down and proceeded to introduce himself. His name matched his persona. With skin the color of onyx, the contrast between it, his full head of stark-white wavy hair and dazzling turquoise eyes made her heart jump. Tall and muscular, he gave jogging all the credit for his physique. She remembered thinking, thank God for jogging. He appeared almost too pretty with a magnetism she couldn't deny. He took her breath away, literally.

At the end of the auction, he politely invited her to lunch and she jumped at the opportunity to spend more time in his presence. The meal ended with her giving him her number, something she'd never done since she'd spoken her marriage vows, some forty-eight years ago. When he sent her flowers the next week, then later called and invited her to dinner, she gave a prayer of thanks and quickly accepted.

And now, here we are. She realized she'd been silent for a while, picked up the menu to hide her embarrassment and peeked over it to see if he'd noticed. He seemed engrossed in the menu. She placed hers back on the cream linen tablecloth and watched him do the same. He removed a clove cigarette from its thin, silver case. She watched him lean back, close his eyes and take his first drag. Although she hadn't smoked in a year, she could feel his enjoyment. She saw how he turned his head, just slightly and carefully blew the smoke away from her. Helene smiled because even though she disapproved of his smoking, his actions were always so thoughtful.

"Have you decided, ma petite chérie?"

She loved when he called her that.

"I'm leaning toward the Poulet au Jambon, although the Filet De Porc Rôti sounds delicious." *Besides, at my age, a little prune sauce couldn't hurt.* Sometimes, I crack myself up. She noticed she did that a lot since becoming a widow. She hoped he could tell she'd been practicing her French.

"Ah, your French is très bon. The improvement is quite impressive. Reward yourself, splurge, order whatever your heart desires."

She pictured the two of them in bed, taking care of all sorts of desires. Suddenly, she lost her appetite and dinner didn't seem so important, yet she didn't protest when he refilled her champagne flute. Slight intoxication would come in handy for her late night plans.

"I've been thinking about you...us, more than you'd imagine," he confessed as he placed the bottle back into the silver ice bucket.

Her heart raced.

"You know, at our age, it isn't wise to waste time. Don't you agree?"

Don't I agree? God, yes... Yes... YES! Sweep the dishes to the floor and take me on the table, right here, right now in front of everyone, please, oh, PLEASE. She could blame her imagination for sending her straight to hell. Silently, she vowed to give up secretly watching her late husband's small collection of porn tapes. She hoped that after tonight she wouldn't need them. It had been her only form of release for quite some time.

"Were you thinking we should take this to the next level?"

She couldn't believe she'd voiced her wish aloud. Guess there are advantages to being a senior citizen.

"Well, for now, let's enjoy our meal and each others' company. Later, we'll see what develops, so to speak."

His smooth bass voice and perfect smile melted more than her heart. In fact, for the first time in years, she felt that all too familiar moisture.

She barely remembered the meal. He kept the innuendo-filled conversation and the champagne flowing, teasing her with hints of things to come. The intense, verbal foreplay definitely aroused her.

Finally, dinner ended. The epitome of a gentleman, he retrieved her wrap from the coatroom and helped her put it on. Leaving Napier's, he gave the valet his parking ticket and held her hand as they waited for him to bring the car around. When the attendant pulled up in his black 1981 Corvette coupe, he let the valet open her door, then took over and shut it. As she sank into the red leather interior, she realized her dizziness didn't come from the champagne, it came from what she knew would happen next. *Oh, God, I'm so ready.*

She watched him concentrate on the road and when he let go of the stick shift to reach for her hand, she squeezed back, hoping he'd know her answering pressure meant yes to anything he wanted. He brought her hand to his lips and the sensation of them touching her skin produced a mini-orgasm. Helene wondered how she would keep herself together until they got to her place. When he let go to shift gears, she folded her hands in her lap, closed her eyes and feigned sleep.

She dozed off and next thing she knew, they were pulling up in front of her home.

"Would you mind if I parked in your garage?"

You can park in my garage anytime.

Everything he said translated to sex. She watched him as he turned off the car, got out and came around to the passenger side.

He helped her out of the low car and she gave him her keys. Opening the door, he politely stood back and let her enter first.

Turning on the light, she walked down the peach colored hall into her foyer, past the family pictures of her daughter, Phaedra, grandson, Tyler and Frank. *Oh, Frank.* She still missed him so.

Helene checked the thermostat on her way to the hall closet. Although she felt warm, the temperature registered at a comfortable seventy degrees. She carefully hung up her silk shawl, right next to the Christian Dior calf-length sable and took a moment to stroke the soft fur. The coat represented her only splurge from the insurance money. Frank had frequently told her he wished he could cover her with diamonds and sable. She finally made part of his wish come true. She forced herself to stop thinking of her late husband. Too bad this late autumn night made it too warm for sable. She would have loved to go back in the living room with nothing on except the coat. The diamonds reference made her think of the sexy man waiting for her. After all, they were the hardest mineral on Earth, hard being the operative word. Her body told her to stop reminiscing and get down to the business of making love. She hurried back to him.

"I'll be right back," she said, touching his lips with her index finger. "If you want, you can make us a drink while you wait."

"Don't make me wait too long."

She didn't need any encouragement, even though his impatience made it all the more appealing.

Once she entered her cottage blue bedroom, Helene went to her closet and took out the brand new sheer black lace peignoir that she'd purchased last month in anticipation of this very night. She laid the gown out on her oak mission-style bed that she'd made up so carefully this morning. She'd chosen rose-colored satin sheets, wanting everything to be perfect. After all, she'd been waiting three long years for this night. Helen lit the candles in the non-working fireplace, went to her bathroom, took a quick shower and put on the gown. Standing in front of the vanity mirror, she ran the brush through her hair a few times and stood back to check out her appearance. *Not bad for a little old lady.* She applied mascara, a tiny bit of rouge and lipstick. Satisfied with her reflection, Helene dabbed a bit of her Nina Ricci L'Air Du Temps behind each ear. The perfume was a twenty-fifth wedding anniversary gift from Frank. Nothing could stop her, not even the small twinge of guilt she brushed aside. Helene hurried back to the living room. The thought of him waiting for her made her heart flutter. She'd forgotten that feeling a long time ago.

He'd made himself at home. Walking across the living room filled with clean-lined, modern Scandinavian furniture, she came around the navy blue pinstriped Bellini couch and stopped in front of him. When he stood up, she discovered he had undressed down to his briefs.

She could see his obvious desire. He'd even turned on her radio. She heard the Eurythmics "Sweet Dreams" softly playing in the background. She noticed how neatly he'd folded his clothes and placed them on the coffee table. Always the gentleman...

Spellbound, she rushed to him, acting more brazen than she ever remembered. He stopped her, held her at arm's length and slowly looked her up and down. The lust in his beautiful eyes washed over her and matched the heat she felt emanating through her lower body. She moved towards him and he enveloped her, kissing her softly on her forehead and eyes, then traveling down, lightly kissing her nose and then her lips. She felt his hardness prodding at the center of her lust, closed her eyes and kissed him back with all the experience she'd acquired during her long marriage. The next thing she knew, he scooped her up and carried her into the bedroom.

He gently laid her down on the slippery sheets and began a trail of kisses that traveled down the front of her body to the spot. *Oh, yes, that's it.* She felt him taste her with quick flicks of his tongue. The jolt of electricity that shot up her spine surprised her. It felt so good she should have been afraid for her heart, however right now, not even the possibility of a heart attack scared her. *I could die right now.* For the first time, she realized how much she missed having a man in her bed.

"I'll be right back."

"Why, where are you going?"

"Safe sex, ma petite femme impatiente. It'll only take a minute."

She watched him walk to her bathroom as she caught her breath. *It's not like I can get pregnant.* That showed the thoughtful side of him again, especially since rumors were spreading about some new sexually transmitted disease responsible for making Rock Hudson sick. Knowing he thought enough to put on a condom for her peace of mind made her even more grateful they'd found each other. He came out of the bathroom, nude, and she caught a glimpse of his dark, magnificent instrument before he turned off the light. Her body quivered.

He came to bed, brought his lips to hers and kissed her, deeply, then lifted her head by putting his hands under the pillow and began kissing her neck, her breasts and her navel. As his kisses traveled down her body, he took up right where he left off by going deep inside her with his tongue. Before she could recover, he grabbed her ankles and his hands traveled down to her calves, raising her legs until he placed himself firmly inside her. Her muscles contracted, holding him and they both stopped to enjoy the sensation. He slowly withdrew, teasing at first, and then pushed forward, firmly. He began a rhythm that she blissfully followed. *This is so good, dear God, so good.* She eagerly answered his every stroke.

He stopped and gently turned her on her stomach, straddled her and began to massage the small of her back. She could feel his tip lightly brush her buttocks as he put pressure on her spine. She didn't know how long she could handle feeling this good, she just knew she wanted everything he could give her.

He grabbed both her wrists with one hand and entered her from behind. She closed her eyes, feeling every glorious sensation. Engulfed in the moment, she didn't notice him reach under the pillow. He bit her earlobe as he placed the chloroform-laced hankie over her nose and mouth.

Helene found herself smothering in a sickly, sweet scent she didn't recognize and violently shook her head to avoid it. He seemed to anticipate her every move, never letting up.

"Shhh, ma petite chérie, shhh, just let it happen. Let go. Enjoy the ride."

His term of endearment didn't thrill her like it usually did. A wave of dizziness and nausea struck her. Her heartbeat accelerated and became irregular.

Suddenly, she found herself drifting. A strange calm came over her even as she realized, this is bad.

He lunged forward, jabbed the syringe in her underarm and quickly pressed down the plunger. Holding her down by her shoulders, he began to take her, roughly. Her body trembled and began to convulse.

When he felt the growing tremor of her first seizure, he rode it like a wave. He began to pound her body with his and it seemed as if she matched his moves with reckless abandon. When she suddenly stopped, his motions increased. He reveled in the feeling, losing himself in the roar that erupted within his body. For a while, he became lost in the heart-wrenching, pumping sensation of his orgasm. When he finally withdrew, she had slipped into a coma.

He flicked the light switch on with his elbow, found the hypodermic needle amongst the sheets, after wetting one of her washcloths, thoroughly wiped it down, and dropped the syringe into the bathroom wastebasket. Not really concerned about his fingerprints, he knew years of playing his vintage Manzanero guitar built up calluses that distorted them. He also knew you could never be too careful. The syringe wouldn't arouse suspicion since she'd been an insulin dependent diabetic for years. He'd thoroughly researched every aspect of her life.

While in the bathroom, he carefully removed the condom so as not to spill any of its contents and flushed it along with the tissue. As he watched them disappear, he reflected, rather pleased with himself. He'd left nothing to chance. He flushed again. *Better safe than sorry, I always say.*

Everything went according to plan. She'd been so caught up in the moment she hadn't noticed him slipping the hankie and small syringe under the pillow when he'd lifted her face to his for that final kiss.

This became his ultimate gift to her. He'd blessed her with the gift of exquisite pleasure and the ecstasy of feeling so alive just before he took it all away. Not one of his chosen ever complained. *I never give them time to do so.*

He grabbed a washcloth from the towel bar over the sink and ran a tub of cold water, adding a large amount of jasmine scented bubble bath he'd found on her green marble counter.

He returned and stood over the bed, watching the imperceptible breathing motion of her sunken white chest. That she actually thought he found her attractive would have almost been funny, if it weren't so pitiful, almost as pitiful as her attempts at French. From her blonde-dyed, straw-like hair to her cellulite-puckered body, she resembled a caricature of the woman she used to be, a very unappetizing caricature. Well, at least he'd brought some excitement to the last moments of her dreary life. Good thing money was his aphrodisiac. Enough of this maligning, he cautioned himself. He could afford to be gracious, especially after her contribution to his cause.

He lifted her from the bed like a sacrificial lamb and carried her to the bathroom. Slowly laying her in the tub full of sweet smelling bubbles, he washed her as gently as a mother washes her infant.

Satisfied that he'd removed all evidence, he stood in the tub, positioned his feet between her legs. The cold water jarred his senses and he never felt so alive. He took a quick lukewarm shower and washed her scent from his body. Toweling off, he went to the living room, dressed and got the straight razor from his inside jacket pocket. Before returning to the bathroom, he turned the air conditioning on high. Then he went back to Helene, flicked open the straight razor and, with loving care, slit both her wrists.

Portsborough, NY, 1985

Chapter One

DETECTIVE SHEVAUGHN ROBINSON ended her stellar day with a sigh of satisfaction. She'd just wrapped up the Roland Johnson domestic homicide case. At first, the coroner diagnosed the woman's death as cardiac arrhythmia. The police were suspicious, continued the investigation and requested Dr. Spencer test for toxins. The results led to the arrest of the so-called "bereaved" widower. Turns out, he'd poisoned his wife with tainted wine, thinking it would give him full custody of their two kids, their joint bank account and the freedom to be with his mistress of eight months. It almost worked, except they'd been sloppy and left a string of evidence that led the police directly to them. The mistress, a smart licensed practical nurse, cracked under Detective Robinson's relentless questioning. In less than an hour, not only did she confess to her involvement in the crime, her testimony gave them enough to arrest the husband when she revealed they'd planned the murder together. She admitted to personally cultivating the monkshood in her basement and extracting the aconitine for his use.

Captain Frederick Campbell, "pronounced CAMP – Bell and don't you forget it," called her into his office to commend her performance in front of several reporters.

Campbell became Shevaughn's boss when Captain Bowen accepted the position of Chief of Police. An ambitious man, he focused on overcoming the bad rap that hung over the prior administration like a gray cloud. The public's memory was amazing when it came to the dishonesty of their police force. He wanted to give them only positive things to talk about during his reign.

His office emulated a masculine sanctuary. All the chairs were made of thickly padded burnished leather and his treasured gold vintage Eames Park Sherman desk accessories, a gift from the Mayor, were displayed proudly all over his desk. A cigarette burned in his large orange and brown ceramic ashtray. You could see Captain Campbell found himself stuck in a couple of eras.

You could hear the pride in his voice as he stood beside her and told the press how Detective Robinson, with her extensive experience, got the witness to confess during the intensive interrogation. She'd come a long way since the public doubted her effectiveness. Right now, she claimed the temporary title of top cop. Shevaughn knew the press would turn on her like a pack of rabid wolves, if any doubt about her performance crept back in.

After the announcement, she went back to her desk and made a quick phone call before she packed it in and headed home. She made note to pick up some juice and milk on her way.

It turned out that when Tony O'Brien's psychic friend, Ariel Knight, predicted it wasn't over, she'd been so right. Thinking back, Shevaughn remembered the moment she realized she might be pregnant. After her fourth morning in a row started with a terrible nausea like she'd never experienced before, she knew. It didn't take a detective to figure it out her future would now include a baby. She'd fallen to her knees and prayed and cried and decided their baby's future, right there on the spot, with no hesitation. Abortion would never be an option. She almost felt her love for Tony physically transfer to their unborn child. She'd been unable to save him, however she would save their baby.

"Our baby," she'd said aloud, touching her stomach in wonder. Her mind flooded with unwanted questions as she wiped the tears from her eyes.

What's everyone at the precinct gonna say? How am I going to provide all the time and money it takes to properly care for a child? What will I say to my child when he or she asks about Tony? She'd never thought she'd be a single parent, but life had a way of hitting you with the unexpected. Determined to stick to her decision, she said a short prayer.

"Thank you, heavenly Father. You have blessed me with this baby. I know You will stay with me during this time as always and help me through this unexpected blessing because in my heart I know I'm making the right choice. Thy will be done. Amen."

So, as it turned out, Tony gave her more after death than he'd given her in their short time together. She remembered him telling her she would no longer face life alone. He kept his promise.

A week later, the doctor confirmed her suspicions and gave her the due date. It convinced her they'd conceived their child on that beautiful day so long ago, under a Maui waterfall.

With no one to confide in, she'd called Tony's mother and explained her situation. At first, Lorraine O'Brien sounded sad and Shevaughn knew she wished her son could have shared this moment and then she quickly warmed up to the idea of her first grandchild. They'd spent hours on the phone, planning and dreaming. She offered Shevaughn her home, thus eliminating the future problem of day care. Later that same night, Ariel called Shevaughn out of the blue. During the conversation, she slipped and said something vague about "she" and Shevaughn knew she was referring to the future, to their child. That's when she knew it would be a girl.

Shevaughn moved in with Mother O'Brien two months before her due date. During the move while digging in the attic, she'd come across her Black Raggedy Ann rag doll. She hadn't seen it in years and had forgotten all about her favorite childhood doll. After getting it professionally cleaned, she placed it in one corner of the crib. The following week after she saw the doll sitting in the crib, Mother O'Brien placed a Sebino Cincina doll in the opposite corner. They completed the nursery with dolls of various ethnicities. Shevaughn even managed to get one of the first Black Barbies and she put it away, keeping it for when their child got older. She wanted to introduce diversity to her daughter from day one. It would prepare her for reality.

The day of Toni Shevaughn O'Brien birth, Ariel Knight and Mother O'Brien were at her side. Shevaughn watched the older women come alive again through her daughter. The three of them shared a maternal joy. That night, Mother O'Brien presented Shevaughn with a scrapbook that contained every article written during Tony's short career. It went as far back as his junior high school days and took her through college and then up to and including the articles he'd written about her last year. She felt so close to him while she read his words, his thoughts. It was as if he were in the hospital room, by her side.

As she read the last articles, she saw herself through his eyes. She felt his pride and remembered his love. At the end, while closing the album, she cried for him for the last time. She vowed her daughter would know how special her father was and how much he'd meant to her.

Later that night, the nurse brought Toni in for a feeding. Her daughter's tiny hand grabbed her finger and her heart. Shevaughn felt overwhelmed with a love unlike anything she'd ever experienced. It seemed like ages since she thought she could be happy again. Now, this perfect tiny human being proved her wrong.

Chapter Two

HIS MORNING STARTED out with a brisk jog around the park. When he worked up an appetite, he'd returned home to his gourmet kitchen and concocted his remedy for overindulgence. Mixing sparkling water with Framboise, he sipped the potion while he whipped up his great tofu scramble; a combination of tofu, shiitake mushrooms, yams, chard, ginger, sesame seeds, caramelized onions, roasted red bell peppers and tamari. He enjoyed his meal, eating slowly while glancing through the newspaper.

Satisfied that his world held more excitement, he folded the paper neatly, placed it on the dining table and went to his bedroom to dress. He'd made it his haven. With his impeccable taste, he'd personally decorate every inch from the gold-beige walls to the antique gold Persian Tabriz Mahi rug under the bed. He loved the fireplace on the wall opposite the foot of his massive mahogany Charles P. Rogers king-sized sleigh bed. He'd filled the room with antiques that he acquired "for a steal" and then tastefully added a solid gold satin bedspread with gold and cranberry chevron-striped pillows to match the striped drapes on the bay windows of his sitting alcove.

His next acquisitions were a pair of sage and gold easy chairs. He positioned them under the window with a small mahogany Norfolk, Virginia writing table, circa 1785-95, in between. It looked rich.

Toweling off after his shower, he started his new Grecian Formula daily regimen to darken his hair and walked nude to his large closet to pick out his clothes. Today the hunt began.

Dressing casually in his black Banana Republic Australian jeans, turquoise Le Tigre shirt and black leather jacket, he topped it off with a gray tweed Trilby hat. He knew gray, especially tweed, highlighted his unusual coloring, so he coordinated everything, down to his gray Hush Puppies. Then he put in his brown contact lenses. The last part of his ritual included a modest dab of his signature cologne, Aramis, on his neck and face. He barely glanced in the mirror. He knew he appeared to be his usual cool, distinguished self.

As a young man, he saw and recognized the salient effect he had on women, all women, no matter what age or race. How just seeing him or hearing his voice made their knees weak, made them wet. They couldn't help it. And he saw nothing wrong with using that power and then eliminating the problem after he'd financially sucked them dry. He thought the world owed him the best things in life and would get them by any means necessary.

He'd studied women all of his life, as if working on his Masters. His above average I.Q. allowed him to absorb facts and then later use them to his advantage. He knew women found his intelligence sexy. He always paid close attention and they loved that he listened so well, not knowing it was more research than interest. A loner, he wanted everyone to see him as he saw himself, the knight in shining armor, the lead in one of those romance novels women were so fond of. He related to the one character whose paragraphs were reread several times simply because it turned them on. He knew...

Born in Haiti, late in his mother's life, he'd never seen his father. His mother told him about her secret affair with the son of a very wealthy man. It made him the grandson of an Italian sugar plantation owner who once lived in a mansion on the other side of the island. Strangely, his skin color hid the fact of his mixed blood. His eyes were the only hint. The youngest of five and the only male, his mother and sisters doted on him from his first breath. They indulged his every whim, denying him nothing. Sometimes, he didn't even have to ask. They were always thinking of ways to make him happy.

When he turned sixteen, they even looked the other way as the neighbor's pets began to turn up missing and his sister's defended him when his mother found a bloody dog collar between his mattress and box spring. She'd quietly paid off the neighbors and sent him to New York to live with Uncle Lucien, a good friend of the family who'd done quite well in life. Everyone knew his "uncle" in their section of Little Haiti because he owned and operated the popular Kompa Club, where fellow Haitians drank Hard Eights and played Casino, a gambling card game. He also owned the adjacent taxi stand, thus making money twice from the same patrons. There were once rumors that he belonged to the Haitian Mafia, although they could never be proven.

They never questioned what happened when Lucien died a little more than six months after Jacques' eighteenth birthday, leaving all his assets to his "nephew". When he suddenly changed his name, they all agreed with his great choice. This new one fit him to a tee. Whatever he wanted, they agreed. That's how much they adored him. They'd just commented on his good fortune and advised him to use his windfall wisely. He hadn't. That's why he needed to get busy again.

He left for his day at the library. Today is research day. When he got there, he went directly to the microfiche machine and began looking through the newspaper obituaries for married men who died between 1980 and 1983. Their widows would be due for a little romance by now. He stayed there for hours, searching for her. His meticulous search netted seven names that merited further investigation. If some husband died and it made the first five pages of the paper, well, that meant a definite bonus because the dead man was powerful and with power came money. Their widows made excellent prospects for his future plans. Further investigation knocked five of the women off his list. He eliminated all the social butterflies, their disappearance wouldn't go unnoticed. The first four were surrounded by way too much family and another one died last year. Now, he whittled it down to two.

He seemed to be always looking for his one big score, the one where he could retire from his life of crime and settle down. He greedily anticipated what he knew would be his biggest challenge. Helene represented a minor tidbit, a temporary fix for his extravagant tastes. He hoped it would be enough to tide him over. *Wouldn't do to have to stick to a budget.* He lived by indulgence and intended to keep up his familiar and hedonistic lifestyle. Then he saw it...the headline and the article that explained how her husband died.

He felt a connection.

Engrossed, he read all he could find about the "Ace of Hearts" case. Fascinating…

This man, Eric Becker, appeared to be a kindred spirit, even though he lacked a sense of style. While reading, Becker struck him as lazy predator. Most of his victims seemed like they were chosen only by convenience since they were his co-workers, nevertheless he admired the man's appetite. He didn't seem to have any method to his madness and that's what made him extremely unimaginative, in his opinion.

Ego turned out to be his downfall, naming himself, flaunting his passion in everyone's face. Stupid fool, he should have tried to remain nameless. When he reached the end of the story, he found a surprising bonus, a childless, young widow. He forgot all about the second woman and Ace's widow became his priority. This definitely merits some looking into.

Further investigation rewarded him with a picture taken of Terri being admitted to The Blackstone House. She looked no older than thirty-five, maybe a well-preserved forty at most. *Tasty morsel compared to what I've dealt with lately.* Lately hell, fifteen years had passed since he'd slept with a woman younger than himself. Admittedly, she looked quite haggard in the black and white photo. It showed a pale woman with black stringy hair and no makeup. He could tell that with a little work, she'd be a knockout! He especially liked the fact that she didn't look like one of those hungry models. No one wants a bone, but a dog, he'd heard his uncle say many times. And he buries it.

Yes, it had been a long time since he'd made love to a woman under sixty. He closed his eyes, gave into the impulse and licked his lips at the prospect.

Next, he went to the phone books along the far wall to see if he could find a current address. Before concentrating on his objective, he tried to check out the second widow whose two sons lived in another state, according to the obit, and found out her number wasn't listed. Guess it's just you and me, babe, he thought and began to search for the one he wanted all along. After systematically going through all the boroughs, he got to the Suffolk County directory and yep, there she was, like she'd been waiting for him. He jotted down her address, impressed to see that it was in a very expensive part of town. This might be the one I've been waiting for. The thought made him feel great.

He returned to the research section of the library and began to hunt down every fact he could find about her. He found out she loved animals, since she owned several dogs and cats and was on the Board of a well-known charitable animal rights organization which was having its annual gala in a couple of months. Timing is everything. Maybe he should get a cat or older dog. He didn't have the patience for a puppy, even though he knew if he did, it would make it a done deal. Women always went for a good-looking man with a puppy.

He wondered if she already had a date for that evening. *Probably, with a body like that.* Either way he'd bet his last dollar, no matter what, in the end it would be him. The thought of future sex with this woman boosted him into high gear, giving him even more incentive. For the first time in ages, he found himself lusting after the prospect of bedding a woman. That fact alone made her intriguing. He swore to himself that she'd never know how much the thought of her thrilled him.

He glanced at his watch, surprised to see the morning had flown by. Pleased with his work, he decided to treat himself to a nice light lunch. He always worked better slightly hungry. It gave him an edge.

He drove to Kanchana, his favorite Thai restaurant and the hostess seated him at his customary table, in view of the doorway and near a window. He stayed on guard and hated surprises.

He ordered Yum Yai, a combination of calamari, crabsticks, scallops and shrimp, tossed with cucumber, onion and tomato and sprinkled with a blazing hot chili peanut sauce. He never bothered with the limejuice on the lettuce leaf crap the restaurant always served with it. He ate his lunch and enjoyed every burning second of it. It seemed like a metaphor for his attitude toward life, spicy and satisfying. Every third bite, he would stop and savor a sip of his 1969 Hugel Gewurztraminer. The manager stocked it for him alone because no one else requested it or could afford it, for that matter. Swirling the golden liquid in the oversized wine glass, he took one deep whiff of the fruity and light fragrant bouquet, recognizing the aromatic combination of acacia, frangipani, freesia, hawthorn, mullein and rose and relished the moment. Sipping, he swished it around in his mouth. It tasted refreshingly clean and dry on his palate. He took in a little air and let it trickle down his throat. *Magnificent.*

After he finished eating, he leaned back and enjoyed an Indonesian Djarum Black clove cigarette. Content from catering to his every whim, the only flaw in this idyllic moment were his thoughts of her. They seemed to hinder his feeling of complete satisfaction.

"Give my compliments to the chef," he commented, while paying his bill. Taking his change, he smiled and tipped his hat at the hostess. It was his best imitation of friendly.

He left the restaurant and decided to check out his future neighborhood, so to speak. He would enjoy the drive to Southampton on such a beautiful day.

When he got close to her home, he saw opulence reflected in the nicely manicured front yards, the docks in the back, clean driveways and well-maintained homes. As he drove pass her two-story white Colonial with the wrap-around porch, he saw the sleek 1987 Abbot 22 out back and actually salivated for the second time that day. He fancied himself quite the sailor. The sailboat looked neglected. Probably not since they'd killed off her old man, he guessed. *Damn, this is my kind of neighborhood.* He estimated the net worth at over half a million dollars. *All that money.* One day soon, he hoped to have his hands on her liquid assets, amongst other things. He just had to be the perfect gentleman and he had that down to a tee.

He saw a sign indicating he was close to a golf course and decided to swing by to take a look, although he knew this would probably never become part of his reality – a black man on a golf course? Yeah, right. If he'd investigated further into Southampton's history he would have been surprised to find that a Black man by the name of John Shippen, Jr., not only played golf there, he actually entered the second U.S. Open with an American Shinnecock Indian partner in 1896, taking fifth place and winning ten dollars. It wasn't until 1948 that another

Black man, Ted Rhodes walked in his footsteps. These facts didn't merit investigation since they weren't associated with her.

Hell, it was 1985; maybe he could make a change. His common sense told him he shouldn't draw attention to himself. A Black man in Southampton was probably suspicious enough.

The next day he began his in-depth study of the woman and the area she lived in. He drove back to the library, his mind full of ideas. He mentally started his to do list. First, he checked Southampton's real estate listings. The property value seemed to be better than he imagined. He found a comparable home that went for over three quarters of a million dollars. That definitely made it worth his while.

He double-checked her marital status by painstakingly flicking through all the engagement and wedding announcements stored on microfiche for the past three years. Her widowed name appeared in the phone book listing. He noticed it wasn't this year's edition, so he decided to be extra cautious. *No sense getting my hopes up if she's remarried.* Even though she wouldn't be the first woman who'd left her husband for him, he knew her being single made life easier.

Satisfied that he'd found no mention of a current man in her life after a couple of hours searching, he read on. When he discovered she'd been institutionalized until last year, he reveled in the knowledge of how easy this might turn out to be. His instincts told him he could do this, he could get this. *Ripe for the picking.* He planned his next move.

The time had come to find the perfect dog. On his drive to the North Shore Animal League, he thought about life's inequities and this made him even more determined. Finding her became an omen that destiny owed him more in life. And he wanted to collect.

When he got to the shelter, he felt slightly overwhelmed with the sight of all the helpless animals waiting for rescue. They reminded him of his benefactors.

Then, at the end of the very first row of kennels, he saw him. A young, blonde, black-tipped Afghan stood quietly and looked him straight in the eye. He advanced toward the cage in awe and returned the stare. It seemed like looking into a reflection of his soul. This dog appeared to be a prince among orphans. Hit with an impulse to own him, he immediately named him Khan.

When he inquired about the dog, they told him he'd been donated by a breeder because of a small black spot above his nose. Poor Khan would never make it in the show dog world due to that imperfection, although his loss could also be his gain. He eagerly filled out all the required forms and paid the relatively small fee and the dog belonged to him. He couldn't believe how excited he felt bringing Khan to his new home.

He worried about how the large puppy would respond to the long ride back to Portsborough. He watched the dog enjoy the ride with a dignified air, occasionally sticking his head out of the slightly rolled-down window to catch the breeze. This is a match made in heaven.

After stopping at a pet store and picking up a leash, a chewy toy, some dog food and treats and a couple of bowls, he headed for home. When they got to his building, Khan led him through the tastefully decorated lobby, past the comfortable cranberry divan and pair of argyle patterned armchairs that flanked the oak wall encasing the fireplace. He went right to the elevator, like he'd done it a hundred times before. He even sat and waited for the doors to open without being told.

He spent the rest of the day learning about his new companion. They both enjoyed the cool breeze that wafted through the living room window and Khan even paid attention to "Night Court", his favorite TV show. Before going to bed, he took his new sidekick for a long walk and Khan took care of business within the first fifteen minutes. When they got back, he placed a blanket on the floor at his bedside, watched Khan rearrange it and after walking around in a circular pattern several times, the dog laid down and went to sleep to the sound of his classical guitar. You would have sworn they'd been separated at birth.

Chapter Three

PHAEDRA DAVIS HUNG up the phone, unaware that the heavy, sinking feeling in her stomach matched the troubled look on her face. She hadn't heard from her Mom in over three days! It was unusual since they always communicated with a short phone call between them on an almost daily basis. They gossiped about the Brooks and Foster families on "The Young and Restless", their favorite soap, like they knew them personally. Then her Mom would talk about her new beau.

Phaedra knew her mother hadn't been this happy in years, not since Dad died. You could hear the joy in her voice, especially when she spoke of him, an excitement that until now Phaedra refused to recognize because it meant her mom had a new love.

"I can't wait 'til you two meet."

She not only remembered her saying it, she could actually hear her mother's voice.

They'd been planning a Labor Day weekend visit. They hadn't seen each other for a couple of months. Time had a way of getting away from you while you dealt with everyday life. The last time they'd spoken her Mom confessed that she missed her, although she made it quite clear she missed seeing her grandson most of all. Phaedra promised they'd both be there soon and they hung up with a mutual "Love you."

She snapped back to the present, stopped, concentrated and realized no matter how hard she tried, she couldn't remember the man's full name. Her mother referred to him only as "J." or "Jay". She couldn't be sure which. In fact, come to think of it, she really didn't know much about this guy. Phaedra dialed her Uncle Allen and although she didn't want to alarm him, she told him she hadn't spoken to her for days and asked him to stop by Mom's house and check up on her.

Terri Becker sat in the psychiatrist's waiting room. She looked at her watch, annoyed. Her weekly session should have begun already. *He's got a lot of nerve keeping me waiting.* She'd wasted enough time here already.

She thought about all the months she'd spent in that damn institution. She didn't remember much of the first year, other than the horrible experience of drug withdrawal. There'd been times when she'd been so sick, when she'd been in so much pain, she didn't think she would live through it. Afterward, when all the drugs and alcohol were out of her system, she'd been exhausted, almost catatonic. After she finally rejoined the living, the doctors diagnosed her, saying she suffered from neurotic depression. They attempted to treat it with tricylic antidepressants and the very unpopular electroconvulsive therapy. Now, almost four years later, she only went to bi-weekly outpatient visits. She'd taken everything they'd thrown at her and fooled each and every one of them.

Terri never let on that her perception of life was now permanently altered. She took pride in the fact that she'd made it out of there without any of them ever being suspicious.

Should have brought my blanket with me, at least it would have kept me occupied. She leafed through an old, well-read magazine, flipping pages, seeing nothing.

Dr. Callaghan hated being late. He checked his gold pocket watch and quickly concluded his conversation, hung up the phone and rushed out of his office to begin their session.

He came across as a fastidious man. At six feet even, he kept his posture as straight as possible to make himself look taller. He wore an extremely expensive burgundy three-piece tailor made suit with a beige Armani shirt. Since his wife left him seven years ago, he didn't have anyone to spend his money on. To celebrate her running off with that pretty-boy pilot, he'd bought a top of the line toupee and he'd been spoiling himself ever since.

There's something about him that reminds me of Eric. Not physically, Lord no, Eric had been far more attractive. Except for the toupee, Dr. Callaghan resembled Santa Claus, although his jolly exterior didn't fool her. Truth be told, she knew that his self-indulgence could be the only thing they had in common. He did things only to make himself feel and look better, just like Eric.

While he escorted her into his office, she once again remembered the starkness of the hospital wards in contrast to his luxurious surroundings. Terri saw where all the money went and that added to her distrust.

"So, Terri..."

"It's Mrs. Becker to you. How many times must I remind you?"

"My apologies, Mrs. Becker."

Her arrogance always amazed him. He couldn't understand why any woman would still want to remind people of that psychopath. He assumed she would have reverted back to her maiden name as soon as she could.

"So have you been keeping the journal as I asked?"

"Not really. I've been busy taking care of my pets, working on my blanket."

"I'm curious, who is the blanket for?"

"Don't know yet, maybe you, maybe not."

"Instead of the blanket, what I want you to do for me is record your thoughts."

"I have no thoughts."

"Yes, you do, everyone does."

"I'm not everyone, Doc. Wanna know why? Because I can take it."

"Can take what, Mrs. Becker?"

"Whatever life has in store for me. If I could survive Eric, I can survive anything."

"Surviving and living are two different things. When you were with Eric, you were surviving, not living."

"And I'm living now?"

"Well, it has to be an improvement."

"If you say so," she whispered, not willing to admit that he'd hit the nail on the head.

"Excuse me?"

"If you say so it must be true, right?"

"There's no need for the sarcasm, Mrs. Becker."

"What do you want from me, Doctor? You want me to say I put my past behind me? I turned over that proverbial new leaf? I have. You want me to say I can forgive my husband and forget what he did? I refuse to forgive and I'll never forget how he tortured me."

"You know, sometimes I wonder what turned him. Something changed him into a dark soul, if he ever possessed a soul. Maybe it started when we lost our first baby and the doctors told us we'd never have children. I know he blamed me. I'm the one with the damaged fallopian tubes." She saw him write something on his legal pad. I'll give him something to think about...

"Once he told me a story about his childhood and although he didn't say it, I got the impression his relationship with his mother had an incestuous quality. Did I ever tell you he used to dream about her? Nasty dreams...I know because he would always come before he woke up. Yeah, ain't that a bitch? He wanted his own mother like that, sick bastard. He grew into a monster, someone who only cared for himself, only thought about what made him happy, no matter whom it hurt. You know, he hurt me almost as badly as he hurt his murder victims. They were lucky. Their pain ended with death, unlike me, I have to go on, even though I know no matter what I did for him or what he did to me, he lusted after another woman for weeks, maybe months before he died."

She tried to remember when it all began, except the years of drugs and alcohol stole chunks of her memory and tossed it aside. There wasn't a remnant of the good days left, although she knew who helped him descend into his obsession. She knew who to blame.

"I take it you're referring to Detective Robinson? Are you telling me you feel she is somehow to blame for your husband's behavior?"

He came so close to the truth, it frightened her. If he even suspected, she'd be on her way back to Blackstone so fast it would make her head spin. Yes, she blamed the woman who conveniently forgot her as soon as she felt it wouldn't look bad for her to do so. Terri felt Shevaughn hadn't even come close to paying her debt, by any means. She owed her. She just couldn't let him ever find out.

"Of course not, Doctor. Detective Robinson killed him and saved me from whatever future horrors he planned. She even helped me after Eric died. You know no one else ever paid me a visit in all those years. If not for her...I don't know...in a way, I owe her my life."

She kept the secret that Detective Robinson had ignored her since she'd been released to herself.

"Good. We both know that harboring resentment won't help, don't we?"

"I'm sure we do. Can I go home now?"

"This session isn't over."

"It is for me. Look, Doc, let's compromise. If you end the session now, I'll start the journal. Deal?"

"We'll make up the time next week when we take a look at what you've written."

"It won't take long. It's just the beginning."

"Exactly, Mrs. Becker, the beginning."

Dr. Callaghan went to his desk and pulled out a black and white composition book. It reminded Terri of childhood, of innocence lost. He offered it to her. Their hands touched. He became uncomfortable when he realized the touch lingered a little too long. He watched her leave and wondered if her gesture meant a sign of trust.

The session ended with both of them thinking they'd won today's battle. Terri took the notebook and drove back to her home. Her two dogs and three cats greeted her at the door. She ruffled the fur behind their ears, gave each dog a treat and poured some milk in the cats' bowls, went to the sofa, stretched out and put her feet up on a couple of charcoal Ralph Lauren cashmere throw pillows.

Even though she secretly enjoyed the verbal sparring with the good doctor, it tended to wear her out. Not as tired as usual, she still closed her eyes, folded her arms and imagined her favorite daydream, the one where she's holding her baby. Someone she could love without ever being afraid. That wouldn't just make her life better. That would make it perfect. She realized she needed a couple of plans to make this dream a reality. She may have to go as far as seducing the good doctor. *Can't put all my eggs in one basket.* She giggled softly at her play on words and then opened her eyes. Terri cautiously glanced around with a small smile on her face, a little habit leftover from Blackstone. Satisfied that she was alone with her pets, she got up, found her blanket and went back to crocheting.

She'd gotten so good at it that she didn't have to pay close attention to the stitches anymore and her mind wandered...

When they released her last year, she sold the majority of Eric's possessions and collected every penny. She'd been paid very well for the torture he put her through. Her lawyer set up an annuity that more than covered her monthly expenses, insuring she'd never have to work again. She then moved to a new exclusive neighborhood far from Portsborough. She remembered the first time she laid eyes on her house. It almost looked like something from the TV show, "Dynasty" and even came with a boat! Though she never considered sailing, it impressed her. Maybe one day, she'd find a man who'd enjoy taking her out in it. Who knew what the future held? Putting her blanket aside, she got up, stretched and stood in front of her picture window.

"What a day," Terri thought as she looked up and marveled at the sky. There were pretty, fluffy white clouds slowly drifting past her realm of vision. The panoramic view contrasted with the scenery from the security-barred window of her cell-like room in her other life at The Blackstone House.

Blackstone, in association with the Friendship Hospital, hailed as an asylum for the mentally ill with an advanced program for neurotic depression. Terri squeezed her eyes shut in an attempt to make her memories disappear, although she knew she would never be able to forget her treatment there.

She looked across her spacious bright living room with the cheerfully painted saffron yellow walls and vowed she would never return. To get into a better mood and take her mind off of the years she'd spent there, Terri sat back down and spent the next few hours quietly crocheting. She took great care with the fifty-eight round aqua, yellow and pale green mohair patches that she created with an elegant bullion stitch. She started the slow process in her last few months in Blackstone. Now she worked on attaching them with a simple chain stitch to create her baby blanket. She closed her eyes for a second and suddenly experienced the sharp aroma of antiseptic that almost concealed the smell of ass in the hospital's Recreation Room. Unable to block out the memory of the constant wails, moaning, chattering and crying of the other "guests", Terri covered her ears and tried not to remember her last scary incident in that horrible place. What happened that day almost got her stay extended...

While in the Recreation Room, another female inmate walked past her and ripped the newly started blanket from her hands. An animal-like snarl rose from the center of her very being as Terri leapt out of her chair, tackling the woman to the floor. She'd grabbed the fellow patient by the throat and choked her as hard as she could. Nurse Cooper heard the commotion on the other side of the room and rushed to Terri's side.

She talked her down, slowly.

"Let her go, Terri, just let her go."

Nurse Cooper quietly repeated the phrase as she pried Terri's fingers from the other patient's throat.

"She's gonna give you back the blanket, now aren't you, honey?"

She'd quickly removed the blanket from the patient's hand and returned it to Terri. As Nurse Cooper stood in front of her, blocking out everything except the two of them, Terri felt intimidated by her size and although she tried not to, she cowered. An intense surge of a hatred pulsed through her. She didn't want to fear anyone. The memory of all she'd been through filled her with conviction. She'd never be at anyone's mercy again.

Suddenly, the hairs on the back of her neck stood on end, interrupting her thoughts. *Didn't that same car pass by a few minutes ago?* For a split second, she got the uncomfortable feeling of being watched. Terri shrugged it off and decided it would be nice to go out for dinner, something she usually did on her therapy days. It lightened her mood a bit and the fresh air always helped her sleep.

♥♦

Allen tried calling his sister several times, however after not hearing from her by the next day, he decided to take a long lunch, stop by and check on her. Maybe he'd ask her out to lunch. He figured he could use it as an excuse plus he thought maybe she would enjoy getting out of the house for a spell. Right then, he promised himself he'd be a better brother and make an effort to see her more often.

He pulled up into her driveway and saw several plastic-bagged bundles of rolled up newspapers, lying randomly on the lawn. They were wet from last night's short rainfall. That indicated something wasn't right. Helene read the paper with her Sanka every morning. She would never have left so many outside to clutter up her landscaping. Allen knew if she'd had been planning to go somewhere, she'd have made arrangements to stop their delivery.

His hand trembled, just a little, as he got the key from under the imitation rock in the terra cotta planter under the doorbell. The tremor got worse as he tried to place the key in the hole. He heard Helene chuckle, "Put some hair around it," and the sound of her laughter reminded him of how much he loved her off-the-cuff evocative comments. He couldn't remember the last time he'd told her he loved her. Sometimes, one should take the time to let people know just how important they truly are.

"Helene?"

His voice came out as a raspy whisper.

"Hey, where are you?" He spoke a little louder this time.

It felt so cold. Allen went directly to the thermostat, turned it up to seventy degrees and proceeded to walk past the living room, down the hall toward her bedroom.

The bed looked like someone had just gotten out of it, rumpled sheets pulled down, pillows scattered. Not at all like Helene, in her world, everything had its place. That condition worsened after Frank died.

When he got to her bathroom, the closed floral shower curtain seemed ominous. She never kept the curtain closed. He remembered she'd told him it had something to do with reading "The Shining", even though she told her lady friends she thought people who kept the curtain drawn were probably hiding a dirty tub. She always kept her shower curtain open.

He pulled back the curtain and although he thought he'd prepared himself for the worst, it turned out more horrible than he could have imagined. He saw Helene, except a bloated, disfigured version, lying in the tub surrounded by what looked like thick blood. He heard a soft wheezing sound and didn't realize it came from him. Allen backed up until the doorjamb jarred the center of his shoulder blade and stopped his retreat. He unintentionally took a deep breath, filling his nostrils with the stench of decomposition and jasmine. He melted to his knees and began to retch, however, since he didn't eat breakfast all he could manage were painful, dry heaves. Trying to regain his composure, he stumbled to her phone and dialed "911". It all seemed surreal and he didn't snap out of it until he heard the operator's voice.

"Send the police to 15 Essen Drive, my sis...my sister's dead."

The morning started out so quietly that, when the phone rang, it startled her. She quickly grabbed the receiver.

"Detective Robinson, Homicide."

"So how's my little superhero?"

She hated that she still immediately recognized his voice, however she couldn't deny it. It belonged to her ex-husband.

"What do you want?"

"I wanted to call, to let you know...my Mom died. Guess it got me thinking about family...about you."

She'd never liked his mother. The woman condoned her son's promiscuous and abusive behavior. He'd grown up, well gotten older anyway, to be a total Mama's boy.

"You have my condolences. Just don't ever call me again."

"You cold ass bitch, you could have at least acted like you cared. You think that because you're the police department's "Golden Girl" you can say whatever you want to me? I should have killed you when I had the chance back in the day."

"I know you're not threatening a police officer? It wouldn't take much for me to look into what you've been up to these past, what, ten years? Call me again, so I can see how easy it is."

"Now who's threatening?"

"No, see, now, there's your problem. You never recognized a promise. I think it started with your marriage vows. Good-bye, Parker."

She hung up before he could retaliate.

Immediately, the phone rang again.

"Don't test me," she whispered as she lifted the receiver.

"Detective Robinson, Homicide."

She was relieved to hear the voice of Captain Campbell's secretary. He wanted to see her right away.

Shevaughn stood up and took a deep breath, calming herself before heading to his office. It wouldn't do for him to see her angry. He'd want to know why.

Every time she walked through his door, she thought, Man, someone's got to tell him it's 1985. The cigarette smoke that hung in the air also reminded her of her first husband and she closed her eyes for a moment, making sure she'd regained her composure. When she opened them, her former partner, Detective Jared Benjamin, sat in front of Campbell's massive mahogany desk. They weren't working together anymore due to Captain Campbell's theory. He believed it served the department better if every three years partners rotated. It stopped them from getting too attached. The two still saw each other outside of work, however lately their schedules seemed to conflict and they hadn't seen each other in months. He looked great. She wondered why some smart sistah hadn't snatched up this fine espresso specimen of a Black man in uniform a long time ago.

"Jared...what?"

"Von..."

"It's so good to see you, man. How've you been?"

"Doin' fine, considering. How 'bout you?"

"Keepin' busy, catching the bad guy or girl, as the case may be, you know..."

"Yeah, I do."

"How's the baby?"

"You mean my little woman?" She couldn't keep the smile from her face. "She's fine, growing like a wild flower."

She felt as if they were excluding Captain Campbell from the conversation and when she glanced his way, she noticed him watching the two of them with a strange expression on his face. She had a hard time reading him.

"Captain Campbell wants us to work together on this new case," Jared said, explaining his presence.

"Which case?"

Why am I the last to know?

"The brother of an elderly woman just found her body. All the evidence points to suicide, however he and her daughter are insistent that's not possible. Find something to prove them right," Captain Campbell replied, handing the single page report to Shevaughn.

Her heart sunk when she read the victim's age. *Dear God, she's probably someone's grandma, someone's nonna. Why would someone murder a woman of that age?*

Chapter Four

IN THE CAR, Shevaughn quickly and thoroughly read the report and then turned to Jared.

"So, partner, it's been a while, huh? How's your love life?" Shevaughn asked to get a conversation going.

"Where'd that come from?" He answered her question with one of his own.

"Don't get all defensive on me, I just wondered."

"Well, honestly, I guess it's pretty nonexistent, still waiting for the right one to come around."

"Don't you mean come along?"

"Yeah, you know what I mean," he said as he pulled up in front of the Elliott's home.

It didn't look like a crime scene. You could tell someone took care of it with a lot of love. The home resembled a grand scale Tudor dollhouse. What disturbed this picture of this "American dream" was the yellow police tape forming an "X" across the white vinyl front door, making it look like a badly wrapped present, and the hordes of reporters, cameras, mikes and vans.

She thought that maybe, after a while, it wouldn't bother her so much, however she never got used to how death found everyday people and turn their families' lives upside down in an instant. Death came with the job description. Hurrying to get inside, she brushed the press aside like flies at a picnic.

"Excuse me, people. I need to get busy in there."

As soon as she entered, she noticed a slight chill in the house. Shevaughn wasted no time and got right to it. She began to supervise the collection of fingerprints and other evidence.

"Make sure everything is photographed and dusted, especially the window casings and the bed. Pay particular attention to the bathroom."

Even though they'd covered every detail, there wasn't anything to suggest murder. It did look like a simple case of suicide. Pulling on a pair of latex gloves, she stepped closer and carefully lifted the victim's left arm to examine the incision on her wrist. Something wasn't right. She concentrated on the wound so hard she didn't notice Dr. Spencer quietly enter the room. As soon as he came close, she cornered him, a puzzled look on her face.

"Something bothering you, Detective?" Spencer asked as he slipped on his gloves.

"The incision, what's wrong with it?"

"Give me a sec, I'll take a closer look," he answered, pulling his glasses from the left jacket pocket of his freshly pressed black mortician looking suit. He instructed his assistants to remove the body from the tub and into the body bag on the stretcher. She stepped back and waited.

After a quick examination, he nodded affirmatively and beckoned Shevaughn to come closer.

"Your instincts are right on. Look at her incisions. Most suicides cut horizontally across the wrist, not vertically on the vein. In the couple of cases where I've seen it done vertically, the cut usually gets deeper as it goes up the arm, possibly because the person becomes more determined in their conviction that it's their only way out, that they're doing the right thing. Here you can see the opposite is true, the wound starts deep and gets more superficial as it travels up the arm. To me, that suggests it wasn't self-inflicted. I'm afraid most of the surrounding evidence has been diluted by prolonged water contact. She definitely bled out. I'd also venture an educated guess that she recently engaged in sexual activity since I found some bruising of the vulva."

"So, what are you saying? That it's possible she committed suicide after the rape?"

She thought of Nonna and knew that tough cookie would help the police catch the rapist, not kill herself.

"Possible, not probable, I don't have enough to come to that conclusion, not just yet, however I am leaning towards murder."

Shevaughn thought as much. She agreed. The poor woman must have been murdered. She wondered what other horrors she'd faced before death. The big question that loomed in everyone's mind was why? She couldn't have posed much of a threat to anybody.

"Get me your complete workup as soon as possible. I need to know everything, everything this woman went through."

"I'll get right on it and try to have some answers by early tomorrow afternoon."

"The sooner, the better, please. I know you'll do your best."

She turned to one of the attending policemen.

"I want you to canvas the neighborhood, see if anyone saw or heard anything out of the ordinary. Who found her?"

"I believe her brother did, he's outside in one of our cars."

"Good, I need to talk to him. Detective Benjamin and I will get his statement at the station."

She walked around the back of the police car where the shaken man sat crouched over in the back passenger seat. He sat up a little straighter when she rapped on the driver's side back window. Shevaughn opened the door and got in.

"Sir, I'm Detective Robinson, I'm told you found the body?"

"The body? That's my sister in there, not just some damn random body."

"I understand, sir. I apologize for your loss. I know this is very difficult for you, yet there's no way around it. Would you mind answering a few questions?"

He shook his head no.

"Let's start by telling me her name."

"Helene, Helene Elliott."

"And yours?"

"Allen Singletary."

"Mr. Singletary, please, I need to ask, did you touch anything when you first went into her house, maybe before you realized what happened?"

"I felt so cold in there...so cold. I turned on the heat."

"OK, so you touched the thermostat, anything else?"

"The shower curtain, dear God, I wished I hadn't...and then the phone."

"Thank you for your help, Mr. Singletary. Now, if I can impose on you to go to the precinct and give us your fingerprints? We'll need them so we can rule them out."

He nodded affirmatively.

"I need to call my niece. She's the reason I stopped by to check on Helene."

"Give the information to the officer and we'll have someone from the precinct contact her."

Shevaughn tapped on the bulletproof glass barrier that separated the front and back seats. The officer opened it and she instructed him on what to do next.

"Take him to the station, get his statement and fingerprints and see that he gets home. Also send a patrolman to Mrs. Elliott's daughter for notification."

She walked back into the house and sought out one of the police technicians whose job included fingerprint collection.

"Make sure you dust the thermostat, phone and shower curtain and you're taking the linens back to the lab to test for blood and semen, right?"

The tech nodded and began to relay her requests to the others that were busy collecting evidence.

Shevaughn and Jared left the crime scene, got back to the precinct and filed their preliminary report. She got ready to leave for the day when someone knocked on her door.

"Come in."

"Detective Robinson? I'm Phaedra Davis, Helene Elliott's daughter. I need to talk to you, please."

"Of course, Ms. Davis, sit down." Shevaughn pointed to the empty chair with her open palm. First, let me say how very sorry I am for your loss. What can I do for you?"

"You can find who m...murdered my mother," she answered, softly.

"Can you tell me why you're so sure it's murder?"

"If this happened years ago, right after Dad passed, well, maybe then I'd think she may have committed suicide. She'd gotten so depressed, like...she'd died with him. Here lately, she'd changed. There was a new man in her life and she seemed so... happy. I could hear it in her voice." Phaedra's own voice cracked. Obviously, she was having trouble holding it together. "I'm telling you, lately her outlook on life changed. I think she actually loved him."

"Him who, do you have a name?"

"I've been wracking my brain, all I remember is she referred to him as Jay."

"Jay? Is that his name or initial?"

"That's just it. I'm not sure. I don't remember her ever mentioning his last name. She did say something about his beautiful eyes. She said they were turquoise. I'm sorry, I wish I knew more. I wish I could be more helpful. Look, Detective, you've got to find him. If he's not responsible, he knows something, I know he does. He's the only one she ever mentioned, the only person in her life. I should have been there for her."

"Hon, don't start blaming yourself. That'll only end up creating more problems, trust me." Shevaughn thought of how she'd blamed herself for Tony's death, *if we'd never met...*

"Sorry, I need to ask you, could she have been trying not to worry you?"

"Lying?"

"No, acting."

"I seriously doubt it."

"I believe you."

Dr. Spencer suspected that there was a man involved.

"And I can assure you my partner and I will be concentrating solely on this case. We all need the truth. Please leave your name, address and phone number with the desk sergeant. I'll be in touch."

"Thank you, Detective Robinson."

"Don't thank me 'til the case is solved."

On her way home, Shevaughn stopped at the A & P and then started to go to "The Book Nook" to pick up a book for Toni. Shevaughn changed her mind when she remembered what happened the first and only time she'd been there. It happened last spring at the bookstore's grand opening...

While looking through the shelves, she came across a rare copy of one of her favorite childhood books, "Olaf Reads." One of the few early memories was of her mother reading it to her and the two of them laughing after the line, "You want me to call you Shirley?" No one could use the word "surely" around them for a long time without them sharing a look and a chuckle. She wanted to create that memory with her daughter, so she picked up the book and got in line to pay. While there, she'd noticed the attractive Black man at the cash register. She first saw his profile and her heartbeat quickened just a little bit. Third in line, she'd found her hormones putting her through an array of emotions. She couldn't deny she felt something happening. It suddenly got very warm. To give herself a moment to get it together, Shevaughn walked off, went to the bestsellers' display, hurriedly picked up "Twilight Eyes" by Dean Koontz and then got back in line. Her little side trip put her back to the end of the line and gave her more time to check him out. He stood tall, maybe 6'4", 6'5" with a dusky, old world sepia complexion, reminding her of a tanned Egyptian. His features were smooth except for his slight five o'clock shadow. His short jet-black curly 'Fro looked so soft, she wanted to reach out and touch it.

He wore a black sports jacket, teal T-shirt and wide leg jeans and had a tiny diamond stud in his left ear. He resembled a combo of that "Miami Vice" cutie, Philip Michael Thomas and Omar Sharif in his "Doctor Zhivago" days. He faced her and she saw his cleft chin. What were the odds? She'd always had a thing for them. Growing up, all her favorite actors sported cleft chins,

Robert Mitchum, Kirk Douglas, Cary Grant, Stephen Boyd, Jeff Chandler, Jack Scalia and even that Travolta guy. She wondered why it turned her on. Funny, she couldn't recall seeing a black man with a cleft chin, until now.

He hadn't given her a second look as he rang up the sale. When he asked cash or credit, she fished her credit and membership cards out of her purse and put it on the counter. He reached out, took it and for the first time, looked directly into her eyes. The bookstore suddenly got hotter and she'd become confrontational.

"I noticed your selection. So you're a Koontz fan, I take it?"

"I'm becoming one, you?"

"I think the world is scary enough without adding the supernatural."

"You may be right, except sometimes the only way you can escape is through fantasy."

"I see you've given this some thought."

"Not really, it's just that I've found it's a good thing to immerse yourself in a book. It's a kind of getaway."

"And what do you need to get away from?"

Shevaughn thought about all she'd been through. She bowed her head and mumbled.

"Life."

He saw the pain in her eyes before she lowered her head and instantly wanted to comfort her. She looked so... vulnerable.

"Don't we all," he said as he held out her bag. Then he pulled his arm back and attempted to start a conversation. *Something about this woman…*

"Hey, I'm getting off in about an hour. Want to grab a cup of coffee, dinner maybe?"

"Why? I don't even know you."

"That's easy enough to fix. I'm Marcus, Marcus Williams. My friends call me Marc."

He held out his hand.

She ignored it and spoke to cover the awkward moment.

"Nice meeting you, Mr. Williams. I'm…"

"I said my friends call me Marc."

"Well, we hardly qualify as friends. We just met."

"Touché… and you are?"

"Shevaughn Robinson. My friends call me Von."

"Von, I like that, short and sweet."

"Are you flirting with me, Mr. Williams?"

"You know, I think I am!"

He flashed his beautiful smile.

"Do you flirt with all the ladies that frequent this store?"

"Actually, no, the majority of women that come here are either little silver- haired ladies or moms with a bunch of kids."

Shevaughn's stomach flipped.

"You don't have anything against children, do you?"

"Of course not, especially when they're not mine. Why, do you have kids? I did notice the other book you bought."

Although tempted to tell him the truth, something made her decide against it. After all, she didn't even know this guy.

"No."

"Want some?" Marcus chuckled, not even trying to hide the smirk.

"'Scuse me?"

She "saw" him flick the imaginary Groucho cigar and tried to appear offended, except damn, this man looked good. Then Tony's face flashed before her and guilt swept the smile from her face.

What man wants a ready-made family?

"You're pretty damn bold, aren't you Mr. Williams?"

"And here I'm hoping you'd think I'm just damn pretty."

"I don't usually classify men as pretty."

"Okay, handsome, attractive, good looking, stop me when I hit the nail on the head."

"How 'bout cocky?"

Good thing he didn't mention cute.

"Uh, oh, that can't be good. Seriously, why don't you have dinner with me? I could show you my humble side."

He raised an eyebrow and flashed that effective smile at her once again.

"I think it would be a lot more humbling if I refuse."

"Ouch, that hurts."

"And it should."

"Damn, you're heartless, woman."

Shevaughn felt a rush of anger that quickly boiled over before she could stop it.

"Don't say that, don't you ever say anything like that to me again."

Her tone suddenly turned ice-cold.

"Shevaughn, I'm sorry. I...I've obviously struck a nerve or something and I apologize. What did I say?"

"Never mind, just give me my books. Oh, and by the way, I have a beautiful daughter, so I don't need any help in that department either." *OK, now, listen to yourself, girl, you're trippin'. Just get out of here.* She followed her instinct.

"I need to go."

She tried to control her feelings, knowing she needed to get out of there before he saw her cry.

He handed her the books with a puzzled expression on his face.

"Look, I'm sorry if I said something to dist..."

Shevaughn cut him off.

"Oh, please, you don't even know why you're apologizing. Good evening, Mr. Williams."

She hurried away, leaving him with a quizzical look on his face.

♥◆

Damn, what the hell...?

Marcus couldn't figure out what suddenly went so wrong. Ms. Shevaughn Robinson seemed definitely touchy about something. *Wonder why she denied her kid at first?* He tried to think back on what he'd said that bothered her, and couldn't figure out what caused such a reaction. He couldn't ignore the hurt in her eyes. It made him want to do something to comfort her. Thinking he'd never understand women, Marcus shrugged and began loading the new books onto the cart and placing them on the shelves. Good thing he had mindless work to do because now she occupied his thoughts. So much so, he located her membership registration card that listed her home and job information, called a florist and arranged a delivery. When she got back from lunch the next day, there was a tiny bouquet of yellow carnations waiting for her on her desk with a note attached that asked, "What am I sorry for?"

As upset as she'd been at her response to his harmless remark, occasionally Shevaughn found herself remembering his smile. However today, she decided not to stop at the bookstore and instead, drove straight home.

When she got to her door, she didn't even have time to fish her keys out of her purse before it opened and there stood the most important person in her life.

"Mommy, Mommy, I help Nonna make dinner. I pop peas, huh, Nonna?"

"No, mia piccolina, you snapped beans."

Mother O'Brien, the feisty quintessential picture of a Sicilian grandmother, with her salt and pepper hair, horn-rimmed glasses and plump cheeks, laughed as she came out of the kitchen, drying her hands on her favorite prayer apron. Shevaughn loved the prayer's sentiment and memorized it years ago:

"Lord, warm all the kitchen with Thy love,

And light it with Thy peace.

Forgive me all my worry,

And make my grumbling cease."

Nonna interrupted her thoughts. Shevaughn never felt comfortable calling her Lorraine. It just wasn't respectful enough.

"She's pretty good at it, too, even pulled out a few stringy ones."

"Nonna says we're goin' to a fetsival."

"Festival," Shevaughn corrected as she put her keys on the wall hook next to the door and swept her daughter up in her arms. She held her close, buried her face in her daughter's tiny neck and reveled in her sweet Ivory soap smell. Holding their child at arm's length, she felt blessed by the constant reminder of the man who'd taught her about love and sunsets. She had just a hint of cocoa in her complexion. At birth, her hair matched the exact shade of brown as Tony's. Each year it got darker and now it looked almost black. She was the spittin' image of her Daddy, right down to her tiny cleft chin. Shevaughn playfully wiggled her forefinger in the small indentation. Toni giggled and made a joking attempt at chomping her finger. Shevaughn joined in and they laughed together.

Nonna spent her days planning an outing to Little Italy's Annual Feast of San Gennaro, an authentic buffet of Italian delicacies and entertainment. This would be

Shevaughn and Toni's first time. When Nonna told her about it, they all were practically drooling as she listed the various delicacies they would encounter. Shevaughn anticipated it almost as much as Toni. They talked more about it during dinner and all three of them showed signs of excitement. Later, Shevaughn had difficulty getting her little one to go to sleep and then she had trouble dozing off too. However, it was more than the festival on her mind. She also worried about this latest case.

The next day, when Shevaughn read Dr. Spencer's report, she saw the coroner had a hard time pinning down the exact time of death for two reasons, the lowering of the room temperature and the body being submerged in water for so long. He could guess Mrs. Elliott died on or around August twenty-third after being brutally raped or she'd engaged in some unusually rough sex. Sadly, due to her age, they were inclined to go with the first option. The time of death could have been off by as much as forty-eight hours. The fingerprints didn't give them much either, since after eliminating the family, they were only left with a few strange smudges.

Shevaughn called the lab and asked to speak with the good doctor.

"Hey, Spence, since they found the Elliott woman in the bathroom, did anyone collect and tag the wastebasket contents? Great, can you have it sent to me?"

"Sure, I'll have someone bring it right over."

When the evidence bag arrived, Shevaughn put on a pair of latex gloves and dumped everything out onto a metal evidence tray. There wasn't much to look at, a few tissues, Q-Tips and a couple of syringes. She picked up a syringe and twirled it around between her fingers, thinking. What if...?

She called Spencer back

"Hey, I've gotta few questions for you. We found out Mrs. Elliott suffered from diabetes, right? Suppose the killer knew about her condition and used her insulin to kill her. I guess what I'm asking is what are the symptoms of an insulin overdose?"

"Well, there's several, the most common symptoms of severe hypoglycemia include sweating, extreme weakness, blurred vision and speech, tremors, some stomach pain and convulsions. It can lead to a coma."

"Did you look for injection sites other than the norm? I guess a better question is where would someone hide an injection?"

"My best guess is probably the pubic area, armpits, maybe under the breasts for an older woman."

"Have you checked those areas?"

"Yes, however I could have missed a minuscule puncture wound. I take it you want me to look again?"

"Yes, I do. So it's possible she may have been in a coma when her wrists were slit?"

"Yeah, that's a feasible scenario."

"Check it out and let me know if you find anything."

Shevaughn and Jared left the precinct and drove to Phaedra Davis' home at the edge of town. On the ride over, she got the idea that maybe she could actually get the press to help her on this case. She knew Mrs. Davis would be agreeable.

Phaedra, who'd obviously been at the window, opened the door before Shevaughn touched the bell.

"Detective Robinson, Detective Benjamin?"

"Hello, Mrs. Davis, may we come in? Is there anyone here with you?"

"My son, Tyler, is upstairs in his room. Why?"

"Let's go sit down in the living room."

They followed her to the tan leather couch and waited for her to sit. Shevaughn sat diagonally across from her and reached out for her hand while Jared stood to her left.

"Please, tell me what is it? Just say it."

"I'm afraid there were signs of a sexual attack."

They watched the blood drain from Phaedra's face. She turned so pale you could see the small blue veins beneath her skin.

"Oh God, someone raped my mother? Oh God, oh my God..."

Her voice went up in pitch and her son, Tyler came running down the stairs.

"Mom, you okay? What's the matter? You scared me."

Phaedra looked at her and without saying a word, Shevaughn knew her thoughts were of how, when or even if she'd ever tell the whole truth to her ten-year-old son.

"I'm okay, Honey. Go back upstairs. We'll talk later."

Tyler shot Shevaughn and Jared a very mature warning look and went back up to his room without a word.

"Could you give me a recent picture of your mother?"

"Yes, in fact, she just had "Glamour Shots" done a couple of months ago. I think she did it for him."

"I'm thinking, if they were dating, they had to go out in public together sometime. Maybe we could find someone who's seen them."

"Yes, a few times she mentioned they'd gone out to dinner and she told me they both liked old Hitchcock movies. Give me a minute, I'll be right back."

While waiting for Mrs. Davis to return, they both looked around the tidy home. Shevaughn found it hard to accept depravity and murder as part of reality in such an orderly existence. She also saw that Mrs. Davis and her mother shared the same feeling of pride in their homes.

Phaedra returned with an eight by ten in a silver frame and a Polaroid. She removed the print from the frame and gave them both to Shevaughn.

"We took this snapshot on our last vacation, so it's older. I think it's more like her every day look, you know, without all the makeup."

Shevaughn looked at the smiling woman in the photos. Mrs. Elliott looked as if she didn't have a care in the world. She carefully placed them in the file with her report.

"We'll let you know if anything turns up."

When Shevaughn and Jared got back to the precinct, he grabbed the movie clue and ran with it by calling all the theaters in town, trying to locate one with Hitchcock on their schedule in the past six months.

♥♦

Black Jack

Back in Southampton, he'd parked his car and sat down for an early dinner at the Baker's Dozen, an outdoor café known for some of the most mouthwatering pastries that ever left an oven. He wanted to check it out because of a review he'd read in a culinary article that raved about their herb encrusted sirloin, burgundy gravy and boursin mashed potatoes. They declared it the best this side of the Mississippi and he couldn't wait to taste their claim to fame. Another reason was the café's location. It sat on the corner of Adams and Main Street and provided a good cross section view of the quaint downtown area. The tree-lined street looked like something from a movie set, right down to the pastel striped awnings with matching solid umbrellas and white wrought iron furniture. The additional benefit of the location, he'd probably see her if she came to town.

He noticed all the women's attention focused on him and his dog, while most of the men glanced at them with jealous curiosity. Khan lay peacefully at his feet. He and his new partner were really working it.

The waitress brought him a menu.

"Beautiful evening for outdoor dining, isn't it? Even if I have to dine alone," he commented, giving her a bold once over before mentally dismissing her. He watched as the sound of his voice made her blush. *I could have her, right here.* Then he thought of his new widow and although the waitress happened to be a cute, petite little thing, financially the girl didn't fit the profile. There were bigger fish to fry. He ordered his steak medium well and added a Greek salad. Reading the wine menu, he found they stocked a 1973 Moss Wood Cabernet Sauvignon. *I could definitely get used to this.*

He ordered a bottle for himself and a bowl of water for Khan. The waitress didn't object and hurried away, eager to please. *Like she has a chance in Hell.* He stopped himself from laughing out loud.

Then he saw her. She walked towards him with a little mop of a dog, dressed in a see-through cream and black zebra-striped oversized shirt with a black tank top underneath. With matching black leggings and flats, the only thing to complete the picture would have been a beret. Then she would have looked like the clichéd French artist. He saw her wavy, jet-black hair had a slightly wild look to it and hung just past her shoulder blades. She didn't look like she wore any makeup and her eyes were hidden behind her Ray-Ban sunglasses. Time on the outside immensely improved her appearance. He wondered if she knew how good she looked. She looked ready for him or at least he hoped so. As he felt himself harden, he knew he was more than ready for her.

Chapter Five

WHEN TERRI NOTICED the striking pair, she inhaled sharply. They gave her goose bumps. She'd seen some eye-catching men in her day, yet none ever came close to this. She hoped he would stick around for a while and wasn't just passing through. She noticed the silver Trans Am parked alongside him at the curb. The immaculate car added to his glamorous presence. Then she realized it looked exactly like the car she'd caught a glimpse of from her living room window. Could he be the one who'd been watching her? She closed her eyes for a moment and made a wish. Please let me get to know this man, whoever he is.

She found herself walking over to his table before she made a conscious decision to do so. She felt more confident with Kayla by her side. The Lhasa apso seemed to be a great judge of character. When the dog walked right up and sat down in front of him, Terri knew he could be the one.

"He's gorgeous," she said aloud, unsure if she meant the dog or the man. It applied to them both.

"You're not so bad yourself."

His velvet voice created a warm feeling in the pit of her stomach as they made their introductions.

"Kayla doesn't take to everyone."

Khan got up to investigate his tiny female counterpart and after several customary sniffs, they laid down together.

"Well, it looks like our companions have found each other. Maybe we should take their cue and do the same. Would you care to join me for dinner?"

Without waiting for her answer, he waived the waitress over. Terri noticed he assumed she would accept, yet it didn't bother her. It would have taken a tornado to stop her from sitting down with this man. She also noticed the look of envy the waitress shot at her when he stood and pulled out her chair. He requested another menu. She sat down with a small smirk on her face and ordered their salmon BLT, a Cobb salad and a diet 7-Up. When she removed her sunglasses, he saw her light blue eyes were beautiful, almost as beautiful as his were behind the contact lenses.

"I take it you don't drink?"

"Not since my husband died."

"I'm sorry."

"Don't be, he'd become a psychotic bastard, if you'll pardon my French."

"No offense taken."

"Let's not talk about him. Tell me about yourself. I've never seen you here before. What brings you to this neck of the woods?"

"I'm just looking around. I'm thinking of moving to this charming town."

"I think I saw your car pass my house yesterday?"

"It's possible, like I said, I'm checking out the neighborhood."

She quickly volunteered her assistance.

"Well, if you ever need a guide, I'd be happy to show you the local attractions. It really is a lovely place to live."

"Have you lived here long?"

"No, it's been less than a year. Still I'm really glad I moved here. It's quiet, beautiful and quite exclusive."

"By exclusive, are you referring to money or race?"

She found herself blushing.

"Well, both, truth be told."

"I wondered if my being here would strike folks as unusual. I figured you don't see many Black men around here. Martin would've been proud of me."

At first Terri didn't get it and then she realized he'd made a little joke, referring to Martin Luther King, Jr. She would have laughed at anything he said.

Dinner went well. He turned out to be smart, well-traveled and quite the conversationalist. Terri really enjoyed herself for the first time in years. She too saw the envious looks they got. *We do make a handsome couple.* She ate slowly, realizing she didn't want the evening to end.

Near the end of the meal, she suddenly felt a soft pressure running up her leg, headed for the place that no one ever touched since Shevaughn murdered Eric. She balked just a little, in shock at first and then tried to ignore the pleasurable sensation as she felt the warmth spread. Small beads of perspiration appeared on her brow. It amazed her that he could still carry on a conversation as if nothing was happening and she became determined to play along.

"What are your plans for the rest of the evening?"

Her question came out in short gasps of air.

"Well, I wanted to take Khan for a walk on Flying Point Beach. Would you ladies care to join us?" As he spoke, his toe found the crotch of her panties and pushed it aside. With what, she wondered before he made full contact. Then she knew. *And what a talented big toe you have, Grandpa.* She tried to concentrate and keep up with the conversation, even as she edged herself a teensy bit lower in her chair.

"It's a good thing we found each other, I have a permit. Otherwise, as a non-resident, you'd pay a hundred dollars for that walk."

The fact that she could complete the sentence amazed her.

"Then I shall pay for dinner, dear lady, it's only fair."

Such a gentleman, she thought and softly bit her bottom lip as she felt her orgasm begin, slowly, deliciously. She inadvertently closed her eyes as the rush traveled to her very soul.

Suddenly, the encounter ended and before she knew it, he stood over her, offering to help her up out of her chair. She hadn't even seen him put his shoe back on! In a slight daze she rose, a bit unsteadily, and stooped to pick up Kayla's leash. She rewarded his good deed with a very nice view of her derriere.

The perfect gentleman, he held the car door open for them, placing the two dogs in the back seat. He then took her hand and helped her into his car, closed her door and drove to the park. By the end of the walk, they were talking softly and holding hands. Neither mentioned their little under the table encounter. Later, he drove her home and although she expected him to accept her invitation to come in, he declined and asked for her phone number instead, leaving her frustrated and confused.

The next afternoon, when the doorbell rang and a deliveryman greeted her with a half dozen pink rosebuds, Terri couldn't contain her excitement. She hadn't been courted in years and it felt good. Smelling the roses, she pulled the small white card out of the bouquet and read his note. He thanked her for a lovely evening and said he hoped to see her again. He promised to call her tonight. Her body flushed with the memory of how quickly he'd brought her to a climax and the fact that it happened in a public place only intensified the heat. She swore she'd keep that fact to herself. She wanted to play it cool.

They began seeing each other on a constant basis. At first, they did the customary dating, going to dinner, movies, a concert here and a play there. In no time they were so comfortable together that renting a VCR tape and ordering takeout suited them both just fine, although she spent the time in constant anticipation, wondering when they'd have their next sexual encounter.

On one of their nights in, he finally made his next real move. After dinner, they washed dishes together, well, he washed and she dried and put them away. It all started when he jokingly reached into the sink and splashed her with some water. Terri took it to another level by grabbing the hand sprayer and dousing him. They laughed as he wrestled it from her hands and turned the tables by spraying her back. The next thing she knew, he kissed her so deeply her toes curled. She eagerly returned his passion. He pushed her up against the edge of the sink and roughly kissed the hollow of her neck, moving her mauve cotton skirt up her thighs. As he reached for the top of her panties, she sat forward, pulling his tan polo shirt over his head. His dark, erect nipples captured her attention. She gave in to the irresistible urge to taste them and teased them with her tongue. Standing straight up, he loomed over her and she watched, panting, as he removed his pants and boxers in one swift move. Next, he discarded her panties. She'd never seen a black man in the nude before and gave thanks that her experience began with such a fine specimen.

He lifted her onto the counter and buried his face in his goal. She responded like a woman who had been on a long sexual drought. He would never know she always gave and never received. She moaned and grabbed him by the ears, keeping him there until her first orgasm. Before the tremor subsided, he placed himself within her, filling her to the point of delicious pain. She rode with him, blissfully, and he seemed to be taken with her enthusiasm. He answered with each thrust becoming faster and harder than the last until she couldn't hold on any longer and let go…

After her second orgasm, she did what she'd been taught to do, in what seemed like centuries ago. Kneeling on the lemon slice kitchen rug, she brought him to a shuddering climax with her mouth.

♥♦

He looked down at the top of her bobbing head and realized this time he felt something very close to love. He found it surprisingly endearing that she seemed so determined to please him. He closed his eyes and wished his past would never come back to haunt him. She had it all, money, looks and a soft young body willing to address his every need. Maybe, if they'd met earlier in life, things would have been different. He thought of all the women he fleeced and murdered to get him to this point. The urge to climax shuddered through his body. He grabbed her hair and guided her to increase her tempo, causing him to ejaculate. As she swallowed, he closed his eyes and wondered how long this good thing could last. When it ended, she stood up, took his hand and led him to the bedroom. Terri willingly gave him a complete performance of all the other little tricks she'd learned in her past. Surprisingly, he kept up with her every move.

Later he woke up, startled that they'd gone to sleep together so comfortably. He felt content with her in his arms and wondered if it was her youth that influenced him so. *This can't be happening, not now.* He watched her sleep and wondered if her dreams included him.

Terri leaned her shoulders against the back of the door with her eyes closed, waiting for the pounding of her heart to subside. She panted slightly from excitement. Standing still, she seemed smaller than 5'4", 140 pounds in her all black jeans and turtleneck.

She looked like a cat burglar with her black gloves on and her hair hidden in the black wool hat. She could still hear her heart pounding in her ears. She took a deep breath, held it, opened her eyes and waited until they adjusted to the dark. Oh God, this is happening, this is really happening!

Exhaling, she looked around. The only relief from the darkness came from a small nightlight on the far wall and she barely made out the outline of the sunny yellow crib. Once her eyes were accustomed to the dark she spotted the baby monitor on the dresser. She tiptoed over, shutting it off. She couldn't risk waking anyone up. Terri then proceeded to lean over the crib and patted the top of the baby's head. She marveled at the extreme softness of the hair.

Such a beautiful baby, the perfect child. She reached over the crib railing, just missing the Winnie the Pooh mobile and gathered up the caramel colored baby and her blanket. The baby woke up and began to whimper. Before she could silence it, she heard noises coming from another part of the house. She grabbed the baby and the blanket and began to run away from the sounds. Suddenly, a man came out of nowhere and began chasing her down the hall. When she got to the kitchen, he tackled her causing her to fall, dropping the baby. The soft thud of the baby's delicate skull hitting the linoleum seemed like the worst thing she'd ever heard. She watched a shrieking woman run over to the baby, who lay motionless, on the floor.

"NO," she screamed from within, clenching her lips together to prevent the sound from escaping. She felt a crushing sadness descend upon her that quickly turned into anger. Swaying slightly, she stood up and ran at the man, arms flailing. She fought him as if defending her life, got away and ran out the house. She tried to reach the gravel road below. Before she could, she stepped on a rock or something, twisting her ankle. Crying out, Terri sat up and frantically looked around. She realized she was in bed, next to him, safe. It had seemed so real. Relief washed over her as she realized it was all just a dream!

She remembered how good it felt when she thought she'd gotten her baby. Somehow, this is going to happen. She didn't know how or when. She did know the dream warned her of how very wrong everything could possibly go. She slowly drifted back to sleep in his arms, confident that she would have the patience and intelligence to pull off whatever she needed to do to obtain what she wanted most of all.

Later that morning, Terri woke up in a better mood. It was probably because she was still in his arms and it felt so warm, so comforting. It dawned on her that the caramel baby she'd dreamed about could have been theirs. Maybe that's what it meant?

He woke up ready to take on the world. Hearing the running water, the thought of her young, nude body, glistening under the water gave him an erection that he gladly took into the bathroom. He opened the shower door with a look he hoped would relay his message without words and then he quickly noticed her attention wasn't focused on his face.

Chapter Six

DR. SPENCER CONFIRMED he'd found one puncture wound under the murder victim's arm and then informed her how impossible it is to trace insulin in an autopsy.

"Insulin breaks down in the body post mortem and since the victim died several days before her brother found her, it's not viable that we'd be able to come to a concrete conclusion, nevertheless you made a good call."

"So we're no further ahead than we were before you found the injection site?"

"Well, it's likely he gave her the insulin to render her unconscious. This way, he could murder her without much of a fight. I'm sorry, Von, unless we can talk to the perpetrator, all we have is speculation."

"Damn...well, we tried. Hey, you think we could get an estimate of the dosage missing from her current prescription?"

"And see if there's a difference between what should be left according to her prescribed dosage and what's actually in the vial?"

"Yeah, at least that way we'd know if the murderer used her own insulin."

"What if the killer brought his own supply? Then it would prove nothing."

"I guess I'm grasping at straws. So all we have is an idea of how he killed her, not that it helps much. If you find anything else, you'll call me? "

"You know it and I will check to see if any of her insulin appears to be missing."

"Thanks, Doc."

Days passed without any leads on the Elliott case. Shevaughn knew the longer the case dragged on, the harder it would be to find whoever's responsible. All of Mrs. Elliott's insulin was accounted for, so it turned out to be another dead end, just like she'd expected.

She felt pressure from the media. They expected her to perform a miracle once they'd made the victim's face headline news. Shevaughn felt her time running out like sand through an hourglass.

On a hunch, she requested that the Elliott woman's financial records be sent to her office. Working backwards, it didn't take long for her to come across a very suspicious cash withdrawal of exactly one hundred thousand dollars in the form of a cashier's check. The withdrawal left Mrs. Elliott with a balance of less than seventy grand. The completed transaction happened approximately six weeks before they'd discovered her body. She shared her discovery with Jared and they spoke to Mrs. Elliott's daughter and brother. Neither could shed any light on where the money went. She hoped if she found the recipient, she'd find the killer.

She heard a light tap on her door.

"Come in."

"Detective Robinson?"

"Yes, can I help you?"

The young Black man sat down in front of her desk, nervously wringing the rolled newspaper tighter and tighter. His normal latté complexion seemed pale. He cleared his throat and said the three words Shevaughn wanted to hear.

"I saw them."

"Who? "

"The murdered woman and her date. I recognized her picture. They came in for dinner at Napier's a couple of weeks ago. I wait tables there. I remember 'cause we don't get many elderly interracial couples."

Jared and Shevaughn shared a hopeful glance.

"If I sent you to a sketch artist, do you think you could give him a good description of her companion, Mr....?"

"Name's Otis, Otis Brewster. Sure, I can. A good-looking, older brotha like him is hard to forget."

She couldn't help the feeling of optimism that flooded her. Maybe they could finally put a face to this guy. She pushed her luck.

"He didn't happen to pay by credit card, did he?"

"Sorry, cash. Great tipper, though. That's another reason why I remember."

"How 'bout I have Detective Benjamin escort you to the sketch artist and we'll see if the two of you can come up with someone."

Jared waved to the young man indicating he should follow him and they left. She prayed that this might be the break they'd been waiting for.

It only took the sketch artist less than an hour to produce a likeness of the man seen with Mrs. Elliott. Looking at it, even Shevaughn found it hard to imagine that someone so handsome, so dignified could be responsible for such a scandalous crime. She knew only too well how deceiving looks could be, look at Becker or that Bundy guy. At first, when just looking at their picture, nobody could believe they were responsible for their crimes either. The only thing she saw in her favor, she didn't think it would be too difficult, finding a Black man with turquoise eyes.

Ariel put off calling Shevaughn all morning after her rough night. After only sleeping a couple of hours, a nightmare invaded her dreams. In it, she saw a small, platinum-haired woman wearing a black nightgown. It wasn't frightening until she saw her face. It resembled Edvard Munch's infamous oil painting, "The Scream". In the far left corner of her dream, standing behind the woman, stood a shadow, the dark silhouette of a tall man. She tried to hone in on his face and the effort forced her to wake up. Flushed, she checked the clock on the nightstand. It said 3:03 a.m. Ariel realized her gown felt wet. She thought it was the remnants of a night sweat until she began choking on the cloying stench of jasmine and death. It smelled so bad, she opened all her bedroom windows, although letting in the cool, night air didn't lessen the nauseating, rancid odor, forcing Ariel to leave her room and go to the kitchen. She sat down at the round glass dining table, wringing her hands, unsure of what to do next when suddenly she felt a burning heat she knew she couldn't blame on menopause. She hadn't felt like this in ages, although she recognized it immediately.

Good Lord, I'm horny! What the hell's going on?

Going back to sleep seemed impossible, like having an itch you can't scratch. For a second, she wondered whose sensations she'd experienced. *It has to be connected to Shevaughn's current case, that Elliott woman.* Ariel got up and went into her bathroom. She ran a cool shower and started to feel better as the streaming water flowed over her body, that is, until a cloying odor of a substance she didn't recognize overcame her. She got light-headed and the first thought that came to mind told her the smell resembled chloroform or ether, something that would render a person unconscious. She closed her eyes and ran her hand over them and her forehead. When she opened her eyes, she look down to watch the water drain. Her alarm increased when she saw it turn blood red. Trembling, she got out of the shower, grabbed a towel and went back to her room. Ariel sat down on her bed, slowly rubbed herself dry and tried to get herself together.

She wondered what linked her to this victim. She couldn't remember the last time she'd had a dream or vision about someone without the use of a personal belonging. Usually that only happened with family. She knew she'd have to tell Shevaughn about her experience. It frustrated her that it hadn't revealed much. What good did she do if she couldn't help? Distraught, she got dressed, sat by her living room window and waited for sunrise. During that time, she decided to go to the precinct and see Shevaughn in person.

On her way to the police station, she stopped at her favorite diner for toast and tea, hoping it would help settle her nervous stomach. Instead, it gave her indigestion. All of a sudden, she felt pressure building under her sternum and pain radiating through her jaw. The room spun once and went black…

She found herself floating and looked down on a scene from her first psychic experience. At the age of eleven, Ariel experienced her first menstrual period. Her mother gave her a sugary-sweet "you're becoming a young woman" speech with the new 'm' word. She never forgot the feeling of pride that filled her small body. So much so, she couldn't wait for her Dad to come into her room and tuck her in, as he did every night. When he kissed her good night, she leaned up and whispered, "Daddy, I got my minestrone."

She watched his face go from puzzled to surprise. Then he lifted an eyebrow, cracked a smile and quickly left the room. She went to sleep listening to her parents' muffled laughter and it felt good to know she lived in a happy home. Years later, her mother told her she'd been the reason why.

The next thing she remembered, she woke up with the feeling that someone had entered her room and stood close, watching her. She looked around and in the corner, right by her small white French provincial vanity, stood her Nana. The elderly woman smiled, blew her a kiss and gradually faded into the darkness. When she disappeared, the phone rang. Ariel heard her mother cry out and knew someone called to inform her that Nana had passed away. She cried herself back to sleep without going to her parents' room for confirmation of her fear. It hurt to know she'd been right, yet she felt grateful for the chance to see her grandmother one last time. Even now, her Nana occasionally came to her in dreams, sometimes warning her of things to come, although most of the time she came bringing comfort.

The next part on her journey took her back to the first time she'd laid eyes on the man destined to be her husband. She'd accompanied her parents on a trip to Boston to see Rowland Sturges, the concert pianist who played Brahms as if possessed by the composer. During intermission, someone bumped into her, causing her to spill a bit of sparkling cider on her beautiful periwinkle gown. She'd angrily turned around and the sight of a rather striking young man knocked her for a loop. Ariel instantly knew that she wanted to look into his eyes for the rest of her life. Six months later, they were pronounced husband and wife. The irony that his last name happened to be Knight wasn't lost on her. He definitely rescued her from her parents' constant scrutiny.

As she calmly hovered over her body, she realized she'd lived a pretty charmed life. Proud and pleased with all the people she'd helped along the way, she felt contentment. In the immeasurable distance, she could see her Nana, standing within a bright white light, waiting with open arms. She could go now, with no regrets...

Shevaughn got on the phone and requested a press conference. It always amazed her how quickly the media could assemble. In less than an hour, there were a dozen reporters, some with their photographers, all waiting to hear her statement. She felt a quick, nervous flutter in her stomach, swallowed hard and stepped up to the platform, stopping behind the mike in the center of the mahogany podium. The room was completely still, except for someone clearing their throat or the occasional cough.

"Ladies and gentlemen of the press, first, I want to say, this is a short announcement only. There will be no questions asked or answered, for that matter. I'm sharing this information with you in the hopes that someone who's seen this man will come forward. I'm giving you all a sketch of a man who may or may not be connected to the Elliott murder case. The department has issued an All Points Bulletin and will be posting this sketch in airports, hotels, motels, train and bus stations and car rental agencies. I know you're all familiar with the story, so I don't need or have the time to give you details. I'm asking you to publish this picture under the caption 'Do you know this man?' or something similar and front-page it as soon as possible. Let him know it's just for questioning, don't speculate, just report. Am I asking too much?"

When she first heard the grumble, she thought they were disagreeing. It sounded angry. Then the sound became louder as more and more people joined in and she realized they were answering her question with a resounding "NO." For the first time, it dawned on her that maybe the press wasn't always the enemy. Shevaughn knew this was a milestone she'd never thought about reaching and it felt damn good.

"Copies of the sketch with the hotline number are on both sides of the door, so you can pick it up as you exit. Please only one per news crew. We need to spread this as fast and far as possible. I don't have to tell you, time is of the essence. Now I have to get back to work. Thank you, thank you all. This press conference is over."

Amazingly, the crowd began to quietly disburse, their demeanor a little more subdued than usual. Jared stood in the back of the room watching Shevaughn in action. It surprised him, how calm and confidently she'd covered everything. Years as a detective gave her a maturity he'd never seen in her before. He realized she made him proud.

"What did you think?" she asked, flushed with her success.

"Impressive, I think you handled them very nicely, very nicely indeed," he cheerfully admitted. "Well, I guess your work here is done. Wanna go for a drink to celebrate your victory with the press?"

"No, I think I'm heading home. Tomorrow's probably gonna be a long day. We'll be getting calls from God knows who. Hey, before I forget, got any plans for next Saturday? Nonna, Toni and I are going to that San Genarro Festival in the city. Care to tag along?"

"Sounds like fun, sure. Give Toni a hug for me, okay?"

"You can do that yourself next Saturday, 'Unka Dred'?"

He loved Toni's rendition of his name. It made him smile.

"I miss the little brat, it's been months."

"Brat? I beg your pardon. I know you're not referring to my angel."

"Yeah, remember that the next time she gets into your makeup."

The last time he'd visited, they'd gotten so involved in their conversation, they'd lost track of time and Toni. Neither knew how long they'd left her unattended in Shevaughn's room. They found her sitting on her mom's bed with makeup all over her face. All the right colors were on all the wrong places. She'd used the eyeliner pencil around her mouth, eye shadow on her cheeks and lipstick on her eyelids and sat there with a lopsided grin, proud of her accomplishment. Shevaughn tried to fuss, however one look at Jared and they'd both burst into laughter. Now they chuckled at the memory.

"Have a good night, then."

"Yeah, you, too."

She went back to her office, collected her things, put one arm in the sleeve of her jacket and the phone rang.

"Detective Robinson, Homicide. Yes, what? Oh, no."

The admitting nurse from Memorial Hospital told her they'd admitted Mrs. Knight for chest pains and it didn't look good. They'd found Shevaughn's card in Ariel's wallet and called her, suggesting she get there as soon as possible.

"I'm on my way."

When she got to the hospital, she rushed up to the desk and gave Ariel's name. A nurse confirmed that Ariel was in the ICU. Shevaughn hurried to her bedside and Ariel's appearance shocked her. Five feet tall and maybe a hundred pounds on a good day, the white-haired woman looked tiny and pale as she lay there, so still. She appeared dead except for all the beeping and blinking machines surrounding her.

Shevaughn sat at her bedside and held her hand.

"Don't you dare die on me, Ariel. You fight this. Nonna, Toni and I need you."

Damn, I've got to call and tell her, she thought, referring to Nonna. It would be difficult telling her of Ariel's condition. Shevaughn always hated being the messenger with bad news, yet it always seemed to come with the territory.

Nonna answered the phone and Shevaughn tried to hide the worry in her voice as she conveyed what little she knew.

"As soon as you get home, I'll go sit with her. I think Toni is too young for this, so we can take turns. I'm going to take Toni with me and go to St. Peter's to light a candle."

"Please light one in Ariel's name for me," Shevaughn requested.

She went back to sit with her dear friend, wiping her brow and holding her hand, speaking softly to her, telling her about today's press conference and funny stories featuring Toni. After being there for almost two hours, Ariel's eyes fluttered and she came back to them.

"Nana," Ariel whispered, licking her lips and looking around the room. She blinked several times and Shevaughn came into focus. "What happened?"

She could see Ariel's disbelief that she'd rejoined the living. Her next words confirmed it.

"Geez, I thought I was done for. Shevaughn, I swear I saw "the light". Guess He isn't finished with me yet."

Shevaughn nodded, picked up the cup of ice from the hospital tray table and gave her a few chips.

"The doctor said you need to rest, save your strength. We'll talk later."

"I have to tell you about last night's nightmare, no, last night's vision. I think it shook me up more than I realized," she whispered.

"I said later. I need you to just concentrate on getting better."

"Listen to me. I think I saw the Elliott woman. Do you know what she had on when she died?"

"Ariel, if the only way I can keep you quiet is to leave, I will."

Although she sulked like a child, Ariel didn't argue and brightened up when a call from the nurse's station announced Nonna's arrival. A hospital worker watched Toni during the quick changing of the guards. Shevaughn drove her sleepy daughter home, tucked her in, gave her Eskimo kisses and, after leaving the door slightly ajar, went to her room. She took the Elliott file out of her briefcase, wondering if she missed something. She didn't think so. This mystery man was their only lead.

Chapter Seven

THE NEXT MORNING, he woke up early with an intuitive warning bell going off in his head just minutes before the alarm clock. Tightening the belt of his silver silk robe, he went to his front door, opened it, bent down to pick up the folded Portsborough Journal and saw half of his reflection staring back at him. Instinctively, he quickly began to step back into his apartment, except he looked down the hall and saw all the other copies of his profile lined up in front of his neighbors' doors. He began to scurry like a trapped rat, picking his likeness up from every doorway. His arms full, he ducked back into the apartment, at first relieved no one spotted him in his petty theft and then he realized he couldn't get rid of all the copies they'd printed. Furious, he sat at his kitchen table and quickly read the accompanying article. When he saw Detective Shevaughn Robinson's quote, he felt a chill of uneasiness run down his spine. *It's the same bitch cop that took Terri's husband down! This doesn't bode well, not well at all. She's fucking up my game.*

He got up and paced around his kitchen until he realized the futility of his actions. This didn't do him any good, so he stopped, sat back down, took several slow, deep breaths and tried to calm down. When his heartbeat finally returned to normal, he dialed Terri and nonchalantly invited her to lunch. As soon as he got off the phone, he hastily packed his duffel bag and got ready to run. At the door, he stopped for a moment to collect his thoughts. He went back to his closet and got the gun he kept hidden in the right corner of the top shelf, underneath his sweat suits. As he reached for it, he reflected back on a time when he'd been so sure that one day he would be famous. At first he thought he would get recognition for his musical talent, although the late Justin Holland seemed to be the last black classical guitarist the public acknowledged.

Now he stared down the barrel of his future and that alternative still seemed better. He knew he would never allow himself to be arrested. He couldn't go to prison, much less Death Row, especially since in New York that translated into a life sentence without possibility of parole. The thought of being imprisoned forever with those common criminals, with society's sewage, became unthinkable. *It will never happen.* He'd rather chat with Satan first.

Hoping he wouldn't be forced to use it, he burrowed the gun in the bottom of the bag under his clothes. *I've got to get out of here before someone turns me in.* If his luck ran out and he eventually got caught, well, he'd just have to cross that bridge when he came to it.

He hastily leashed Khan and left his place in an upheaval for the first time in his life. Before stopping at the local branch of his bank to withdraw two grand, he made a quick detour for one last glimpse of his club and taxi stand. He chose the route that took him past the gas station and saw everything appeared as it should. He didn't know how long his secret would be safe. He just knew he should leave before they found out. Escaping Portsborough, it took all his restraint not to push the speed limit.

The red and blue blinking lights in the rearview mirror grabbed his attention and he glanced at the speedometer to make sure he couldn't be getting pulled over for speeding. Even though the speedometer indicated he'd beat the limit by only five mph, he slowly raised his foot, no more than a quarter of an inch and slowed the car down. He realized he'd been holding his breath and exhaled deeply when the police car sped up and went around him. He could feel and hear his accelerated heartbeat and this time it didn't come from excitement. It came from sheer terror.

He saw the look of surprise on Terri's face when he showed up at her door so early. He knew she probably expected him to show up closer to noon and he'd prepared for her questions.

"What's wrong?"

Too early for the loan scheme, he'd thought of an alternative twist to his story during his ride over.

"Terri, I know we've only known each other for a relatively short time, yet I need to ask for a favor. I don't want you to think of me as a cad or an opportunist and I'm embarrassed to admit I need your help. Wait...," he said when she started to speak. He came to her, gently took hold of her shoulders and looked directly into her eyes. "I don't want to frighten you. I've made a couple of bad decisions lately and there are some pretty disreputable people out there looking for me. I know it's seems presumptuous, nevertheless I wondered..."

He paused at exactly the right moment.

"If you'd allow me to stay here with you for a few days, a week tops, just until I can get my finances in order and see what I can do to fix this situation. I need to get these people off my back. Do you think you could stand to have me as a roommate for a while?"

Who the hell says cad or opportunist in a real conversation? She couldn't remember the last time a man asked her for help, yet Terri still recognized bullshit when she heard it. He talked as if he lived in the roaring 20's, too many black and white flicks. She smiled, trying not to let him know her suspicions. The only reason Eric got away with deceiving and controlling her were the toxins he'd constantly given her. Well, she'd been drug and alcohol free for almost four years, so she had a clear mind. If he thinks he can get over on me, he's got another think coming. She'd always wanted to think that. She found it difficult not to laugh and almost choked holding it down. You wanna play? I can play.

"Of course, you can stay. You'd do the same for me, wouldn't you?"

"Definitely, I'm glad Kayla and Khan get along so well, that would have been a problem."

"Do you need to go home and get some of your things?"

"No, I packed a small bag. It should do me for a while."

You were that sure of yourself, weren't you? Maybe she could use his ego to her advantage. If she could get something out of it, that would make it worth her while. She instantly knew what she wanted.

"Okay, put your bag in the guest room. And since we're talking about favors, I do have a small one to ask as well. I need an escort to the Humane Society Gala next month. Would you care to join me?"

With him on her arm, she'd be the talk of the event.

He knew she couldn't say no. Not only did she agree to let him stay, she freely gave him what he'd thought he would have to work for to achieve. He made note to be the most helpful and considerate roommate possible.

"Of course, I would be honored to. We do make a striking couple, don't you think?" He continued before she could answer. "Why don't we stay in and I'll make us brunch? I'm sure I can find something to whip up."

He opened the door with its new-fangled automatic ice cube and chilled water dispenser and quickly found some eggs, chives, broccoli florets, Swiss cheese and Canadian bacon. He spotted an opened quart of orange juice on the top shelf and a bottle of champagne on the bottom shelf of the door. A half loaf of cinnamon raisin bread sat on the counter.

"See, this'll work just fine. I can make omelets, raisin toast and mimosas."

The first time he'd seen her kitchen he'd thought he'd died and went to gourmet heaven. It would have made a chef drool. He'd never seen a kitchen that large outside of a store display. Then she'd confessed she didn't like to cook, she just wanted the top of the line. He remembered the sizzling sex they'd shared right there and felt himself harden. Talk about if you can't stand the heat...

"After brunch, would you mind if I took a look at your sailboat? Maybe I can do a little maintenance, get her up and running. Have you ever been out on it?"

"No, would you believe the previous owner moved to Manhattan and included it in the sale of the house?"

"Well, his loss, your gain. I'll take a look at it. I bet we'll be sailing in no time."

Ever since their first volatile encounter, Shevaughn deliberately avoided The Book Nook, thus avoiding Mr. Williams. That's not to say she didn't think of him or his smile. She'd been without a man for such a long time and although her family and job kept her occupied, she missed the companionship she and Tony briefly shared. She always faced life on her own, yet lately she wished she could confide in someone.

She'd never been very good at making friends. People acted strange and kept you at a distance when they found out you were a former foster child. Shevaughn thought they feared she would try to steal their family's affection. So to protect herself, she put up an emotional wall, convincing herself that others would just interfere with her goal of becoming the best police officer possible. That's why she'd devoted all her energy to her career. She only needed herself to prove her capabilities as a good detective and a good mother, hell, a great mother to their child. Her parents would have expected nothing less from her and she expected no less of herself. That's just how she lived her life.

Every morning, Shevaughn stopped at the newsstand located in the office-building lobby across the street from the precinct. It always looked pretty deserted at that time in the morning. Shevaughn picked up her newspaper, pleased to see the reporters made good their promise. They'd followed her instructions from the previous day. She handed the cashier a quarter and hurried to leave. She didn't notice the man next to the card stand until he touched her arm as she brushed past him.

"Excuse me," she mumbled when something in the touch caused her to stop and look up. There stood Marcus!

"Are you following me?" she asked, not hiding the annoyance from her voice.

"No, hey, look...we've seemed to have gotten off on the wrong foot."

"We're not 'getting off' anywhere."

Her animosity even shocked her. Something about him seemed to bring out the worst in her.

"Okay, okay, no need to get your drawers in a bundle."

"My drawers aren't your concern."

As the words left her mouth, she realized she sounded asinine and couldn't keep the embarrassed smile off her face.

"Ah, so you do have a sense of humor."

"Sure, when something's funny."

"Okay, can we end this war and play nice?"

"I didn't realize we were at war."

"Then why do I feel so wounded?"

"Oh, please…"

"No, look, I said something that made you angry, though I don't have a clue what. And I've already apologized. Didn't you get the flowers I sent?"

Am I being too hard on him? He couldn't have known his statement brought back terrible memories. He sounded so sincere and the message with the flowers had made her smile …a little.

"Yes, I did. Thanks."

She still didn't want to give him too much credit for the gesture.

"Okay, I admit I may have been a little over sensitive," she confessed. "And I'd really love to stay and chat, except I've gotta get to work."

"If you really mean that, maybe you can explain it all to me over dinner tonight?"

"You are the persistent one," she said, while thinking she actually liked that quality in him.

"I'm only talking about dinner. What harm could it do?"

"I don't think it would be a good idea, Mr. Williams, at least not tonight. Now if you'll excuse me, I really have to go."

Marcus sidestepped her and blocked the aisle, preventing her exit.

"Come on. Why are you being so difficult, really?"

"Honestly, I don't even know if I could handle telling you the whole story."

"All I'm saying is...if you need someone, a shoulder, I'm willing."

"Why? You don't even know me?"

"I want to, Shevaughn Robinson. I want to know everything about you. Come on, please reconsider. I'll be on my best behavior, promise."

Just the thought of letting go brought her a sense of relief. She hesitated for a moment and then relented.

"Can I get back to you on that? I have to check on a sick friend. She's in the hospital."

It even sounded weak to her, although it was the truth.

"Maybe I can call you later this afternoon? We could set something up then?"

"I know, after you check on your sick friend. What do you say to us meeting here at six or I could meet you at your job?

Shevaughn thought of the looks and comments her fellow officers would give her if this fine man came to her office. She didn't need to be the subject of gossip right now. It would only make life unpleasant.

"No, I ..."

She realized she didn't know what to say.

"It's okay. I'll be here at six on the dot."

"No, wait for my call, I can't promise," she answered, rushing to the door. Shevaughn glanced back in his direction, relieved to see he wasn't following her. Then she saw him talking to an attractive young Black woman and watched as she smiled up at him with adoring eyes. *Oh, so that's how it is? Like I'd let some apprentice Romeo test his game on me.* Right or wrong, Shevaughn decided she would not be calling Mr. Williams today and hurried across the street to the precinct.

When she stepped off the elevator, she could actually feel the undercurrent of excitement. She didn't have a chance to wonder why before Jared met her at the door.

"Waiting for me?"

"Lady, the phones have been ringing off the hook since the morning news went out. EVERYONE has seen this guy EVERYWHERE! I swear there have been at least fifty calls."

"Any good leads?"

"I'd say...at least two of them, one is an apartment building on Dygan, he lives there, the other is a Thai restaurant on McMath, he's a regular. They've both positively identified him, said they've known the guy for years."

"His name, Jared, what's his name?"

"Jacques Diamante."

"Jacques...J. or Jay," she thought aloud.

Hey, hold on, just wait a damn minute, this coincidence is a little too bizarre for me. Jacques Diamante, that's Jack Diamond, Jack of Diamonds, Ace of Hearts... what the...the game continues? Could there be a possible connection between him and Eric Becker? Does he know about me? She wondered if she suffered from a case of paranoia which led her to leap to the wrong conclusion. After all, what were the odds? She knew if they could find a connection, the press would have a field day. She'd have to keep this to herself and not to let them know her suspicions. *Well, not really suspicions, you're just speculating, there's probably nothing to it, there can't be, can there?*

"Jared, I need you to go talk to those two. Get me everything you can on him, I want to know his entire life story from birth up to and including what he ate for breakfast this morning. In the meantime, I'm going to take a good look into his bank records. They may tell us something."

Jared quickly left, a man on a mission. He went to the apartment building first and talked to Mr. Colón, the building's lone security guard. When he showed him the sketch, Mr. Colón recognized their tenant right away and didn't object to letting the police into his penthouse apartment.

Jared looked around and couldn't help noticing that the apartment, although decorated in excellent taste, seemed to lack any personality. He noted the only picture on the fireplace mantle showed three Black women in some kind of native Caribbean attire. He wondered if they were his family. It quickly dawned on him that all the walls were blank and the place seemed rather cold and impersonal. It reminded him of an unfinished model home. Jared walked around and noticed hints of someone leaving in a hurry. There were clothes hanging out of the armoire drawers, dishes on the table and in the kitchen sink.

"It certainly looks like he got the hell out of here. What does this guy do for a living?"

"He owns a club down in Little Haiti."

"You wouldn't happen to have the address?"

"Not offhand, but I can get it for you. I'm sure it's in the building manager's files."

Jared followed the guard to the small, closet-sized glass security room. It was hidden behind the elevators, at the back of the lobby. He watched the guard dial the manager, who must have wanted to speak to him directly because he immediately handed him the phone. Jared explained why they were looking for Diamante and the manager gave him the address of his club.

"Thank you, sir, you've been very helpful."

He handed the phone back to Mr. Colón and heard him say, "Sure, no problem," before he hung up.

"Boss says I should help you any way I can."

"Well, you've been great. Look, I gotta get a move on. Here's my card, if you think of anything, call me. I really appreciate your help. Thanks."

"You're welcome, sir, no problem. I wouldn't feel right if I didn't tell you I think the police are barking up the wrong tree this time. It's hard to believe that Mr. Diamante would have anything to do with this...sort of thing, he's such a refined gentleman."

"We just want to question him, not arrest him."

Jared thought they both heard the "yet" at the end of his sentence.

"If I see him, I'll call you."

"I'd appreciate that."

On his way to the restaurant, he thought about the apartment. *Something wasn't quite right with Mr. Jacques Diamante.* He could feel it. Realizing he'd pass the club on the way to the restaurant, he decided to stop there first.

The Club Komba didn't look like much more than a storefront from the outside. The protective metal grate that covered the front of the building must have been broken since it still blocked a small portion of the door even when the club opened for business. Three blacked out windows and a matching blacked-out glass door broke up the brick exterior. You couldn't see inside. When Jared walked in, the patrons who were boisterously laughing and slapping cards on the table instantly stopped and silently waited. They knew a cop stood in their midst and they knew why. They'd all seen "Diamond" in the news. Well known in Little Haiti, they believed the police were railroading him. Everyone knew how much the police hate a legitimately successful Black man. The fact that they'd sent another Black man to ask the questions added insult to injury.

"May I help you?" the bartender reluctantly asked as he wiped down the fake black granite counter. The Haitian flag colors were represented by the black and red imitation leather quilted bar front which didn't have quite the luxurious Caribbean look Jared thought the owner tried to accomplish because quite a few of the gold metal studs were missing.

"I'm looking for Mr. Diamante, is he here?"

"No, we haven't seen him at all today."

The bartender kept his head down and concentrated on an imaginary spot on the Formica.

"Hey, sir, would you mind looking at me while we have this conversation or would you like to continue it down at the precinct?"

He stopped cleaning, rested his forearms on the counter and stared Jared directly in the eyes, showing him the police didn't scare him. Jared stared back.

"Is that unusual, seeing as it's his club and all?"

"Is what unusual?"

"The fact that the club is open and he's not here."

"No, sometimes he doesn't show up until sundown. Most nights he's here to close the place up at 2 a.m."

"Well, if you see him, give him my card and tell him to give me a call or you can call me yourself. We'd like to ask him some questions."

The bartender took the card and without looking at it, placed it in the cash register drawer slot under the twenties.

Jared drove to the taxi stand next. Neither the dispatcher nor the mechanic could help him with any pertinent information regarding the owner. He gave his card to the dispatcher, wrote down the stand's number and left for the Thai restaurant.

When he showed her his picture, the hostess recognized Diamante immediately. She could only tell Jared what his favorite lunch consisted of. Heading back to the station, he hoped Shevaughn ended up finding something a little more concrete.

Chapter Eight

SHEVAUGHN CALLED ALL the head branches of the major banks in the tri-state area. After identifying herself, she asked for the records of a particular depositor named Jacques Diamante. Eleven or twelve calls later, she got a hit and a woman transferred her to their bank manager. He confirmed Mr. Diamante as one of their customers and then refused to discuss anything more with her over the phone. Though she tried to convince him otherwise, he vehemently stuck to his decision.

"Then I guess I'll be there as soon as possible."

"With a warrant, I hope."

"So do I. Goodbye, sir."

She scribbled down the address and made a call to the court. She explained the circumstances and requested the warrant. When Jared returned from setting up the twenty-four hour surveillance of Diamante's apartment, she held up her index finger, indicating that he hold on a minute and finished speaking to the court clerk. Jared sat at his desk and waited for her to hang up.

"Jared, we need to get moving. I'll explain in the car."

While driving, she told him about locating the bank account and the manager's insistence that they obtain a warrant before coming to see him. He told her about visiting the slightly peculiar penthouse apartment and the club that must have seen better days. He also told her that the officers who'd been canvassing the Elliott neighborhood didn't find one neighbor that could give them any pertinent information.

"She pretty much kept to herself. A couple of them said they only saw her in the morning when she got her paper or sometimes she'd leave in her car, usually coming back with groceries. The only visitors who stopped by were a young lady and a younger boy. The neighbors assumed it was her daughter and grandson. No one remembers seeing anyone else, especially a Black man."

Shevaughn pulled into one of the courthouse parking spots reserved for official visitors and Jared hopped out, taking the stairs two at a time. He returned in less than twenty minutes, warrant in hand. By the time they pulled up in front of the bank, she knew they were on the right track. They needed to determine if Mr. Diamante made a healthy deposit around the same time as Mrs. Elliott's withdrawal.

The tall building loomed in front of her and Shevaughn stretched her neck like a tourist to look beyond the endless rows of shiny windows until she could see the top of its thirty-eight floors. In the small park area to the left, the branches of the trees seemed to be extending themselves as if they were reaching for the roof. She saw a few of the leaves were already starting to change to the bright oranges and reds of fall. She took a deep breath and they walked through the impressive glass and aluminum doors. The bank took up the whole first floor.

Dapper in his navy blue double-breasted suit, Mr. Pittman, the bank manager, waited, nervously pacing in the entrance and quickly ushered them past the customers and tellers' counter to his office. He closed the door and with a wave of his hand indicated, they should both take seats in the two leather maroon barrel chairs in front of his large, executive Burl desk. Before sitting, Shevaughn handed him the warrant. He carefully looked it over, sat down and placed it on the corner of his desk. When he started speaking, he leaned forward, resting his clasped hands on the file in front of him and whispered as if he were telling a secret.

"I find it a tad distasteful speaking to you when it's in regards to one of my most loyal customers."

"Not as distasteful as murder of the elderly, I'm sure."

"I read the news and find it hard to believe he did what you're accusing him of. Mr. Diamante has been one of our best customers for close to forty years and his uncle before him."

"We've been hearing that a lot, what a nice, distinguished gentleman he is. Nonetheless, I need to know if he made any unusually large deposits lately, say, within the last two to three months."

Mr. Pittman opened the bulky file containing Mr. Diamante's account history.

"Yes, this shows one large deposit early last month for one hundred thousand dollars. Admittedly, it's considerably larger than the norm."

Shevaughn and Jared shared a glance. Bingo! They had him.

"Now I want you to go as far back as possible and identify any other large deposits he may have made."

Mr. Pittman examined the account and after several minutes, came up with another seven deposits. They started over thirty years ago.

"I'll need copies of all eight deposits."

"I think I should speak to legal before releasing this."

"Talk to whomever you'd like, just know I'm not leaving here without them. You looked at the warrant. Did you happen to notice the attached subpoena for specific records or do you wanna explain your hesitance to cooperate to Captain Campbell? And then there's always the charge of obstruction of justice."

"There's no need to threaten me or involve your Captain. I'll be right back, excuse me." Mr. Pittman hurried out of his office.

Someone must have instructed him to be as helpful as possible because he came back almost immediately with the copies in hand.

"Has there been any recent activity, like in the last day or so?"

"He did make a withdrawal in the amount of two thousand dollars this morning."

So he's probably already on the run.

Shevaughn and Jared went to Captain Campbell with all they'd found so far, knowing he'd say they could issue an arrest warrant. He didn't agree.

"I think there's enough for probable cause," she argued.

"Well, it's a good start, but it's still all circumstantial, you both know that. What do you really think you have? There's no witness, no fingerprints, no weapon, no motive and the list goes on. You need to get out there and find me something concrete, something we can nail this guy with when we find him. Once he's caught, we can't let him get away due to insufficient evidence."

Disappointment made them even more determined. They went back to their office and worked overtime; going through the little evidence they'd accumulated, trying to find something to solidify their case. It seemed the Fates were against them. Tired, they decided to call it a night and start fresh in the morning.

As they were about to leave, the door opened without a knock and there stood Marcus.

"You weren't going to call me, were you?"

"Excuse me...how did you find me?"

"Locating the famous Detective Robinson isn't a difficult task. Besides, I saw you enter this building when you left me this morning."

Shevaughn caught the puzzled look on Jared's face.

"Left him this morning? You know this guy?"

Jared's reaction bordered on comical. He took a deep breath and seemed to puff up before their eyes, like a blowfish. He looked Marcus up and down, as if sizing him up for a beating.

"Jared, Marcus. Marcus, this is my partner, Detective Jared Benjamin."

"Nice meeting you, Jared," Marcus said tersely and turned back to Shevaughn.

"Detective Benjamin," Jared informed him, stepping between them.

"Look," Marcus said as he sidestepped Jared and stood facing Shevaughn.

"All I want to know is why you stood me up?"

"Can we discuss this some other time, preferably at some other place?"

"No, I think I deserve an answer right now."

"She said 'not now'."

Jared's temper started to show.

"This is none of your business."

"Well, I'm making it my business," Jared countered.

"Boys, boys, come on, cool it. Jared, I can handle this, please. I'll see you in the morning."

Shevaughn and Marcus watched Jared leave and saw him shoot Marcus a "you-better-watch-yourself" look. Then they turned their attention on each other.

"I'm not sure why you insist in chasing me. It looks like your schedule is pretty damn full."

"I have no clue what you're talking about."

"Well, let me refresh your memory. I didn't get out the store before you redirected your attention to some other woman."

"Huh? Who?"

He surprised her when he broke into unexpected laughter. That really rubbed her the wrong way.

"What's so funny?"

"You're jealous...of my sister!"

"Jealous? I think not...your sister?" She rolled her eyes. "Is that the best you can come up with?"

"I'm telling you she's my sister, Kennedy. She's a senior at LaGuardia Community College. Even if we weren't related, she'd be a little young for my taste. We ate breakfast together this morning. We try to do that at least once a month. If I need a witness, I can give her a call right now. You can talk to her yourself. May I use your phone?"

He picked it up without waiting for her to answer.

As she watched him dial, she began to feel a little silly. *Maybe I did jump to the wrong conclusion?* When someone answered, she heard him say, "Hey, Girl, I want you to say Hi to a friend of mine," and then he handed the receiver to Shevaughn.

"Hello?"

After introducing herself, Kennedy chattered on about what a special man her big brother grew up to be and how much he needed a good woman in his life. She even warned her that she'd have to pass inspection from the other members of their family. Obviously, he'd been talking about her. When the conversation ended, she hung up, embarrassed at how apologetic she felt.

"Okay, so you're telling me a fine man like you is single and available?"

"Why's that so hard to believe? Hey, you think I'm fine?"

Shevaughn ignored the last question.

"I get your point. I made a mistake, sorry."

"Yes, you were and I think the only way this fine man will accept your apology is over dinner."

He wouldn't let her comment go.

"I really need to call home first."

"Do what you gotta do."

She called Nonna and tried to explain why she would be late. The woman wouldn't budge. She suggested Shevaughn come home as soon as possible so she could spend time with Ariel at the hospital.

"Hold on."

She turned to Marcus.

"I can't do this tonight. I need to go home to my daughter, so her grandmother can visit our friend."

"The friend in the hospital? Have to admit I thought you were giving me the business."

"Guess we were both wrong."

"So you're asking for a rain check?"

"Yes, Mr. Williams, I think I am."

"Apology and rain check accepted on one condition. You start calling me Marc."

"Fine, Marc and call me Von."

"Well, Von, it looks like we've just gotten over our first hurdle."

He took out his business card and wrote on the back.

"Here's my home number. Why don't you give me a call when your friend gets out of the hospital and you have some free time?"

"I will."

Shevaughn took the outstretched card and placed it in the zippered compartment of her black leather purse.

"Sorry, I really gotta go."

"May I walk you out?"

She nodded affirmatively. When he opened the door for her, she looked up into his face and realized, at her five feet seven inches, she felt petite. *He's taller than Tony.* Stop comparing, she admonished herself.

When they got to the parking lot, she looked around.

"Where's your car?"

Marcus gave her a sheepish grin.

"I didn't drive. You made me so mad that I walked here from the Nook. Double time, I might add."

"That's over a quarter mile away!"

"I guess anger gives me motivation."

"Are you sure we're cool now?"

"We're cool."

"If you'd like, I can drive you back."

"I'd really appreciate that, feels like I've run out of steam."

"I can relate. Hop in."

Shevaughn drove him back to his store, sneaking glances at him the whole way.

When she pulled up to the bookstore, he hopped out and looked into the car window.

"You sure we're okay? I know the ride lasted less than ten minutes, but you didn't say a word the whole way." It was important to her that this ended on a positive note.

"Well, neither did you, and yeah, I'm fine"

Yes, you certainly are.

"Thanks, I owe you."

"No, I'd say we were pretty even."

"Well...get home safe."

"Thanks, night, Marc."

"Night, Von."

On the drive home, her mind wandered and she found herself fantasizing about how competent Marcus would be in bed. Something told her she wouldn't be disappointed and she smiled at the prospect. When she arrived, Nonna and Toni were ready to go. They'd been discussing why Toni couldn't see Ariel in the hospital and she didn't agree with what Nonna told her.

"Don't like her one bit."

"Don't like who, Puddin'?" Shevaughn asked and knelt in front of her daughter. Toni was wearing the cutest little pink and brown patchwork jean set. It consisted of a matching brown tank top with a pink organza butterfly on the front and brown denim pants with pink straps. When Nonna combed her hair, she'd parted it in the middle, made two pigtails and then brushed them around her finger until they were spiral curls. She looked too adorable to be so unhappy.

"I don't like Rules. Nonna says Rules say I can't see Auntie Real. Rules should mind they business. I'm mad to Rules. She's my Auntie Real."

To emphasize her position she pouted and crossed her arms.

"Honey, Rules isn't a person. It's a...umm, people make rules to guide..."

Shevaughn looked at Nonna for help and noticed her conspicuously looking up at the ceiling, deliberately avoiding her silent plea for help. She knew she wouldn't get any help from her. How do you explain rules to a three year old? She decided to try another tactic.

"Besides, it's only until she leaves the hospital and then you can visit her as much as you want."

"She's gettin' out soon?"

The news seemed to lessen her pout just a little.

"I hope so. I promise to ask the doctor tonight. Now come on, I'll go up first and after I see Aunt Ariel, Nonna will visit for a while and we'll be on our way home. You feel like pizza and sarsaparilla tonight?"

Currently, pizza topped Toni's list of favorite foods and she immediately forgot how upset she'd been a moment ago.

"Just cheese, no funny stuff."

Toni referred to mushrooms, pepperoni, sausage or anything other than cheese as "funny stuff".

"Half with, half without 'cause Nonna likes just cheese too."

"Count me out," Nonna answered. "After I go up, you two go ahead and have dinner. I'll stay and eat with Ariel and catch a cab home."

"You'd give up pizza for hospital food?"

"I made us a little Bistro Chicken with Fresh Asparagus."

"Dang, that's almost worth the heart attack. Did you clear it with her doctor?"

"Of course, Von, and I made it practically salt free. I know what I'm doing."

"Well, I know Ariel will be grateful. Come on, ladies. Let's get this show on the road."

Chapter Nine

THE NEXT MORNING, she and Jared were going through his notes, when Shevaughn saw a detail he neglected to mention in their previous conversation.

"He owns a taxi stand?"

"Yeah, it's right next to the club. Why?"

"Well, say you have a small fleet of cabs. Would you send them to any gas station or would you usually have, like...a contract with a certain company?"

"I'm sure some do either one," Jared answered.

"Let's find out which one Mr. Diamante preferred."

"What difference would it make?" Jared looked puzzled.

"I don't know, maybe we'll find someone else who knows him, someone he did business with?"

"I think you're grasping at straws, but I'll give the taxi stand a call."

When Jared hung up, his expression resembled the proverbial cat that caught the canary.

"They have a contract with Safeway and primarily use the one about five blocks from the club."

"Okay, let's get a search warrant and go take a look around."

They rode to the gas station and talked to the attendant. He couldn't tell them much and didn't really care. At the age of seventeen, he considered it just a job. He'd only been there for the last five months.

"Mind if we look around?"

"Sure, help yourself."

Around the back of the station in the far left corner, behind some high, dry weeds were several oil barrels. They looked like they'd been abandoned there for ages. Assuming they were empty, Jared attempted to move one of the fifty-five gallon drums. Its weight surprised him. He called to the attendant.

"Hey, man, what's in these?"

"Hell if I know, they were here before I started working here."

Shevaughn came over and shook the oil drum. She heard a sloshing, liquid sound come from inside.

"Open it."

Jared attempted to pry open the first rusty oil drum cap with no success. He couldn't open the other four either.

"I'm radioing the lab to send a truck. They'll get into them."

While they waited for it to arrive, Shevaughn took a closer look at the barrels. She ran her finger under the rim and felt a small welt.

"Hey Jared, it looks like someone may have carefully cut the entire top of these barrels off and then soldered them back on. Let's see if we can find a cutting torch or soldering iron inside and test them for prints."

The lab truck arrived while they were searching inside the gas station. Unable to locate the tool used to cut the barrels, Shevaughn instructed the lab tech to open one of the barrels. Using an acetylene torch, the technician made quick work of it. As soon as he finished, the smell of decay filled the air. She watched the tech put on the long rubber gloves that went way past his elbow. He reached in and slowly stirred the barrel's contents. Feeling contact with something solid, he stopped and pulled it out. He'd found a rather large bone, covered in used motor oil.

"God, is that human?"

"Yeah, looks like a femur. The size of the femoral head is small, so I'm thinking female or maybe an adolescent. We'll know more after we get it back to the lab."

"How soon will you have the results?"

"Well, it's gonna take some time to assemble the skeleton. If we locate the pelvic bone it would help a lot. I'm assuming the other barrels contain body parts too, so you're gonna have to give me at least a couple of days. Once we get the results, we'll immediately fax them to you."

"Do you think you'll find enough for us to identify the victims?"

"At this point, we can only hope. Look, they've finished loading the drums on the truck. I need to get a move on."

"Before you go, try some luminol on the back room. Hopefully, we'll find evidence that supports my suspicion that he dismembered his victims here. Something tells me he used this as his dumping ground."

The tech went to the lab truck and came back with a spray bottle. He, Shevaughn and Jared went into the gas station's back room and watched as he pulled down the tattered shades.

"Anyplace in particular you want me to start?"

"Try the worktable and the floor under it."

He sprayed both areas and the faint light blue glow showed the splatter pattern. They weren't ready for the copious amount of blood it revealed. It looked like a virtual slaughterhouse.

"Good Lord," Shevaughn whispered. "Guess that about says it all. I want you to photograph this and see if you can get some samples. Maybe we can match the blood type?"

"Considering how old some of this is, I can't promise."

"And you'll let us know if you find anything concrete?"

"You know it. We'll be talking soon."

As Shevaughn and Jared watched them leave, she reinforced what they both were thinking.

"Everything points to Mr. Diamante. We just have to wait for the coroner's report. Hopefully, we can finally arrest him. In the mean time, let's see what else we can find on this man."

However, no matter how far back they looked, the investigation into Diamante's past seemed to indicate it didn't exist. His history didn't go any further back than his mid-teens and since then it looked like he'd been a model citizen. Shevaughn found his uncle's death certificate dated two years after Jacques arrival in New York. Something told her that wasn't a coincidence. The problem being, to exhume his uncle's body would be almost impossible without some really hard evidence. Judged didn't grant exhumations on a whim.

Shevaughn thought she'd go crazy waiting for the lab results. She called the lab and demanded an explanation for the delay. They told her it would take them longer than they'd estimated. Somehow, the ratio of skeleton to barrel wasn't one to one. It turned out to be a massive, macabre jigsaw puzzle and they wouldn't release the results until they were sure they'd gotten it right. The various stages of decomposition became the key to solving the puzzle. Add that to that the fact they'd been soaking in oil for decades made it all the more difficult. There was nothing to do, but wait. Thank God, the hospital released Ariel the next day.

After work, she drove to the hospital, picked up Ariel and her few belongings and drove her home. Nonna and Toni were waiting at the door and when Toni first saw her godmother, she took a step back and silently ran to Shevaughn. They could see Ariel's drawn appearance frightened her.

"Mommy," she whispered. "She looks better now?"

"Yes, Puddin', she does. It'll take a while for her to get back to her old self and now that she's home with us, she'll get better every day."

"Rules was right. If she looked worser yesterday, I'd be scared to see her."

Shevaughn didn't bother to correct Toni's grammar. She knew exactly what she meant.

After she and Nonna got Ariel settled in, Toni got over her fear, hopped up on the bed and snuggled close to her godmother. Shevaughn made a quick phone call, changed clothes and checked on them a half hour later. Ariel and Toni were fast asleep. She stopped by Nonna's door and lightly knocked.

"Come in", Nonna said as she put her Bible down and patted the bed, indicating Shevaughn should come and sit next to her.

"Nonna, would you mind if I go out for a bit?"

"Go out, where?"

"I need to talk to a friend."

"You never mentioned a friend. Who is this new friend?" She put her Bible down, cocked her head and gave Shevaughn a curious look. "Why are you being so mysterious?" Then she answered her own question. "It's a man, isn't it?"

"What, you've got a crystal ball hidden somewhere? Yes, Nonna, it's a man. I'm sure you know him, Mr. Williams, he owns the Book Nook."

"No crystal ball, just noticed you changed into something more comfortable, as they say. So what's your friend's first name? I'm sure you don't call him Mr. Williams."

"What happened, your crystal ball got cloudy?"

Shevaughn dodged the question.

"Don't get smart with me, young lady."

"Marcus, his first name is Marcus."

Sometimes Nonna made her feel like a kid. Shevaughn wouldn't let her do it this time.

"I'll be back in a couple of hours."

"Just don't come home pregnant."

"Nonna!"

"I'm just saying it's been a long time since you've enjoyed a man's company."

"We're just catching a bite together. Jeez, you're making more out of this than it's worth."

"No, I'm not. Hey, I know you have good judgment. You go have fun, just remember to be careful."

"It's a good thing I love you."

"I love you too, that's the point."

Shevaughn smiled, kissed Nonna's cheek and left.

Traffic made the drive into Manhattan a little longer and parking turned out to be a little farther away than she'd anticipated, so Shevaughn ended up arriving late. As she walked up to the brightly lit restaurant marquee that announced Tad's, she saw Marcus patiently waiting next door in front of Sbarro's. He didn't complain about her being late.

"You look great," he observed and opened the door to the 42nd Street steak house for her with a flourish. Always one of Shevaughn's favorite restaurants, she loved the sight and smell of their fresh meats grilling in the front windows and the succulent chickens spinning on their rotisserie. The gauche interior with its red and black velvet T-patterned wallpaper and barrel chairs with red imitation leather cushions looked more like a dancehall or cheap bordello than a steak house, yet once you started eating you were inclined to forgot about the decor.

♥♦

He watched her as she walked towards him and it took all his resolve not to start grinning like some lovesick kid. Ever since they'd resolved the issue of her standing him up, she'd been sneaking into his thoughts. After her conversation with his sister, Kennedy gossiped to all their family members about Shevaughn, they were all waiting to meet her. She even found articles about her illustrious career. They told him they were hoping he'd introduce them to her soon and he totally agreed.

Now here she stood, looking better than he remembered. Up until now, he'd only seen her in a conservative business suit. Tonight, she wore a pair of black acid washed jeans and a sexy sheer white button down ruffled blouse that showed off her black lace push-up bra. She looked even sexier than he thought she could. She'd pulled her hair back in a neat ponytail with a few ringlets surrounding her beautiful dark chocolate face. As he quickly looked her up and down, he wished her outfit left a little more to his imagination because what he saw made it run wild.

She fascinated him. The old adage that you should be twice as good as your White counterpart to get half as far in your career rang true. He couldn't understand how this strong, intelligent, beautiful Black woman didn't have a man in her life. Maybe tonight she'd open up and let him in. He hoped so, in more ways than one. That thought brought a smile to his face.

♥♦

Going inside, she brushed past Marcus, turned slightly and looked up into his gorgeous smile. Every time she saw it, her mind would see his face just touching hers as he leaned in for a kiss. He looked like he could, mmh, mmh, mmh. *Girl, get your mind out of the bedroom.* Her mind refused to listen, so she tried to ignore it and began to tell him how they ran things at Tad's. Handing him a couple of red trays, she started giving him instructions.

"You need to get in line, pick the number of the dish you want and tell it to the cashier when he yells 'next' at you. Get me a # 6 with gravy on the side. I'll go find us a table."

He reached out, grabbed her hand and prevented her from running off.

"And a good evening to you too, Von. Why are you in such a rush?"

"Well, I did get here late. Sorry, I didn't mean to...I guess my social skills are a little rusty. It's been a while since I've done the dating thing."

"You don't need to apologize. It's just that nice and slow always works for me. Let's take our time, eat, talk and try to get to know each other. I'll be right back with our steaks."

As soon as she heard the words nice and slow, she imagined them together, gently making love. This guy really flustered her. Twice tonight she'd been made to feel like a teenager. Shevaughn found a table, grabbed a napkin and nervously wiped it off. She realized that her anxiety may be the reason her defenses were up so high.

If I could stop my heart from racing so fast, I'd be fine. She watched him walk towards her with the tray balanced on his right arm and two glasses of the house red in his left. *He's got skills, bet he's waited tables before.* She wondered what else he did well and felt warm from the thought that came to mind. *It has been a while...*

He put the glasses and the tray down and after placing the plates on their table, took the tray back to the counter. While alone, Shevaughn reached for her glass, took a sip of wine and prepared to accept the inevitable.

As soon as he returned, she said, "Okay, so what do you want to know?"

"Well, let's start with how you got into police work? Did you always want to be a cop?"

His question started a conversation that, between bites, lasted almost an hour. She told him about losing her parents, her childhood as a foster kid and why she'd decided to be a cop. By the time they finished eating, she'd told him about Tony and lastly, their daughter. Then she got to his "heartless" comment and what it meant to her.

"Geez, I'm so sorry. I would have never..." he started and reached for her hand.

"It's okay. I know you didn't say it to hurt me."

She finally let it all out and shared stories she'd held close to her heart. Admittedly, she felt better for it. As she told Marcus how she and Tony met, she remembered the first time they'd argued in the Chinese restaurant and realized verbal sparring might just be a part of her mating dance. Sort of like in elementary school when the boy with a crush on you made your life miserable. She then thought of her first confrontation with Marcus. Had she put up barriers to what she now recognized as an instant attraction? She watched him get his last piece of steak and followed the small morsel of meat to his mouth. He licked his lips and suddenly she wanted to do the same.

"Ever been here before?" Shevaughn changed the subject. She wanted out of this dangerous territory. Marcus didn't cooperate.

"No, I think I understand your choice. Guess it wouldn't do to pick someplace with a romantic atmosphere, would it?"

"That's not it. I just know a man usually appreciates a good steak at a good price."

She didn't mention she'd also wanted to go somewhere she hadn't been to with Tony.

"Know what I'd really appreciate?"

Somehow, she thought she did. She hoped he couldn't read her expression. She knew he'd missed it when he kept talking.

"A place with a touch more ambience, maybe a little privacy."

"And why is that?"

"Because then I could kiss you."

She pretended to be shocked.

"Mr. Williams, we don't know each other that well."

"Oh, so now it's back to Mr. Williams? You're killing the odds of a good night kiss."

"Not necessarily, we won't know 'til our evening ends."

"Well, then let's get the hell out of here. The suspense is killing me. Ready?"

"Yes, Marc, I think I am," she answered, referring to more than just leaving. She saw him hesitate and give her a questioning look and then he got up, took their plates and glasses, disposed of them and proceeded to walk her to her car.

A chill permeated the air. Without a word, he took off his denim jacket and placed it around her shoulders. The warmth from his body heat and his sexy Lagerfeld cologne surrounded her. She took a deep breath and let her senses enjoy his scent and how it made her feel. She closed her eyes for a second.

That's how he kissed her before she saw it coming. Shevaughn hesitated, remembering the last time a man kissed her by her car and the consequences she'd endured. *Cut it out, that's over and done with, thank God.* She put her reaction in check and responded. It quickly went from a get-to-know-you to a get-to-know-all-of-you kiss. He backed her up against the driver side and slipped his hands under his jacket, pulling her so close she could feel their rapid heartbeats. She also felt his hardness pressed against her and her body responded with a flash of heat. She nibbled his upper and lower lip and felt his tongue brush her lips. Shevaughn teased him with a tongue touch of her own, enjoyed the sweet melting sensation of the moment and then gently, reluctantly pushed him away. She didn't want this to happen so fast. She wanted to follow his lead and "take it nice and slow".

Marcus cleared his throat before continuing.

"Guess that answers the good night kiss question."

"I have a question of my own. Can we do this again and next time you pick the restaurant?"

"Of course."

"I enjoyed myself."

"So did I. Get home safe, okay? Call me when you get in."

"Will do."

On the drive home, although she didn't want to admit it, Shevaughn recognized this new feeling. For the first time in years, she felt optimistic. "Back in Stride Again" by Frankie Beverly and Maze came on the radio and she sang and rocked to the music. It felt good.

Chapter Ten

DANA DIDN'T SEE the newspaper until a few days later. As soon as she saw the sketch, she remembered the customer who'd snubbed her the week before, the one who wouldn't give her the time of day. *Pretty bastard, if he knew what I'm planning, he'd think twice about ignoring me now.*

Although she worked in the lovely town of Southampton, she lived in Riverhead, a small town less than twenty miles away. She saw her life on a totally different level. Her dad was an insurance salesman and her mom a secretary. Although both were honorable positions, they could never make living in Southampton a reality. Every day she watched people come into the café, sometimes spending more on one meal than she made working an eight-hour shift.

Immediately, she wanted to figure out a way to contact him. *Maybe I could get some money out of him or something.* She'd waited until late afternoon, hoping he might come back to the café. When that didn't happen, she began to ask around, trying to find out about the woman he'd been with that evening. There were plenty of folks who loved to gossip about their new neighbor, Mrs. Becker and some of them were Dana's co-workers. When she first moved into town, the story of her murdering husband and subsequent stay in an institution spread around town quicker than an accelerant assisted fire. After a few questions, it didn't take Dana long to find out where she lived. Maybe she'd drop by and see if he was still keeping company with the crazy Mrs. Becker. He'd seemed interested enough in her that night at dinner, so much so he'd barely given Dana a second glance.

Common sense outweighed her greed. They wanted this man for questioning about a murder. *No amount of money is worth risking my life.* She dialed the number listed in the article and when the police switchboard answered, she told the woman she'd seen someone who resembled the sketch in Southampton about a week ago. The switchboard operator told her to "hold on" and transferred her to Detective Benjamin because Shevaughn's line was busy. On the second ring, Jared picked up.

"Detective Benjamin, Homicide."

"I think I saw the man in the newspaper, only his eyes weren't blue, they were brown and his hair is darker than the sketch." Her words came out in a rush.

"Where and when did you see him?"

"He ate supper at the Baker's Dozen."

"Where?"

"The Baker's Dozen, it's an outdoor café in Southampton, 4290 Main Street. He was there about ten days ago."

"Do you have any idea where he might be now?"

"No, but I think you might wanna ask Mrs. Becker, Mrs. Terri Becker."

Jared almost dropped the phone. Holding his hand over the receiver, he told Shevaughn, "You gotta hear this," and put the call on speaker.

"Could you repeat that, please?"

"I said Mrs. Terri Becker may know where he is."

"What the f...?"

Shevaughn almost lost her professionalism. She managed to stop herself before she blurted out the third word. She rephrased the question and held her breath, waiting for the caller to answer.

"Why would you say that?"

"They were together when I saw him."

"Are you sure?"

Shevaughn felt the room spin and steadied herself by holding onto the corner of the desk. *I knew all along...*

"Yes, I'm sure. Hey, is there some kind of reward for this?"

"There may be. Please leave your name, address and number with the operator and we'll be in touch if the information checks out. I'm sorry, I have to go now. Goodbye."

Shevaughn called the operator back.

"I need you to connect me to the Southampton police."

Once they answered, she explained why they wanted to question Mrs. Terri Becker as a potential witness in the

Elliott murder. They agreed to meet her and Jared at the Becker home in two hours with a warrant.

The last two days were idyllic. She even liked his tofu scramble! They worked together on the boat and she actually helped, listening to his instructions and following them to the letter. She looked so good, his little shipmate. Today her hair was in a ponytail that hung to the side and she looked almost childlike. For a moment, he felt like the luckiest man in the world. Everything he'd done in life brought him to this moment. Somehow, the planets had aligned and brought them together. He wondered if the time had come for him to change his ways. Maybe he could find for real happiness. He knew that without her, he would return to his former life and suddenly, even with all that money, it didn't seem to amount to much.

Each night, although they should have been exhausted, they made intense love. Today, when he woke up late, he found himself actually smiling! This felt so right that, for the first time ever, he thought he might be comfortable enough to open up and tell her a little about his past. He'd never confided in anyone before because never trusted that they would keep his secret safe. Today that would all change. He sat up on the bed and she instinctively followed suit. She smiled up at him and he knew he'd made the right decision.

"I feel our relationship is very special to both of us and I want to open my soul to you."

When he started talking, at first, he purposely left out things he thought she would find repulsive. In order to win her sympathy, he made it sound like his family deserted him when they sent him to the States. When he thought she could handle it, he began to tell her part of his secret.

"I have a confession."

The words gave her a sinking, nauseous feeling in the pit of her stomach and her heart started pounding in her ears. She remembered the last confession she'd heard and how it ultimately changed her life. She didn't want to hear what she thought might be coming next, yet then again, she did. She wanted to know what he felt he needed to share.

"I'm afraid the police may become involved in looking for me very soon. I did some things that weren't exactly legal that associated me with certain people. They found one such associate dead and they think I may know something about it. Hold on, I'll show you."

She watched him put on his robe and leave the bedroom. Terri wondered how afraid she should be of his return and something told her to get up and run. Instead, she drew up her knees, rested her head in an upright fetal position and waited.

When he returned with only a newspaper in his hand, she realized she'd been holding her breath and finally exhaled. She relaxed and cracked a small smile. *What's he gonna do, spank me like a puppy?* Then she realized she never even missed not seeing the paper. *Has he been purposely keeping them from me?* A frown crossed her face as he sat next to her on the bed and spread it out in front of them. She saw his picture and looked up, puzzled.

His expression matched that of the saddest little boy, like one who just realized that divorce is final and Dad would never be coming back and her heart melted... until she look back down at the newspaper and focused on Shevaughn's name in the article. *She's Homicide. Good Lord, they think he murdered somebody!*

"Damn, Jay, what have you done?"

"Please, ma petite chérie, stay calm, let me try to explain."

"Cut the French crap and just tell me."

"Well, I knew this little widow who the police found dead a while back. Look, the last time I saw her..., there's no way to put this delicately..., the sex got pretty rough, especially for people of our age. When I left her, I swear to you, she was fine. Well, they found her with slit wrists. Even I don't believe she committed suicide, I mean, I'd just left her..."

This bastard is actually bragging about screwing this woman..., his associate, my ass. Terri covered her ears with her palms and began rocking back and forth, a low moan seeping out of the remnants of her soul. *This can't be happening, God damn you.* Suddenly, she stopped rocking, grabbed up the paper and began to read. It said the dead woman was sixty-eight years old, for Christ sake. She read Shevaughn's quote and didn't believe it one bit. *They want him for murder.*

"Please don't jump to conclusions."

Her response sounded like a witch's cackle, even to her.

"Conclusions, my ass, Einstein, she's Homicide. The police think you murdered that woman."

"Wait, listen, I can't go to jail, I didn't...I swear to you. I just don't know how to prove it. Mon Dieu, if I were guilty, would I be telling you now?"

She thought about it for a split second.

"Of course, you would. You just said the police might be looking for you soon. Now would be the perfect time."

"I see I made a mistake thinking I could trust you with this, I thought...you cared for me. I thought you'd believe in me."

She opened her mouth to answer when the sound of screeching tires caught her attention. He got up and walked to the window.

"They've come."

He knew she didn't believe him and now that they were here, he didn't have a choice. *I can't let them take me to jail.* He looked out of her bedroom window and watched the Southampton and New York state police cars pull into the driveway behind an unmarked lead car. He recognized Detective Robinson as she stepped out of it. *The bitch may have won again, only I'm gonna get the last laugh.* He ran to the bathroom, stepped into the shower, quickly closed the door and slipped the charcoal gray Ruger 9mm gun from his robe pocket. He saw Terri standing there, watching him from the bathroom doorway. She raised her hand and then stopped when he looked her straight in the eyes. Something in the darkest part of him made him say the one word he knew would get the most reaction out of her, something that would cut her deep.

"Shevaughn," he said, in his beautiful, bass voice. He spoke just loud enough for her to hear him clearly. He cherished the shocked look on her face during his last moments as he placed the barrel of the loaded gun in his mouth and felt the gunmetal rest on his bottom teeth. He angled the barrel up until it pressed against the roof of his mouth, felt the slight pressure of the trigger against his finger as if fighting the inevitable and with only a moment's hesitation, he won.

What he said registered just before she saw the blood splatter onto the back of the glass shower door and the small masses of bloody tissue appeared across the tiles on the back of the shower stall. *He'd said her name!* He'd probably gotten it from the article. Not only did his saying it bother her, the way he said it, as if he'd known her, as if he'd known their connection. It sent a chill down her spine. It sounded impossible, except she knew what he'd said, what she'd heard. Without realizing it, Terri bit down on the muscle tissue between her thumb and index finger until she tasted blood. She thought that would keep her from screaming, yet she could still hear the sound escaping around her or it could have been an auditory hallucination? She tightly shut her eyes and crumbled to the floor.

At the sound of the gunshot, the police burst simultaneously through the front and back doors, their guns drawn. Somehow, she knew Shevaughn would be leading the pack. It all made sense in this twisted scenario. Her familiar hatred flooded in. *She's here to gloat.*

"Terri, are you okay?"

"Yeah, right, like she cares," Jacques' voice whispered.

Terri shivered as she felt the breeze created by his ice-cold breath passing her ear, numbing the lobe.

"Ask yourself, ma petite, how is it she's been there when the only two men in your life died? She always brings you death."

She heard his voice! The trauma of watching the man she'd made love to last night blow his brains out right in front of her sent her from teetering on the edge of sanity back into a sky dive towards the depths of madness.

You're right. She's like a fuckin' curse. I almost forgot how much I hate her. Except you're here to remind me, you're here to keep me from straying from my goal. Keeping my eye on the prize, aren't you?

It took everything she had to keep the fury out of her voice.

"I had no idea...I didn't know..."

Without needing to, Terri pointed to the shower and watched as Shevaughn's attention focused on the blood-splattered glass.

Shevaughn tried to wrap her head around what just happened. She felt like she'd landed in an episode of "The Twilight Zone". *How could this case have led her back to Terri?* After all these years, she'd ended up in her worst nightmare. *This is like something out of a bad movie!*

She had slowly weaned Terri off her visits for both their sakes. Dr. Callaghan agreed that they needed the separation to heal. Terri needed to regain her independence and Shevaughn needed to stop dwelling on her loss. The sight of Terri always brought it all back.

She'd started out by going once a month. However, after the first six months, the visits dwindled down to once every other month then to quarterly visits. Last year, Shevaughn visited two or three times, tops. *I should have kept a closer eye on her, stayed in contact after they released her, maybe I could have seen this coming and I could have helped her avoid another tragedy. I needed to get on with my life, dammit, raise my daughter.* Yet she couldn't help how upset …and guilty she felt. Shevaughn supported Terri's body and semi-carried her to the doorway, turning her away from the gruesome sight.

"I want you to come outside and sit in the car," she said as she led her out of the room. She waved the other police officers off, took Terri to the car, sat her down and instructed her to move over, sitting next to her in the backseat. She made sure she blocked the car window to shield Terri from seeing the other two divisions gathering evidence and removing the body.

"Do you have someone you can stay with for a few days? It'll be a while before you can come back here."

"Come back here? Why the hell would I come back here? I never want to see this place again."

"Where will you go?"

"I don't know…, a hotel maybe. What will happen to my pets?" She didn't tell her Khan belonged to Jay. She knew he'd want it that way. "What's going to happen to them?"

Shevaughn knew where this conversation was going and it scared her. It didn't help that she knew guilt made up most of her motivation.

"How many pets do you have?"

"Six, three dogs, three cats."

Oh, great, the woman has a zoo!

Cat allergies prevented her from offering to look after them.

"Where are they?"

"Two of the cats are somewhere in the house, the other one is an outdoor cat and only shows up for meals. The dogs are out back in their dog run."

"Give me the cats' names and I'll see they're rounded up. I'm afraid they'll have to go to the Portsborough Animal Shelter for a while, allergies. I do have a little yard for the dogs."

"Are you saying I can stay with you until I straightened things out?"

"I'm saying I have to clear it with the Captain and my family, if they're okay with it, it's fine by me." As she spoke, she knew there was no turning back now.

So, this is what Kismet feels like. It made it almost worth losing Jay.

"You've not lost me, chérie. Just get into her house. We have a mission, you and I, don't you worry. I'll guide you."

This time the chill didn't seem as cold.

"Thank you, Detective Robinson, I promise it'll be only for a few days, a week at the most until I can find a place and see about putting the house up for sale."

"Okay, good. I have to go inside and give your cats' names to one of the officers. I'll send someone out to keep you company until I return."

♥♦

Shevaughn went back in, sent an officer out to the patrol car and told Jared what she planned to do. His frown told her he disagreed and his next words told her exactly how he felt about it.

"Woman, have you lost your mind? We both know that would be a big mistake. There's gotta be somewhere else she can go."

"She has no one, no friends or family. I'm the only visitor who came to visit her the whole time she lived in Blackstone and even I didn't go to see her as much as I should have."

"So what, now you're guilt trippin'? If you want my opinion, I think she'd be better off going back to that nuthouse. Watching a suicide couldn't have helped her sanity any. What about a women's shelter?"

"That would probably be worse than Blackstone. She seems fine, a little subdued, maybe she's in shock. She's thinking logically as far as I can tell. I think she's too fragile to be sent back there right now."

"Yeah, and that's just it. You're no psychiatrist. At least talk to hers before you go inviting this woman into your home."

As much as Shevaughn didn't want to admit it, she couldn't disagree. She would give Dr. Callaghan a call.

"Give me a minute," she said and left the room, going back into the bathroom. The attendants were just about to close the body bag.

"Did anyone test for gunpowder?" The attendants rolled their eyes and gave each other an "is-she-kidding-me?" look. Stevie Wonder could see the man committed suicide.

"Humor me, guys. Check both sides of his hands."

The attendant took the corpse's right hand and tested both sides for gunshot powder residue. They all saw the strangely calloused fingerprints.

"Bet that makes for some freaky fingerprints. See if you can match them with any you found in the gas station's back room."

Satisfied, she returned to Jared.

"Okay, I'll admit you've got a point. I'll call her doctor as soon as we get back to the precinct."

Back at her desk, she decided to call Nonna and get her opinion first. Shevaughn knew she wouldn't bite her tongue and she'd tell her how she really felt...and she did.

"I don't think I'd be comfortable with her in my house. Besides Saturday's the festival, is it your plan that she joins you for that too?"

She'd forgotten all about the festival. Since Nonna had already decided to stay home with Ariel, maybe she could talk her into adding Terri to the mix. Terri needed her and she couldn't let her down again. Maybe I can use a little reverse psychology...

"Well, I think Jared and I are capable of keeping an eye on her."

"Did you tell him what you're thinking about doing?"

"Yeah, I did..."

Shevaughn didn't want to tell Nonna he agreed with her. Then again, she didn't have to.

"He said you're as crazy as she is, didn't he?"

"Well, not in so many words and yes, he's on your side."

"I'm not taking sides. I just want what's best for my family."

"Please, Nonna, I'll sleep with Toni and she can have my room."

"And your boss is okay with this?"

Shevaughn couldn't fool this woman, so she didn't even try.

"I haven't asked him yet."

"Get his opinion and call me back."

Nonna hung up on her.

She called Dr. Callaghan before going in to see the Captain. He assured her that although Terri sometimes became verbally combative, he didn't see her as a threat to herself or others. Armed with that information, she felt certain she'd made the right choice. She placed the receiver back in the cradle and went directly to Campbell's office, not giving herself a chance to back down.

Might as well get this over with.

She rapped on his door three times and heard him say "Come in." He smiled as she entered the room.

"Well, you've been busy the last couple of weeks, closing two of your three cases. And I think the score will go higher when the lab finishes deciphering the contents of those barrels."

"I try not to keep score, sir. That would imply we were all playing some kind of game."

"Whew, are we in a mood? What's wrong? You should be proud of yourself."

"You may not think so when you hear my request."

"Well, I'd say you're in a great bargaining position."

She took a deep breath and began her story.

"Captain, I don't know if you heard, somehow Terri Becker is involved in the Elliott case. We found her with Jacques Diamante, the man who resembled the police sketch. She watched him kill himself when we arrived."

"What?"

"You heard me. Mrs. Eric Becker seems to have found another man we suspect may be a serial killer."

"What the hell is she, some kind of psycho magnet? Boy, she sure can pick 'em," he said, shaking his head in disbelief. "Does this have something to do with your request?"

"Well, sir...yes...she's alone and I wanted to see if you'd agree to her staying with me for a few days."

"You've got to be kidding me. And I'd let you do this because...?"

"For both our sakes, besides it could be good PR, I think."

She knew those were the magic words.

"And you really want to do this?"

"Yes, sir, just until she finds a decent place to stay. She'll be out by next week."

"I'm curious, what did Mrs. O'Brien say?"

"She wanted to know if you approved first."

"So she made me the culprit? Smart woman."

"I don't know what the big deal is? I'm doing what I feel is right. It's only for five days tops, promise."

"Alright, alright, if you're so gung ho about this, go for it."

"Terri and I thank you, sir."

She left before he changed his mind.

When she returned to their office, Shevaughn didn't make him wait to hear the decision.

"I cleared it with the Captain."

"Is the whole planet freakin' nuts? He okayed it?"

"Yep, I've got five days to get her situated. We'll start looking for a place on Monday."

"You gonna take time off before the lab gives us their final results?"

"Well, all I'd be doing is waiting on them anyway. I can afford to spend a couple of hours helping her."

Shevaughn called Nonna back and told her the Captain agreed.

"He did? I guess I underestimated your powers of persuasion. Well... since Ariel and I are staying home Saturday, she can stay with us. I'll keep an eye on her. This way, you, Jared and Toni can have a good time with no worries."

If only it were she, Marcus and Toni that were going. Shevaughn remained extremely cautious of the men she let her daughter meet. *Who am I kidding?* Jared's the only man who'd ever been to her house. She hoped maybe that would change in the near future.

She went down to the reception area where Terri waited and told her the good news.

"Let's go home and get you comfortable."

Nonna, Ariel and Toni were all a little apprehensive when Shevaughn brought Terri home. Her daughter picked up on the vibe and stood behind her grandmother, shyly peeking out at the stranger.

"Terri, I'd like you to meet my family, Nonna is Tony O'Brien's mother. Her name is Lorraine. Everyone calls her Nonna."

Ariel spoke up.

"I don't. She's Lorraine to me."

Shevaughn smiled.

"And this is Ariel, my good friend and my daughter's godmother. The little one is my daughter, Toni."

Toni ran to Shevaughn and whispered, "Mommy, is she your friend?"

"Yes, Puddin', she's gonna stay with us for a few days. I'm giving her my room and you and I will have a pajama party in yours."

"She doesn't wanna come to our 'jama party?"

"She's tired, she'll be better tomorrow."

"Like Auntie Real? She feels better today, huh, Auntie Real?"

"Yes, I do, Hon. Von, when you get a minute can I talk to you alone?"

"Sure, let me show Terri to her room and I'll be right with you. Come on, it's right at the top of the stairs. Let's get you settled."

Ariel watched Shevaughn and Terri leave the room. She didn't care what anybody said she knew something dark resided within this Becker woman and it had nothing to do with her dead husband. She was glad to be on the road to recovery. Something told her she'd be testing her psychic strength very soon.

"So what do you think about our new houseguest?"

Nonna asked Ariel's opinion.

"Let's talk later, 'little pitchers have big ears'."

"Huh?" Toni asked. Her brow scrunched up with a puzzled look on her face.

"Exactly, see what I mean? Toni, do you wanna watch The Muppet Show?"

"Yep, that's my favorite."

Nonna turned on the TV to sidetrack Toni's inquisitive mind. The two women chuckled as they went into the kitchen where they could talk without her overhearing.

"I'll leave you to get comfortable and rest. There's a nightgown in the third drawer from the top. Oh, and we'll need to go to the shelter in the morning to pick up your dogs and once they're here they'll have to stay in the backyard. Nonna won't allow them in the house."

"That's fine. I don't know how to thank you, Detective Robinson. You didn't have to do this."

"You could start by calling me Von. I know I didn't, I wanted to."

Shevaughn smiled and shut the door behind her.

As soon as Terri laid eyes on Toni, everything fell into place. Now it all made sense. She knew the caramel baby in her dreams belonged to Shevaughn and something told her that would change.

"Didn't I tell you that you needed to get into her house?"

The chill quickly became a welcome sensation.

"Yes, you did."

"And now you know why. Look at her. She's so beautiful, she could be our child. All you have to do, when the opportunity presents itself, is take her."

"That's not gonna be easy. There's always somebody with her."

"I'll tell you when, just watch and wait. Now you need to rest, ma petite. You have a big job ahead of you."

Terri sighed.

"Will I ever see you again?"

In answer to her question, a small gray whiff of what looked like steam and smoke began to take form, becoming denser, more solid until he slowly appeared to her, looking just like the day before his suicide, strong and sexy in his Levi 501 jeans and tight white t-shirt. He even wearing the Sperry Top-Siders she'd bought for him. She saw the smile on his handsome face and his beautiful eyes seemed even brighter that she remembered. Suddenly she felt safer and not so alone. She put on the nightgown and got under the clean, crisp rust-colored bed linens on Shevaughn's bed. Terri drifted off almost instantly. It had been a traumatizing, emotionally exhausting day.

Shevaughn walked into the kitchen and the two women immediately stopped talking.

"Okay, let me have it, get it off your chests."

They both began speaking at once.

"I think this is wrong and risky..." Nonna began.

"That woman has a dark soul. I see her in a black shimmer, like heat off a summer road," Ariel added.

"Aren't we being a little overdramatic? You two are acting like this is permanent, it's just for a few days."

"I don't know, Von..."

"Look, at least one of us will be with her at all times. I doubt she's much of a threat. Remember, she suffered, too."

"Time will tell," Ariel whispered. "Time will tell."

Chapter Eleven

TERRI WOKE UP with the eerie feeling of being watched. She opened her eyes and saw the one thing she wanted most staring back at her.

"Nonna says you hungry? She made breakfast."

"Good morning, cherié." The French term of endearment came out so naturally, it felt like he now existed inside her.

"I'm not Cherry, I'm Toni."

Terri laughed and thought of all the joy this child would bring to her life.

"Well, Toni, how are you today?"

"Okay. Mommy says come on. She says you're getting puppies today and then we're going to the festival."

"That sounds like fun. Do you like puppies?"

"Oh, yes, never got one though. Had a fish named Bubbles."

"Puppies are a lot more fun, you'll see."

Terri sat up and looked at the clock. It said 7:50! Her "nap" had turned into a full night's sleep.

"I'll be right out and after breakfast, we'll go get my puppies."

Going into the little pink and black-tiled bathroom in the center of the hall, she found the clothes Shevaughn left on the counter for her. Their style and size indicated they were pre-Toni. The teal blouse had shoulder pads and the jeans were wide-legged bell-bottoms. She's gained a little weight since then. As much as Terri hated to admit it, it looked good on her.

As she showered, she imagined her hands belonged to Jacques. She slipped her finger between her legs and began to stroke herself, all the while remembering the last time they'd made love. Made love, hell, they fucked like it could be their last time. Who knew that would turn out to be true? That depressing thought subdued her orgasm. She stopped, rinsed herself off and stepped out of the shower, unhappy and unfulfilled. As she wrapped the towel around her body, he slid behind her, helped her dry off and nibbled her ear before he spoke. She instantly climaxed and trembled from the cold and the heat.

"Now that's better, isn't it? You'll be fine, time and the child will heal your wounds, I promise. Do you believe me?"

"Yes, I do."

"Good, now what you need to do is get a copy of her house key. That's a priority. It's not going to be easy. They're all very careful, very observant. I'll try to help by telling you when. Now you need to finish getting ready and go get our dogs."

Terri dried between her legs and felt a tingle, a small remnant of her sexual excitement. She dressed in the hand-me-downs and went downstairs to the kitchen for breakfast although she'd lost her appetite.

"Morning, everyone," she said and caught the guarded look shared between the two older women. *The feeling is mutual, you opinionated old bitches. I don't like you either.*

Shevaughn stood in front of the vintage white porcelain Magic Chef and turned around to talk to Terri.

"Sit down. I hope you are hungry. We're having French toast and sausage. After breakfast, we'll go get your dogs and check out a few vacant apartments in town. I circled some in the paper, if you want to look." Before handing the paper over to her, Shevaughn removed any mention of the Elliott case or Mr. Diamante.

"I'm sure you found some good places."

The closer to her, the better.

Shevaughn placed the platter of French toast on the table when the phone rang.

"Hello, yes, this is Detective Robinson, yes, give me twenty minutes. Have you called Detective Benjamin? Well, call him and tell him I'll meet him at the precinct. I'm leaving now."

Terri listened as Shevaughn told old lady O'Brien what she'd learned from the phone call.

"I have to go in for a bit. The lab has finally put the oil barrel evidence in order. This shouldn't take long and when I get back, we'll get started on her apartment hunting."

Oil barrel evidence? Terri didn't know what she meant and wondered if it had anything to do with her or Jay. She did know this would leave her with the two old bitties and Toni. Maybe this would be her opportunity to snatch Toni and run.

"Hold on, don't do anything foolish. It's way too soon, ma petite. You just got here. Where do you think you would go? You need to bide your time, listen to me and wait. Have a little patience. I swear it'll all work out in the end. You have to trust me."

She trusted him with all her heart.

As Shevaughn drove to the precinct, she appreciated the weather. On the radio, the weatherman promised the temperature would reach the high seventies by mid-afternoon. The day seemed surreal, especially considering the gruesome details she would soon have to deal with. She hoped they could now somehow prove Mr. Diamante's connection to their shocking discovery. She parked her Audi in a spot closed to the entrance and while deciding if she should wait for Jared, he pulled into a parking space two cars away.

"Morning, Von. I can't believe they called us in on our day off. I guess we shouldn't complain since they've been working around the clock. Hope that means they've come up with something concrete."

"I just want to be able to close this case."

"So, how's your houseguest this morning?"

"Fine, why, what did you expect?"

"Look, since you're so determined to do this, I'll leave it alone. You already know how I feel."

"Yes, I do and I know you worry 'cause you care about us."

♥♦

My God, if only you knew...

He'd been fighting it all these years. That's why he'd jumped at the chance for the transfer, why he didn't visit so often. He thought the separation would fix the flurry of emotions that began when she first told him about her pregnancy. His first reaction to the news was anger and jealousy...and then shame. How could he be jealous of a dead man? That's just sick. He never let on because he feared his feelings would mess up their friendship, even though he wanted more, hell, he wanted it all, the woman, the child, the life...

"Hey, Jared, are you okay? Where'd you go?"

He snapped back to reality, the land of unrequited love.

"I'm sorry, you were saying?"

"I said you worry 'cause you care about us...maybe I'm wrong?"

He could tell his silence confused her and quickly changed the subject.

"Let's go see if the lab found anything we can work with."

♥♦

What the hell is his problem? Shevaughn didn't understand what just went down and she decided to ignore it. She didn't want anything else spoiling the day.

She went directly to her desk, picked up the thick report and began to read aloud to Jared. Suddenly the day didn't seem so beautiful.

"They found seven mutilated bodies in the five barrels, all women, their estimated ages between fifty and sixty-five. Cause of death is undetermined due to the bodies' extensive decomposition. They didn't find a weapon. If the victims were shot, they would have expected bullets in the bottom of the barrels, unless the killer had enough cunning to remove them from the body during dismemberment, so they're guessing stabbing or strangulation. All the victims died somewhere between 1955 and 1983. Damn, the length of time alone means this is starting out as a series of unsolved cold cases and now we have more questions than answers. There's no way the lab can connect them to Diamante. Something tells me it's not a coincidence that seven bodies plus Mrs. Elliott equals his eight largest deposits. You'd think someone would be looking for these women, I mean, family, a loved one, somebody? Let's look into all the cases of missing women in the same age group during that time span, see if we can come up with a match."

"You're talking about almost thirty years of records."

"I know it's a needle in a haystack, I say we put those new Commodore 64s to work. Maybe they can match them up by their dental records and if so, I want them to cross-check their IDs with their bank records and look for any large withdrawals."

Jared placed a call to the computer research department and put in the request, while she read to herself for a bit.

"They said to give them a few days," he told her as he hung up. She then shared the rest of the report results with him.

"It took the lab so long because after the killer dismembered the last two victims, he distributed their parts between the five barrels. That's why each barrel contained more than one body. Wonder why Mrs. Elliott never saw the inside of one of his barrels. Something changed. What happened?"

"Who the hell knows, Von? Maybe he lost the compulsion to hide them in plain sight or maybe the place wasn't as convenient for him as it used to be? Hell, Von, maybe he just got lazy in his old age. We could play this guessing game all day. Let's face it, without Mr. Diamante's confession, we'll never know. We're not even sure he's the one responsible for them all."

"He's the one. I can feel it. And it bothers me that at least one of these murders happened on my watch. Okay, so now what am I supposed to do? Forget about seven Jane Does and go on my merry way to a damn festival?"

"Got a better idea? Not to sound insensitive, but life goes on. Besides, you promised Toni. You don't want to disappoint her, do you?"

"No, I'm going back home to talk to Terri first. Maybe he told her something, who knows?"

"Okay, I can miss that. How 'bout I stop by on the way, say, give you an hour?"

"Yeah, that should work."

As they left the precinct, Shevaughn thought he would have something more to say. He surprised her again when he got into his car without even saying "Bye"! Something was bothering him and she knew he couldn't blame it all on the case. She stopped by the animal shelter, picked up Terri's three dogs and returned home.

Although she worried about having them in her car, she got them home without any problems.

Shevaughn walked in and found Nonna and Ariel watching Terri and Toni working on a giant coloring book.

"Terri, I picked up your dogs. They're out back. After you see them, can I talk with you for a moment?"

"Right now?" Terri sounded like a petulant child. "Can Toni come with me and meet my dogs?"

"Sure, I'll go too. Come on, Puddin'."

Shevaughn took Toni's hand and they all went to the backyard.

"Ooh, puppies!" Toni clapped and ran straight for Khan. The child showed no fear when it came to animals. For a split second, the Afghan made Shevaughn nervous. Then Khan walked right up to her little one and gave her a long lick that covered almost half of her face. Toni giggled, wiped her cheek on the shoulder of her creamsicle-colored t-shirt and gingerly patted the dog on the head.

"What's her name?"

"His name is Khan, she's Kayla and he's Baron," Terri introduced her Toni to the Afghan, Lhasa apso and the Spaniel Terrier mix.

"Oh, he looked like a girl to me."

"Probably 'cause of his long hair and his eyes look like he's wearing makeup."

"Yeah, it does!" Toni giggled. She looked so cute that Terri felt tempted to pinch her. She stood there and watched the child run around the yard with the dogs close behind. Nonna came to the back door after hearing Toni's laughter.

"She's having a ball," she chuckled. "If you two want to talk, I'll stay out here with her."

"Thanks, Nonna, Terri, let's go in."

Shevaughn led her back to her room and shut the door behind her.

"I need to ask you, what can you tell me about this Diamante guy?"

"Not much, we only met last month."

"And he lived with you?"

"No, he just stayed over for a few days. We were working on my boat."

"Good girl, try not to tell her anything I told you, not about Helene, not about me calling out her name before I pulled the trigger, nothing, understand? You wouldn't want me to leave and kill your chances of getting the girl, now would you?"

The thought chilled her more than his icy breath and she knew she had to keep her emotions hidden. She would tell her as little as possible.

"I need you to tell me everything you know about Jacques Diamante."

"Like what? I don't know much. He's just a man I'm attracted to."

"There's got to be more to it than that."

Why does she constantly refer to him in the present tense? She knows he's dead. We were there.

"He just started opening up to me. He talked a little about his childhood in Haiti and his first impressions of

New York. About the only thing I can tell you is he's good in bed. I don't think that helps your case any."

"I'm really not interested in anything that doesn't have to do with the Elliott woman's murder. Your sex life is your own business."

Terri thought back to the first time she'd laid eyes on him, sitting there at the café. She couldn't believe that happened only a few weeks ago. They'd been a regal pair, the man and his dog. Then she remembered the sex, the incredible, gut-wrenching sex and felt her loss all over again. She wanted him back.

"I'm here, ma petite chérie, I promised I'll always be here for you. That's what you want, isn't it?"

"Yes," she answered.

"What?" Shevaughn thought she heard Terri murmur something.

"Sorry, just thinking out loud."

"So, you're telling me you know nothing about him? Come on, how naïve can you be?"

"You think I'm lying to you? Why would I? Look, we were having a fling, that's all, nothing more. We were just beginning to know each other. Haven't you ever done anything like that? You act like you've never slept with a man without a background check first."

"I wouldn't go that far, Terri. I just thought maybe you could tell me something about him that we don't know."

"There's nothing to tell."

"It may have been something small, something you might think insignificant."

"I swear nothing comes to mind. If it does, I promise you'll be the first to know."

"That's all I can ask for. I'm going to get Toni ready."

"For the festival? I'd like to go."

"I'm sorry, I think it's best you stay here and take it easy."

"So, what, now this is my cell?"

"I want you to think of it more as your haven."

"She took you in, don't argue with her. You need some alone time. You're going to have to be at the top of your game to beat her, you know that. So far, she's always won. Don't waste your energy on such trivial things...a festival? Remember your goal, ma biche. Be nice."

For a second, she thought he'd called her his bitch! She then remembered a song from a French class long ago and realized he'd used another term of endearment. Biche meant doe, a deer, a female deer. I'll have to remember to teach Toni that song one day after we start our new life.

"You're right, and I'm sorry, I need to rest. Maybe that's why I'm so cranky. If you don't mind, I'm going to lie down." Terri quickly changed the subject. "Did I thank you for getting my dogs?"

"No, you didn't, it's okay. You go rest and on Monday we'll go back to your house, pick up some of your things and find you and your dogs a new place to live."

Better make it a two bedroom with a yard.

"Will you call Dr. Callaghan for me and postpone my appointment until the end of next week, so he won't think I'm making up empty excuses? I've got a lot to do next week. Hey, can I go get my cats?"

"Sure, I'll let him know and if you find a place Monday, we'll make sure your cats are dropped off there."

"I can't thank you enough. You were the only one I could to turn to. You've really been a friend when I needed one."

"No thanks necessary. I want to do this for you. You just take it easy and rest. I'll look in on you when we get back."

♥♦

Shevaughn left with an uneasy feeling after watching Terri's swift mood swings and her inappropriate comment about their sex life. She chalked it up to her recent trauma. She kept trying to make this as easy for Terri as possible. She'd already arranged for people to come in and clean up Terri's bathroom before the two of them returned late Monday morning to help avoid any additional reminders of death.

She returned to the living room and helped Toni finish coloring while they waited for Jared to arrive. It turned out to be quite therapeutic. Shevaughn decided calling Marcus would be even more beneficial.

"Hi, guy, enjoying your Saturday?"

"I'd be enjoying it more if you were here with me."

The sound of his voice gave her butterflies and she liked it.

"I think I would too."

"We could fix that. What are your plans for the rest of the day?"

"Jared and I are taking Toni to the Feast of San Gennaro."

"My whole family went year before last. We had a blast. Can you imagine a block party reunion with an all-you-can-eat buffet? If I invited myself, would you think I'm being pushy?"

"I like an aggressive man, question is can you handle an aggressive woman?"

"I'd like to take that test as soon as possible. How 'bout starting today?"

"Well, it's a public event. I don't think I could stop you?"

"Yeah, it's not like you could arrest me for showing up."

"Bet you'd like the idea of the handcuffs though."

"Never thought about it. Probably if you're the one putting them on me."

"I think that can be arranged."

"I'm on my way."

He hung up before she could change her mind. She realized she really didn't want to. Jared would just have to handle it. It's not like he's my man or something. She remembered his weird attitude and a light bulb went off. *He'd acted so strange this morning, like a man with a crush.* Now who's being ridiculous? She was laughing at herself when she heard Ariel calling her into the kitchen, their favorite room of the house. She and Nonna were sitting at the round butcher-block kitchen table. As soon as she stepped into the room, Shevaughn knew they were unhappy about something. Her silent laughter instantly stopped.

"Okay, what is it?"

"I want to tell you about last night's dream."

"You saw something?"

"Yes, a small pale woman and a little girl who kept crying. I could hear her. I just couldn't see their faces because their backs were turned. It could have been Terri and Toni."

"And that means?"

"All I'm saying is I saw the two of them alone and Toni seemed miserable. I don't think it's a coincidence that I dreamt this the first time that woman slept under your roof."

"So the solution is to never leave the two of them alone, right?"

"Don't be flip, young lady," Nonna cautioned. "You know Ariel's only trying to warn you. Don't mock her gift."

"It's not just a bad dream, I'd call it more of a premonition," Ariel interjected.

"Please, now you know I appreciate how much you care for us. Look, as long as we all keep an eye on her while she's here, we'll be fine. And today, Toni will be with three adults and with two of us being cops, I doubt there'll be anything Terri can do, even if she could escape you two."

"Three adults?"

"Yes, three, I invited Marcus to join us."

"Does Jared know?"

"What difference does that make?"

Nonna and Ariel shared a knowing look.

"What?"

"You should probably talk to Jared."

"I don't think I need his permission to bring a friend along."

"For a cop, sometimes you're oblivious."

"Can you please stop talking in riddles and just tell me?"

"No, Detective, I think you need to find out for yourself," Nonna said sarcastically.

"Alright, you two, I give. I'll tell Jared on the way. And thanks for volunteering to keep an eye on Terri."

"We're gonna watch her like a hawk," Nonna said seriously.

The doorbell chimed at just the right moment.

"I'll get it," she volunteered, almost running out of the kitchen.

"No, she doesn't," Nonna told Ariel and they smiled, although a hint of worry crossed both their faces. They followed Shevaughn into the living room.

"Unka Dred," Toni squealed as she ran into his arms. He scooped her up and blew "raspberries" against her neck. She giggled and squirmed away.

"We've got puppies, wanna see, Unka Dred?"

"Sure, just let me get a look at you first. Wow, you've gotten big. What are you, in high school now?"

Toni chuckled.

"Nope, Mommy says I'm goin' to 'kinnagarden' next year. I hope they let me pick some. Are kinnas pretty?"

The adults burst into laughter and Toni looked at each one, puzzled. Her expression made them laugh even harder.

"Come on, silly Munchkin, let's show Uncle Jared the dogs and then we can leave for the festival."

Chapter Twelve

TERRI STOOD BEHIND the bedroom window curtains and sadly watched the car pull away from the curb. She really wanted to go. Resigned to her current fate, she got into bed and turned to face the wall. The sheets rustled and she felt the chill of him sliding in next to her.

"Patience, ma petite, didn't I promise you it will be worth the wait? You have to have faith in me. Now, there's only you and the old women in the house and they won't be going anywhere until she and the little one get back. Do you have the keys to your house or better yet, is there a key on your ring that you no longer use?"

"Yes, why?"

"Just trying to think ahead. Maybe you can switch keys with old lady O'Brien. You must be very careful, we don't want her to find out and then you would have to get a duplicate made and return it before she discovers the switch. You keep all your medication in your nightstand, right?"

She never realized how much he paid attention to detail.

"Monday, while you're packing, I want you to grab all your sedatives and put them in your purse, not your suitcase. She may want to help you unpack. And you're going to need someone to make a duplicate key, so find a hardware store or locksmith. Can you do that?"

"I'll try, you know I'll try. I can put the Yellow Pages in my overnight bag, so she won't see that either."

"That's my girl. Now let me help you sleep."

She felt a trail of frozen kisses begin at the nape of her neck and when he reached the bottom of her spine, she trembled with anticipation. He slipped into her from behind and gently rocked her into a slow, sweet orgasm. When it ended, sleep came easy.

Ariel stood at Shevaughn's bedroom door. She wanted to talk to Terri alone, see if she could find out what she was really up to. She started to knock when the sound of Terri's voice stopped her and made her listen. *Crazy girl's in there talking to herself!* A low moan replaced the muffled words. *Humph, playing with herself by the sound of things.* She leaned in closer with her ear cocked and her shoulder brushed up against the door. A deep chill went through her arm. It felt as if frozen fingers reached out and squeezed her heart. Shocked, Ariel backed away. *What the hell is going on in there?* She stood outside the door and listened for a few, careful not to touch the door again, but it was quiet now. Whatever had been happening in there was over. Before she left, she hesitantly touched the door one more time. It had returned to room temperature, although that didn't reassure her. She knew Terri could be dangerous, in fact, Ariel worried that she might be more dangerous than even she could imagine.

Shevaughn couldn't get them to the Feast of San Gennaro fast enough. Although Toni must have asked, "Are we there yet?" a half dozen times, she knew exactly how her daughter felt and although a lot of it could have been the anticipation of getting there, some of the nervous feelings she experienced came from the fact that she still needed to tell Jared about Marcus meeting them at the festival before it actually happened.

Marcus must have been on Jared's mind too because he brought him up before she could.

"So you're not gonna mention it, are you?"

"Mention what?"

"How your date went?"

"Huh, wait…, who told you?" She immediately knew the answer. "You talked with Nonna, didn't you? I swear that woman can't hold water."

"You're stalling."

"It turned out okay."

"That's it, okay?"

"No, I'll admit to nice. Look, before I get into it, I should tell you, he'll be meeting us today on Mulberry Street."

"I see, so when were you going to bring it up? What were you trying to do, ambush me with him?"

"I'm telling you now."

"Only 'cause I brought him up first, Von."

"Do you have a problem with him...or me, for that matter?"

"No problem, I don't even know the guy and then again, neither do you."

"Well, the little time I've spent with him, he's always been the perfect gentleman, so I doubt you need to worry. You think I haven't noticed your little funky attitude lately? If you have a problem with me, it's time to cut the bull. We need to talk it out. I don't think I can take much more of this tension between us anyway. So what's the problem?"

The urge to come clean overwhelmed him and he almost did. He almost told her that he didn't want to see her with another man. To add insult to injury, she looked sexy as all get out, in her one-shouldered psychedelic top and jeans. Her effect on him made him nuts and she didn't have a clue. He almost admitted that every time she entered a room, he got this lump in his throat and couldn't swallow. He almost confessed that he'd dreamt of her, sometimes for nights on end, over and over. That even when he woke himself up and paced the floor, he still thought of her, wondering if she ever thought of him. It got to the point, he couldn't take it anymore. Exhausted, he finally tried to force himself back to sleep, however when he finally dozed off, he ended up right back in the dream he'd just left, the dream of how their life together would be. He wanted to, he really wanted to, he just couldn't. Instead, he ignored the question and gave her a warning.

"Let's just say the jury's still out. You can bet I'll be keeping my eye on him...and you."

"Me? What do you think I'm gonna do, take him down a side street and seduce him?"

"That's exactly my point, I have no idea."

"Well, you know I'll be on my best behavior in front of my daughter, so you don't have that to worry about either."

"So, you're telling me if Toni wasn't here with us, I'd have a reason to worry?"

"Okay, I can see there's no winning with you. Can we just try and enjoy the day, despite everything?"

Again, he almost let her know how he really felt and then he relented. He decided to give it his best shot.

"Yeah, let's go have some fun."

When the three of them hit Mulberry Street, it overloaded their senses. They were overwhelmed with the explosion of brightly colored balloons, streamers, flags and outdoor umbrellas and the delicious aromas from the vendor carts that lined the streets. People were everywhere. Toni backed up. She was a little afraid of the largest crowd she'd ever seen. Shevaughn recognized her nervousness and picked her up.

"You alright?"

"Yes, I just didn't know *everybody'd* be here."

"There are a lot of people, huh? Don't you worry. They're just like us. Everyone's here to have a good time. Come on, you two. Let's go see what we can find."

"Or who," Jared insinuated as they caught a glimpse of Marcus coming towards them. He instantly felt like the fifth wheel.

Seeing Marcus, her mood changed for the better. Ignoring Jared came easy, ignoring Toni did not.

"Who's that, Mommy?"

"Marcus, he's a friend of mine."

"Your boyfriend," Toni snickered into her hand.

Not yet. Thank God she didn't say that out loud.

"What do you know about boyfriends?"

"Nonna says it's 'bout time you got one."

"What?" Shevaughn saw she and Nonna were going to have to have a little talk. "No, baby, he's just a nice guy I want you to meet. He's going to have a fun day with us, too."

She and Toni walked towards him and while she introduced him to her daughter, she couldn't believe how if affected her heartbeat. For a second, she thought they all could hear it. Every time she saw him, he looked sexier than the last. He looked especially cool in his tight jeans and his electric blue Air Jordan t-shirt.

The Indian summer day turned hot and humid and the heat suddenly became uncomfortable. The thick air smothered her and she found it hard to catch her breath until she looked into his eyes. A cool feeling of assurance came over her as she realized he just might be the man she would make love to...and soon.

"Glad you made it," she said and kissed him on the cheek. She turned away just in time to see Jared's disapproving frown and she chose to ignore that too.

Shevaughn tried to cover the uncomfortable moment of silence with a reintroduction.

"Jared, you remember Marcus, right?"

Jared acted as if he hadn't heard the question.

"Yeah, man, how you doin'?" Marcus asked as he held out his hand and offered to shake. Jared sideswiped him, picked up Toni, spun her around and placed her on his shoulders.

He immediately regretted his actions as he watched Marcus take Shevaughn's hand instead. They began walking in front of him. *Great, now I'm giving the two of them their space.* Despite his mood, as the day went on everyone began to have a good time. They went up and down the closed off streets under the green, white and red decorations, looking at art and trinkets and watching a parade. Shevaughn and Toni danced to the music of the various bands that passed by. Jared and Marcus stood back and watched as Shevaughn showed Toni how to play Skee-Ball and won her the cutest teddy bear. Well, it turned out to be more like Jared watched Marcus watching Shevaughn and Toni. Stubborn, at first he tried not to say anything at all to Marcus, however as the day progressed the silence wore thin and so did his attitude. As if by some unspoken agreement, the men shared the time with their two female companions, politely taking turns until Marcus finally broke the ice.

'So, what do you think about that Walker family mess? Although they were convicted, I still have a hard time believing that three former naval officers sold government secrets to the Soviets."

"Yeah, talk about a woman scorned. She took 'em all down."

As they continued their conversation, Jared found his knowledge of world affairs impressive and although he would have denied it if anyone asked, he actually began to like the guy!

The two of them got into a hoops battle with Jared beating Marcus by two points and because he lost the bet, Marcus paid for sausage and peppers heroes all around. Then when Marcus won the football toss, he and Jared devoured a couple of calzones, Jared's treat. Every time Shevaughn offered to pay, the two men refused and told her to put her money away. Next, the men went on to finish off some braccioles. After that, they shared a pizza, bought Shevaughn a candy apple and Toni some cotton candy. Jared walked off for a bit and came back with zeppoles and cannolis for everyone. Shevaughn loved cannolis and after sharing one with Toni, she swore she couldn't eat another thing. She could see all the walking, dancing, playing and eating finally wore Toni out. When they saw her nodding off atop Jared's shoulders, they decided to call it a day. Marcus gently took her wrist and pulled her aside.

"Are we ever going to get any time alone? I've wanted to kiss you all day. Please say I can see you later," he whispered as he nibbled lightly on her ear. "Maybe pick up where we left off without the ever watchful eye of your partner over there?"

She glanced in Jared's direction and saw the look of annoyance on his face. *So, maybe my crazy idea isn't so crazy after all.* She thought about all the hints Nonna and Ariel threw her way and realized Jared just might be jealous!

"Sure, I'll call you after I get the little one to bed. Maybe we can go have a drink or something 'cause Lord knows, I think I've eaten enough to last me for a while."

Although tired, she really wanted to be with him tonight. She knew he could make her feel needed and for a while, it would take her mind off the case...and this new problem with her partner.

Terri woke up around two in the afternoon, reached for him and found him gone. She sat up, sighed and began planning how she would get the sedatives from her nightstand drawer into her purse without Shevaughn catching her. *I've got to fluster her, throw her off. I won't be ready to go when she is and when we get to my house I'll act like it's too difficult for me to go in alone. She'll probably think I'm in too delicate a state to handle it. I'll tell her I can't face going into the bathroom and send her in to get my stuff? I tell her to look for anything she thinks I'll need and give her my carry-on bag. That should keep her for a while, long enough for me to grab all the pills and put them in the bottom of my purse, like he said, in case she wants to help me unpack. He thinks of everything.*

Right now, she wished she could thank him for all his help and the next time he came to her, she would. Terri came downstairs and found Nonna and Ariel in the living room. She heard them talking from the hall and when she entered, they both got quiet. *They were talking about me.*

"Did you rest well?"

"Yeah, what's it to you?"

"Watch your tone, young lady. Show some respect in my house."

Now who's got the attitude?

"No disrespect intended. I'm still a bit on edge. It's been a rough couple of days."

"I'm sure it has, it's still no excuse for bad manners."

You just wait, old woman. I promise, I don't get mad, I get even.

"Unless she snatches that away from you too."

Now even he's taunting me.

"No, just keeping you on the straight and narrow. Make nice with them, NOW."

"Guess that nap didn't improve my mood as much as I thought it would. I'm sorry. Would you mind if I get something to eat and go back to my room."

"I'll make you a plate. You go back upstairs and rest. Maybe a nice hot bath will soothe you."

Terri thought about her last encounter in the bathroom. *That's a marvelous idea.* She quickly went back upstairs with the intention of a repeat performance. She shut the door, started the water, got undressed and stood in the steamy shower, waiting for him to appear.

She stood there with her eyes shut until she heard a knock on the bathroom door. He wouldn't show up now.

"Yes?"

"I'm putting your lunch on the nightstand."

Terri got out of the shower, put on the robe that hung on the back of the door and waited until she heard Mrs. O'Brien go back downstairs before leaving the bathroom. Going back to Shevaughn's room, she found the small tray with a grilled cheese sandwich, salad and Coke on the night table and took a sip from the ice-filled glass. The sight of the food made her ravenous.

She devoured the sandwich and salad with the appetite and manners of a cavewoman. After she drank the last of her Coke, she returned to the bathroom, undressed and got back into the shower. She adjusted the water temperature to lukewarm, reminding her of a summer rain.

"Please, Jay, come to me," she whispered and immediately felt the bathroom temperature drop. She closed her eyes and almost swooned when she felt his presence behind her. He buried his cold face into the curve of her neck and she leaned back, her body growing weak and warm at the same time. She turned to face him, convinced if she could see him standing before her, then all this could possibly be real. When she did and she opened her eyes, there he stood, naked, in all his glorious beauty. Each time he appeared to her, he seemed slightly denser, a little more solid. The phrase 'fine specimen' came to mind and with it she felt the now familiar moisture begin. Light-headed, she took the small step that brought their bodies together and then realized he had her actually floating. *Look at me, I'm levitating. My feet aren't touching the bottom of the tub!* For one fraction of a second, sanity popped in and Terri felt intense terror. Then he slowly and smoothly entered her. She forgot why she'd been so afraid.

Chapter Thirteen

SHEVAUGHN COULDN'T IGNORE the thick silence
that hung in the car as she drove them home from the
festival. Toni dozed off before they got to the Queensboro
Bridge and the atmosphere in the car seemed filled with
attitude. It became especially apparent when he mumbled
"good-bye", jumped out of her car and rushed to get into
his brand new silver blue '85 Nissan 300ZX. He didn't
even look back.

She got back home a little after five. As she carried her
sleeping daughter into the house, Shevaughn looked at
Toni's angelic face and an overwhelming feeling of love
literally struck her like a left hook. Thinking of how much
her child meant to her, she suddenly got an ominous
feeling. At that very moment, she realized she'd do
anything to protect her child or Nonna or Ariel for that
matter. Shevaughn thanked God for her blessings and
thought about Tony for the first time in days. That's how
she measured her grief. The less she thought of him
meant she got better with each passing day. When Marcus
came to mind and she recognized it as another sign she
might be ready for a new relationship. She breezed

through getting Toni bathed and ready for bed and then gave him a call.

"So, what's on the agenda?"

"Well, family started dropping by my folks and it's turned into a Bid Whist party. Care to join me?"

"And meet your family? Isn't it a little early for that? I don't know."

"Oh, come on. Don't tell me that you're tired. What happened to the strong Black woman or maybe you're just afraid I'll whoop your butt?"

"Yeah, right, get ready for school, grasshopper."

"Ooh, that sounds like a challenge."

"Sounds more like a promise to me."

"So confident, all I can say is bring it."

"I will and I'll be there in under an hour."

"I can hardly wait." Then the laughter left his voice. "No, really, hurry up."

His serious tone made her a little nervous and her stomach fluttered because she knew tonight might be the night.

His sister opened the door open before she stepped onto the porch. Shevaughn knew she'd been waiting for her.

"Mama, Detective Robinson is here."

"Call me Von, Kennedy. Where's Marc?"

Before Kennedy could answer, Marcus and his parents came out of the dining room into the foyer.

"Glad you could come by. Marcus and Kennedy have spoken so highly of you. We've all been dying to meet you. Oh, I guess you shouldn't say that to a homicide detective, huh?" She chuckled and Shevaughn instantly liked her.

"I guess not. Hi everyone, I'm Von and...Marcus, aren't you gonna introduce us?

"This is my Mom and Dad."

"I was Kim way before I became Mom." She informed him and then gave him a peck on his cheek.

"And you still are, Hon. Hi, I'm Darien, they call me 'D'."

"It's nice to meet both of you."

"Marcus, get Von a glass of wine and introduce her to the rest of the family."

She met numerous aunts, uncles and friends of the family. They were a boisterous group, joking and laughing, enjoying each others' company. There were two tables, one for Bid Whist and one for Spades with everyone telling lies and talking smack. Shevaughn sat across from Marcus. With him as her partner, she bid a five-lo and made a six. Although they were playing 'rise and shine', the two of them were still playing nearly an hour later.

"So the little lady does know how to play. Nuthin' mo' dangerous than a good-lookin' card shark," D remarked as he left the table.

Although they teased her, or maybe because they did, Shevaughn found she felt very comfortable with his family and time flew by. The next thing she knew, the evening ended and the time had come for her to leave. Saying her good-byes included a lot of hugging and kissing and that took another ten minutes. They were a large, loving family and she had to admit she envied their relationships.

"Would you like to stop by my place before you go home?" he asked as he walked her to her car. "I only live a few miles away."

"Sure, for a little while. I'll follow you." She could hardly wait. Now, if she could only get over her bad case of nerves.

The short drive to his place took another fifteen minutes because of late night traffic. It seemed like forever. While driving, the thought of what would happen next made her a little sick. It also excited her when she realized she'd already made up her mind. Her time had finally come.

His apartment building didn't look very appealing to her because it resembled the interior of a prison. Even the balconies added to the similarity. When they got into the industrial elevator, she stood in the corner as he reached in front of her and pushed the button for the third floor. He turned around to face her and she surprised him by giving him a long sensual kiss. She ended it by nibbling his bottom lip. Marcus responded by placing his knee between her legs and got in close, so close she could feel his heat pressing against her. She forgot everything and let the lust take over. He answered her every move and by the time he got the apartment door unlocked they were both out of breath. A flurry of clothes led from his tiny living room, down the hall and into his surprisingly large bedroom as they hurriedly undressed each other. Nothing mattered, not Terri, Diamante or Jared. She let her body answer the call she'd been waiting so long to hear.

Her first orgasm came as he placed kisses all over her body, starting at her feet and working his way up. When he skipped over her burning need and went further up to her breasts, she pushed his head back down to where she wanted him to be. He willingly followed her lead, causing her second orgasm to erupt before he entered her. When he finally did, she lost all sense of self and time. She'd forgotten how good it felt to let go and enjoy serious lovemaking. He filled her to the point of pain, such sweet pain that she answered his thrusts with an enthusiasm that startled her. When she felt him come, he buried his face in her shoulder in order to muffle a low growl, which turned out to be one of the sexiest sounds she'd ever heard. It brought her to the point of orgasm one last time.

They laid there for a while with him on top and inside of her. Not until she felt the exquisite pulsating connection between them slowly fade did they separate. Marcus rolled off of her and they lay side to side on their backs.

"Damn..." Marcus started.

"...that was good."

Shevaughn finished his sentence, leaned over and kissed his nipple. He shivered and she felt strangely powerful. It caused her to wonder how she'd ever survived without this feeling of satisfaction.

"I'm thirsty, how about you?"

"Yeah, whatcha got?"

"I think some pineapple Slice or ice water. I can make us some coffee."

"It's too late for coffee. Split a can of Slice with me, it's hot in here. "

"Yes, it is and it's all your fault. Bet you come in handy in the winter."

"I'm handy all year round, Mr. Williams."

He chuckled.

"I believe you," he said as he got up, put on his short black kimono and left the room. Shevaughn got up, went to his bathroom and took a quick shower. She noticed all his bottles of aftershave and cologne on the beige onyx counter, picked up the Lagerfeld and took a sniff. The scent brought back the memory of their first kiss and that added to her sensation of satisfaction.

When she came out of the bathroom, he sat in bed, waiting for her. He'd placed a glass of soda on a coaster on each of the golden oak nightstands. From his facial expression, he didn't look too happy.

"You're not coming back to bed, are you? Talk about hit and run."

"Come on, it's not like that. You know I need to get home."

She explained what she'd been through the last couple of days and why she'd allowed Terri to stay with her.

"Is it safe to have her there?"

"I think so, I just feel better when I'm there to keep an eye on her."

"I bet."

Shevaughn took a sip of soda, then walked through his tiny apartment and picked up their clothes. She placed his on the well-worn orange wingback recliner in the corner of the bedroom and proceeded to get dressed.

He watched her lotion her dark magnificent body and felt the stirrings of a feeling he'd avoided most of his life. A woman broke his heart once back during his college days and he'd vowed it would never happen again. He'd made good on his promise for longer than he wanted to admit. *I'm not getting any younger.* He wondered how she could be so unaware of her effect on him. He saw she'd put her hair up to shower. It gave her a regal air. Smiling to himself, he remembered how raw the queen could get. Her orgasmic contractions surprised him. She'd tightened around him like a silken fist and damn...even though he didn't want to admit it, he knew he'd experienced the beginning of an addiction. Sitting on the bed, she bent over to lotion her legs and he lost himself in the smoothness of her back. He noticed there were no vertebrae showing like some of the skinny chicks he'd slept with. She'd been made to order, just for him.

He'd always liked his women comfy and her being so shapely didn't hurt. Then she had that ass, man, talk about amazing. The fact that she had no idea how awesome she truly was only made him appreciate her more. Most women would use it to their advantage, especially in the game of love.

She made him wish he could paint. He wished she would slow down the process of getting dressed because he enjoyed looking at her in the nude. He tried to memorize every feature of Shevaughn's body. Her full, dark breasts with aureoles and nipples the color of midnight, her slender waist and almost non-existent hips were well compensated for by her firm rounded derriere. The hair that hid the part of her he wanted most felt soft to the touch, like black silk. Her legs were sturdy and well muscled, yet shapely. Now he understood why artists felt compelled to capture beauty on canvas. He wanted to hold onto this vision forever.

Marcus thought back to the first time they'd spoken. Her appearance caught his attention and his interest definitely sparked when she got an attitude. Even though he knew it sounded like such a cliché, her anger made her even sexier. He'd actually seen her dark eyes flash fire and at that moment, he knew he wanted to know more about her. Now, months later, here they were, together, in the aftermath of some serious fucking, no, scratch that and call a spade a spade. They made love. *No sense kidding myself.*

When she turned around, he noticed a small scar on her right shoulder.

"What happened here?" he inquired, lightly brushing the spot with his fingertips.

She told him how Becker cut her on that fateful night. The fact that she could have been killed by that maniac before they'd ever met scared him more than he wanted to admit. It made him realize just how dangerous her job could be. He never wanted to think about the prospect of losing her.

"Will you call me tomorrow?" she asked as she pulled on her blouse. Hell, yeah, his mind shouted, yet he kept it cool. He wasn't going to let her peep his hold card, not until he knew she felt the same way.

"Sure, what time's good for you?"

"Afternoon, anytime, I'm just gonna take it easy, spend some time with my family."

"When you say family, does that include Jared?"

"Sometimes..., you know, he's like a brother."

"You need to tell him that."

"Not you too?"

"Why, someone else said something about it? I know he didn't."

"Mother O'Brien and Ariel were hinting around, saying things about his feelings for me. How do you know it wasn't him?"

"'Cause you still don't believe it and if he'd said something, you would. I saw how he watched you today. The brother has a serious jones for you. You should have listened to those two, paid their observations a little more attention. They're smart cookies. I can't wait to meet them. Don't you get it? You're telling me everyone sees it except you...some detective."

Shevaughn remembered Nonna's words. She'd said almost exactly the same thing. *Could I have missed something so obvious?* She thought back on how he seemed to be at odds with any man that interested her. *God, am I really that dense?*

"I guess I will have to bring it up soon," she admitted, mostly to herself.

"Yeah, 'cause he's not gonna take it well coming from me."

"No, I'm sure he wouldn't. I'll handle it, thanks."

"I'm just letting you know, if you need me to talk to him, I will."

"I said I'll take care of it."

"And the sooner the better, okay?"

Marcus got out of bed. This time he didn't bother putting on his robe. He secretly hoped it would entice her to stay.

"Well, as much as I'd like to keep you, if you're ready to go, I'll see you out."

She stopped at the door, turned around, grabbed his cleft chin between her thumb and forefinger and gave him a kiss that rocked them both.

"I'll call you after one," he said.

"You'd better," she said and smiled. "Good night."

"Night, Von. Drive safe."

As she got closer to home, it began to rain. In a matter of minutes, it went from a light drizzle to a full-blown thunderstorm, lightning included. Still nothing could dampen her mood. *If it ain't love, it's definitely lust.*

Chapter Fourteen

SUNDAY, SHE DID exactly what she wanted to do, nothing. Nonna took Toni to church, allowing Shevaughn, Ariel and Terri to sleep in. When they returned, Shevaughn spent the rest of the afternoon with her three ladies. She and Toni did a puzzle together and later she played Scrabble with Nonna and Ariel while Terri spent most of the day outside with her dogs. Marcus called around one and asked if he could come over to meet the rest of her family. Since she'd already met his, she saw no reason not to invite him to Sunday supper.

"Come by around six."

When he walked in the door, Ariel looked him up and down, mumbled, "That explains it," out the side of her mouth to Nonna who smiled and shook her head in agreement. The women watched Toni run to him with outstretched arms and heard her laughter as he picked her up and airplaned her through the air. When he put her down, he magically produced a copy of "Mother Crocodile".

"Got this for you because it reminded me of your Mommy," he joked.

Toni eyes lit up and she snickered behind her hand.

"What do you say," Shevaughn admonished.

"Thank you, Mawcus. Will you read it to me when I go to bed tonight?"

He'd obviously passed her test.

On his best behavior, Marcus charmed all the ladies, well, all except Terri. He got the nod of approval from the two older women when he helped Shevaughn set the table without asking. Nonna outdid herself and made her tasty Spaghetti al Pesto and Ariel made an antipasto salad with roma tomatoes, cucumbers, red onions, roasted garlic and pepperoni, topped with homemade croutons and a virgin olive oil and red wine vinegar dressing. Crusty cheese-garlic bread topped off the meal. It seemed infatuation didn't curb their appetites, although several times during supper, Nonna and Ariel caught the two lovebirds sneaking glances at each other.

Terri kept quiet during supper. When she realized no one seemed to notice that made her even angrier. *I can't believe the bitch gets rid of my men and then flaunts hers in front of me. Talk about nerve.*

"Just bide your time, ma cherié, bide your time. She'll be the loser in the end."

After supper, they all went to the backyard, ate spumoni and watched Toni play with the dogs. Terri watched the 'happy' family scene and fought back the nausea. When Marcus left, she enviously watched

Shevaughn walk him to his car and kiss him good night. She hoped that tomorrow would mark the beginning of the change. She couldn't wait for this day to end. Her future promised a whole new way of life and only time and Shevaughn stood in her way.

Chapter Fifteen

MONDAY TURNED OUT to be a busy day, especially since she needed time off to help Terri apartment hunt. When Shevaughn picked up the newspaper from her usual spot, the Portsborough Journal's headline blew her away: **"Black Jack! Detective Robinson adds Jack of Diamonds to her hand!"** The story went on to tell all about the eight murders and the charismatic man suspected of the crimes. There were hints of payment in exchange for sexual misconduct in the over sixty crowd and of course, a reference to Ace of Hearts. The deaths in this case placed Diamante among the most prolific serial killers in New York history, surpassing Ace's record, just in a much longer time span. The only thing not divulged in the story was the Becker connection. Shevaughn knew it wouldn't be long now. It looked like perfect timing. Terri needed somewhere else to live and fast. Shevaughn hoped Terri's whereabouts would remain unknown for a while. The media should be last thing either one of them had to worry about.

Shevaughn got to work, checked in with Captain Campbell and the lab to see if they'd come up with anything new.

Campbell seemed pleased to see the story plastered all over the news.

"We can never have too much good press."

Shevaughn didn't particularly agree with his sentiment. She didn't want to be some superhero, although she did like the role model part. She wanted everyone to realize that a Black woman could handle any job she put her mind to and not look at her like the exception to the rule.

She resigned herself to the fact that the department would officially close the Elliott case soon, despite the fact that she wanted to hold off until she found something definite to tie Diamante to the other victims. Oddly enough, his calloused fingerprint made them unique enough to be recognized. The match in the gas station's back room certainly said he'd been there, however it still didn't tie him directly to the murders. Then the computer lab came up with two withdrawals that were close to the amount of Diamante's deposits. It all still fell in the circumstantial category. Although she hated to admit it, this just might be the case she couldn't close. She sat down and began tidying up her desk when the phone rang.

"Detective Robinson, Homicide."

"Hi, Detective Robinson, this is Dana, Dana Dixon. I'm the one who told you where you could find the guy in the sketch, remember?"

"Yes, I do, Dana, you were very helpful. What can I do for you?"

"Well, I just saw the article about the case and I remembered the reward, ten thousand dollars and...well, it should be mine, right?"

"If you're entitled to it the department will notify you as soon as the case is officially closed."

"If I'm entitled? Did someone else lead you to him?"

"No, it's just there are procedures that have to be followed. I'm sure someone will be in touch with you within a week or two. You know how bureaucracy works. It takes time."

"Okay, okay, I can wait, just as long as I know it's coming."

"All I'm asking for is a little patience. If you don't hear from someone in the department in a couple of weeks, call me back and I'll look into it, okay?"

"Okay, thanks."

They were saying goodbye as Jared walked in. He'd spent the morning talking to people who lived near the gas station, yet another dead end. She noticed the forlorn look on his face.

"I take it you saw the paper? I'm sorry they gave me all the credit."

"That's not what's bothering me. We need to talk." Shevaughn decided to take the initiative.

"Yes, I think we do, Jared. We've been down this road before." She decided to challenge him head on. "You know I love you, it's just not in a romantic way. You're more than a partner, more that a friend, you're family, like my little brother. I hope you can learn to at least tolerate whoever I chose to have in my life. You have to know that anything between the two of us would almost feel like incest. It's not gonna happen. Don't get me wrong, that doesn't diminish my feelings for you. It just wouldn't be right."

Before Jared had time to let his mind talk him out of it, he quickly walked the three long steps, which brought them face to face.

"This is right," he said, as he grabbed and kissed her with all the pent up emotion he'd been hiding for years. As he reveled in the delicious feeling, Shevaughn, using both hands, pushed against his chest and broke his hold. Before he stepped out of range, she slapped him.

"Shevaughn, I..."

"You didn't hear a word I've said. What the hell's wrong with you? I swear, Jared, if you ever touch me unprofessionally again, no, if you even think about it, I'll have you brought up on charges. I mean it."

Jared looked shocked, like she'd snatched the rug out from under him. For a New York second, he looked down, hiding the hurt in his eyes. When he recovered some of his composure, he mumbled something that sounded like "it'll never happen again" and then, in close to his normal voice, he apologized.

"I'm sorry."

"I accept your apology on the condition that it never happens again. I intend to forget this ever happened and suggest you do the same. I'm trying to be with Marcus now, whether you like it or not. I know you think you're looking out for me, by now you should also know I can handle myself. Besides, he's a great guy."

"I don't doubt that. I apologized, you accepted. End of story."

"Okay, look, we both need some time to cool off, so I'm going to take an early lunch and see if I can help Terri find an apartment. If you need me, call me on the mobile phone. I've gotta get used to using it sooner or later. I should be back in a few hours."

She left him standing in their office with his mouth hanging open in surprise.

♥♦

Hearing her words, his heart sunk with his squashed dreams. *If I need her?* The fact that he would always need her scared him. He wanted to shake some sense into her and make her see the one important thing she always overlooked…him. Instead, he kept his thoughts to himself, picked up the Elliott case file and went to his desk. Even though they didn't have much, the department was prepared to close the case. They were still having a hard time finding out who the other victims were, even after crosschecking Missing Persons, so it looked like this guy actually did get away with multiple murders. He wondered how they all could have disappeared without anyone missing them. Feeling sorry for himself, he wondered if anyone would really miss him if he just disappeared.

The words blurred as his thoughts drifted back to Shevaughn. *Women… always looking for a good man and when there's one right in front of them?* She needed to take the afternoon off. This way he could avoid contact with the one thing he wanted most. *Just let it go, man, let it go.* In order for them to work, together in harmony he would have to keep his feelings in check. From now on, I'm relegated to the friend zone, he thought, unhappily.

Terri woke up late as planned and wasted more time by slowly showering, hoping he would re-appear. While Shevaughn waited in the living room for her to get ready, she slipped out the back door to spend some time with her dogs. Shevaughn found her in the backyard and didn't hide her annoyance. Terri saw her attitude and knew it meant she'd done exactly what she'd hoped.

"Come on, Terri, we don't have all day. You know I have to get back to work. We need to get a move on. I have the paper and a map. Let's go."

She handed the map and the apartment section of the newspaper to Terri and got behind the wheel. They tried some small talk, however once Toni and her pets were discussed there wasn't much else to say. The silence put Terri on edge.

They stopped at her house, where they started by pulling out her suitcases and going through her closet. Terri packed her essentials and practical clothes, since she knew it would be a long time before she'd be socializing again. Shevaughn seemed anxious to help and didn't refuse when Terri asked her to pack up whatever she thought best from the bathroom. After she made sure she wasn't being watched, she stealthily slipped three bottles of sedatives into her purse and went back to packing the rest of her things. Everything went according to plan. A little more than an hour later, they loaded up both Shevaughn's Audi and Becker's old Mercedes. They got back on the road and began the search for Terri's new place.

The first two apartments weren't even close to her standards, not enough yard and too many steps. When Shevaughn pulled up in front of the duplex, Terri knew she wanted it. It needed a little work, mostly cosmetic, however it did have a nice back yard and a second bedroom...for Toni. She hid her excitement until they got to the fourth apartment. Terri pretended to fall in love with it just to throw Shevaughn off and convinced her she could handle it from there. She made arrangements to come back the following day to sign the lease.

"Would you mind if I borrowed the map? I want to try and familiarize myself with local streets around the new apartment."

"Sure, keep it, no biggie."

It was a biggie to Terri. She needed that map. She relaxed on the drive, satisfied with the results of their little road trip. Shevaughn helped more than she'd ever know. She even brought some of Terri's luggage into the living room and sat them by the front door.

"Well, I've got to get back to work. I'll see you all this evening."

"Bye, Mommy."

Toni grabbed her around her legs. Shevaughn bent down, kissed her on the cheek and left.

Terri gave a half-hearted wave goodbye and then quickly took her purse and overnight bag into Shevaughn's room. She closed and locked the door, sat down on the bed, dug the prescription bottles from the bottom of her purse and began to count her stash. *Now, all I have to do is get these into the old bitties' cup of tea or something.*

"*Not so fast, ma cherié. First, get the key. Then we can come back for the girl.*"

"I could test the dosage, you know, see how many pills it'll take to knock them out?"

"*You're putting the cart before the horse again. Don't be so impatient. You need to watch and wait to pull this off. You may never get a chance to use them. I wanted you to take them just in case, you know, for backup. You said yourself that you can't put all your eggs in one basket.*"

"How did you know that? I thought that before I met you."

"*I know you that well, your thoughts, your desires and I'm going to help you get it all.*"

"Well, I can't wait forever. I need to do this soon."

"*No, you need to do this right. The opportunity will present itself.*"

"Oh, I know it will. And I'll do whatever I have to, to make it happen."

"*While you're waiting, go get that map you so cleverly obtained. Let's find someone to make a copy of that key you'll soon have in your possession.*"

"Soon? Well…alrighty then." The word 'soon' brought a crooked smile to her pale lips.

Terri looked up hardware stores and locksmiths in the Yellow Pages so conveniently stored on Shevaughn's oak night table's bottom shelf, crosschecked their addresses with the map and located two hardware stores and a locksmith located near the duplex. *This is all going to work out.*

♥♦

Mission accomplished, Shevaughn thought, as she drove back to the precinct. Tomorrow their lives would get back to normal. She felt good that she'd stuck to her guns and lent Terri a helping hand. Her office was empty, so as soon as she got to her desk, grabbed her moment of privacy, called Marcus and told him how productive her day had been.

"I can tell you're in a great mood, for a moment I thought I might be the reason."

"Well, you do have something to do with it. I'm just happy to get my life back to normal. No more babysitting Terri. She'll be moving into her own apartment, possibly as soon as tomorrow."

"Does that mean you'll have more time for me?"

"How much time do you need?"

"Oh...a few hours maybe?"

"I think I can arrange that. What do you have in mind?"

"How 'bout a romantic dinner, some champagne and we'll take it from there."

"Sounds good, what time?"

"Say eight?"

"I'll be ready."

"I'm ready now."

Shevaughn chuckled.

"So am I."

"Well, babe, then let's get this day over with. I can't wait to see you tonight."

"I'm thinking you'll do more than see me."

"I certainly hope so." She could hear the smile in his voice. "Bye, Von."

I think I've got me a man! She couldn't deny the warm feeling he gave her. Back to it, she thought as she dialed Dr. Spencer.

"Okay, tell me something."

"I wish I could," Dr. Spencer admitted. "I'm afraid we don't have the technology to give you any definite answers. This all happened so long ago. If we could find something to tie him with the victims, if he'd kept something of theirs..."

"Other than their money? I'm sure he used that back room to mutilate his victims. Didn't you find his prints? Doesn't that prove he did it?"

"No, we both know that only proves he'd been there, not that he's the one responsible. It's logical to find his prints there since he did a lot of business with the garage."

"They were found in the blood, right? Doesn't that positively tie him to at least one of these murders? Maybe we could find a witness who saw him with one of the other victims?"

"We aren't even sure when he left it. Who knows, maybe someone will come forward and give us what we need. For now, all I can say is if I find something else, you'll be the first to know."

"I'm counting on that...and you."

"Guess I better get back to work then."

"Yeah, you should. You'll call me?"

"You know it."

Jared walked in and her agitation increased. The warm feeling she'd gotten talking to Marcus vanished in a flash. The tension between the two of them had to end. She really didn't want to lose him as a friend, he just needed to realize she was a grown-ass woman and could make up her own mind.

"Have you heard anything more from the computer lab?"

"They've only come up with one possible lead. It took some time for them to locate what might be a distant relative of one of the victims. He said the story he remembered hearing was the missing woman suffered from Alzheimer's and probably wandered off. Anyway, we haven't gotten a positive ID yet. They're checking her dental records now. You have any luck?"

Shevaughn shook her head no.

"I don't even have anything I could give to Ariel. I thought about taking her to the barrels, except she usually needs something the person touched while they were alive to make a connection. That's probably not the case this time. I'm thinking none of the victims touched the barrels until after death. It's best not to risk it anyway. After all, the woman just got out of the hospital and I don't want a relapse. This sucks."

"The case?"

"Everything, the case, the rift between us...there goes my good mood," she said with a sigh.

"What...when I showed up? I know you don't mean to be intentionally cruel, maybe you should think a bit longer before you speak."

"Okay, did you ever think maybe you're being overly sensitive? You're taking all this a little too personally. You know I would never hurt you. We are still friends, aren't we?"

Friends, Jared thought sarcastically to himself. He walked towards her, looked her straight in her beautiful brown eyes and lied to her and himself.

"We'll always be friends. You know I only wish the best for you and Toni."

He hated himself for saying it. *The best for her would be me.* The fact that she'd named her kid after Tony ended up being a constant thorn in his side. She didn't have a clue how she tormented him. *Come on fool,* he rationalized. *Obviously, it ain't all about you. Snap out of it, be a man and get it together.* He changed the subject.

"Did you eat?"

"No, wanna go grab us something?"

"Only if you're buying."

"I guess that's a small price to pay for friendship."

"Well, then, let's go," he answered and headed for the door. When he opened it, an elderly Black woman, dressed in a colorful full-length dashiki with a matching head wrap entered. She looked like Caribbean royalty, down to her gold hoop earrings and matching bangles. The illusion ended when you got to her feet. She wore a pair of raggedy black Keds.

"Eskize mwen, excuse me, my name is Aniyah, Aniyah Landre. I've been trying to claim my brother's body and they told me I needed to speak to you. I want to tell you the truth about...well, you know him as Jacques Diamante.

"Please have a seat, Ms. Landre," Shevaughn prompted, indicating the chair in front of her desk. "Can we get you anything, coffee, tea, water?"

"No, thank you, I just wanna get this over with." Aniyah began rubbing her eyes and forehead in a circular motion. She looked exhausted. "His real name is, I'm sorry, was Jacques D'arcy Landre. Dre, we called him. At the age of, I guess about fourteen, he told everyone to call him J.D. His "uncle" helped him legally changed it to Diamante after his sixteenth birthday, soon after he got to New York. Looking at him, you couldn't deny his outer beauty, but it hid the lack of beauty in his soul. We protected him, made excuses for him, ever since the puppy incident. He carried death in his heart and we refused to see it. Such a charmer, believe me, so much so my mother denied his guilt to her death, even though she knew. We all knew."

"The puppy incident?" Shevaughn asked. The phrase piqued her curiosity.

Aniyah told them everything from discovering the dead puppy's collar between his mattress and box spring to his move to New York. She mentioned that their family friend, the "uncle" died soon after Dre's eighteenth birthday. They wondered how her brother always seemed to live above his means, even considering his inheritance, yet they never questioned him.

"The doctor called it "manie sans délire". I think it's like insane on the inside, quite the ladies' man on the outside. Jacques never had a conscience and we chose to ignore that, too. We were wrong. I think...no, I know women died by his hands. Mon Dieu, talk about charismatic. On the inside, he hid an animal with a drive to kill. Their lives weren't important to him. Money became his God. It's hard to believe his dark soul has left, however the world's a better place because of it. I believe he's guilty of everything you suspect him of and I'm so sorry. You do understand. All I can do is apologize for all the grief he's caused."

"Is there anything else you could tell us?" she asked, looking in Jared's direction. "Oh, I'm sorry. This is my partner, Detective Jared Benjamin. We're working together on the Elliott case. We suspect she may be your brother's last victim."

Ms. Landre acknowledged Jared with a nod and continued speaking to Shevaughn.

"No, I have no idea what he's been up to since he moved here. All I know is he's been sending us a thousand dollars a month since he took over the club. He took care of us and now that I'm the last of my family, I'm free to tell the truth. There was something defective, something...calmly monstrous about my brother. I wish I could tell you more, I really do, yet I believe we probably don't really want to know the whole truth."

"So you really believe he could be responsible for the eight murders?"

"I'm afraid I do."

"Alright, Ms. Landre, I'll call the coroner and see if we can get his body released. Please wait outside in the reception area...and thank you for your insight." It confirmed what Shevaughn already knew Mr. Diamante had been a classic sociopath.

Jared showed the woman out as Shevaughn dialed the morgue and spoke to the attendant on duty, securing the body's release. She continued talking on the phone after he returned. He stood and waited for her to finish her phone conversation and was about to ask what she thought when she dismissed him.

"Would you show Ms. Landre to the morgue and then pick me up some chicken noodle soup from the corner deli? I've got to touch bases with Dr. Callaghan?"

So now I'm the errand boy?   He'd noticed how Ms. Landre ignored him and it just added fuel to the fire. His anger surprised him. He was only too glad to leave. He needed time to cool down. *This is some BS. I can't go on like this, as soon as this case is over, I'm requesting a transfer and starting tonight, I'm going to start looking for someone who appreciates me. I'm done.* Now if only he could believe it.

Chapter Sixteen

TERRI AND TONI were outside with the dogs when Shevaughn got home.

"Mommy, Mommy, look what Kayla can do," Toni said, excitedly. "Terri, gimme a treat."

"Say please," Terri said.

"Please."

Terri gave her a tiny dog biscuit. Toni held it up as high as she could and twirled it. Kayla stood on her hind legs and began twirling too.

"See, Mommy, she's dancing!" Toni giggled. "I taught her how to dance. I love Kayla."

"Very good," Von answered, clapping. She enjoyed watching her daughter interact with the dogs, although she wondered what would fill the void once Terri left. She thought Toni needed to be a little older before they got a dog. *I'll worry about that later.* Shevaughn laughed, picked Toni up, kissed her, said "hello" to Terri and went inside to see what Nonna and Ariel were up to.

"So, you talked to Jared? He didn't take it well, did he?" Ariel asked, before Shevaughn told them how her day went. Sometimes Ariel's talent unnerved her.

"Yes, we talked. He knows how I feel."

"And you know how he feels?"

Shevaughn refused to say anything about their kiss.

"I think I do. I told him we were family and he seemed to take it okay. He did say he approved of Marc. We're fine."

"I'm glad you cleared the air," Nonna said.

"Speaking of clearing the air, I heard you were talking about me needing a boyfriend ...from Toni. You know she's a little tape recorder."

"Well, I only told the truth. I only want to see you happy."

"So, that means you won't mind watching Toni while I go to dinner with Marc?"

"Are you leaving us with that nut case again?"

"Toni?" Shevaughn asked, innocently.

"Oh, so, now you're a comedienne? You know damn well who I'm referring to."

"Yes, I do," Shevaughn admitted. "It'll only be for a few hours. Come on, Nonna, I'm really starting to like this guy. Please."

"We know you do and yes, we will. Sometimes I just get a kick out of giving you a hard time. Now go change into something a little more casual. You look like an accountant."

"Thanks, you two. I'll be right back."

She went to her room, took off the navy blue business suit and powder blue blouse, and did a quick touch up on her mauve toenail polish. While she waited for them to dry, she got everything else together and took it to Toni's room. There she dressed in her rust dolman-sleeved top and her brocade tapestry print pants. She added her black wedge sandals and purse. Shevaughn borrowed one of Toni's tan ribbons and braided it and her hair into a single French braid. After refreshing her makeup, she checked her image in the mirror. She hoped Marcus would like what he saw.

Shevaughn went to the kitchen and poured herself a small glass of Riunite D'Oro, then went outside to join Toni and Terri. Shevaughn sat in the blue and white striped patio chair and slowly sipped her wine while she waited for her man.

"Von, telephone."

"Coming," she answered, making her way back inside. "Hello?"

"Detective Robinson, Dr. Callaghan here, I got your message. How's Mrs. Becker doing, any problems?"

"She's doing really well, in fact, she'll be moving into her own apartment tomorrow. It's just a short term solution 'til her house sells. I'm really proud of her. She's handling the situation like a trooper."

"Can you tell her to give me a call soon? I'd like her to get back on schedule with her appointments."

"Would you like to speak with her now?"

"No, tell her to call me when she's ready."

"Okay, will do."

She hung up and went back outside.

"Terri, I just spoke to Dr. Callaghan."

"What did he want?"

"He said you should make an appointment to come in soon."

"I will."

"Good, you shouldn't stop seeing him."

"I said I will. Can we drop it?"

"Alright, no need to get an attitude. Toni, go inside. I think Nonna wants you."

Shevaughn waited until her daughter left and resumed the conversation.

"Look, Terri, you need to watch your tone when you speak to me in front of my daughter."

"Oh, sorry, it's just that Dr. Callaghan gets on my nerves."

"That's all well and good, except it doesn't change the fact that you should set a good example in front of Toni."

"OK, I get it. Can we drop it now?"

"See, that's exactly what I'm talking about. Cool it."

"Yes, ma'am," Terri mumbled.

Who the hell does she thinks she is, talking to me like I'm some child?

Terri could hardly contain her anger as she watched Shevaughn go back into the house. She stayed outside a while longer, although Shevaughn had taken all the joy out of playing with the dogs. Disgusted, she started to go inside.

"Bitch," she whispered and kicked the backdoor mat.

And that's when she spotted it. The key, what they'd been planning for since she'd gotten there, had been under the doormat, waiting for her all along! Trembling, she picked it up and tried it in the keyhole. The soft click gave her a rush. She removed it from the lock, slipped the key into the tiny inside pocket of her jeans and placed the mat back in the exact spot, so no one would notice. *Now all I have to do is get a copy and return it before it's missed.* Her bad mood immediately disappeared and she quickly went to her room. He sat naked on the bed, waiting. The sight of him filled her with desire. She wanted him from the moment she walked into the room. Terri quickly undressed, sat in his lap and leaned into him. She felt his arms surround her. His cold breath tickled.

"See, all that planning ended up being unnecessary. I told you this is going to work. Do you believe me now, ma cherié?"

"I always did, it's just patience is not one of my virtues."

"I love your lack of virtues," he said as he lifted her. She grabbed his turgid flesh and helped him make the connection. This time they enjoyed vigorous, triumphant sex. It took all of her composure not to scream aloud when she came. In her haze of satisfaction, she heard him whisper.

"I need you to make sure you move alone. She has to think you're going to move to that apartment. We'll keep the duplex a secret, understand?"

"Of course I do."

"Good, now get dressed and join the others."

When Terri joined everyone in the living room, everyone noticed her obvious good mood. Shevaughn watched her suspiciously, wondering what caused the change. She started to mention it when the doorbell rang. She let it go and went to the door. There stood Marcus with his beautiful smile.

"Good evening, ladies."

"Good evening, Mr. Williams," Nonna and Ariel answered in unison.

"Hi, Mawcus. He's mommy's boyfriend, but I like him, too," Toni informed them. Everyone laughed including Marcus and Shevaughn. They shared a look, hers, a little reserved, his, a little daring.

"Well, I like you *and* your Mommy," he confessed, as he gave Toni a peck on her cheek.

"Von, we've gotta get a move on or we'll miss our reservation."

"Toni, I want you to be a good girl and listen to Nonna and Ariel."

"I *am* a good girl, huh, Auntie Real?"

"Yes, you are. You're the best. Come on, let's help Nonna with dinner. Terri, care to join us?"

"Naw, just call me when it's ready. I'm going back to the room."

"Terri, you could at least set the table," Shevaughn said as she and Marcus went to the door.

"You're right, I should. You two have a great night out."

Terri went to the cabinet and got four plates out to set the table.

Shevaughn raised an eyebrow. Something about Terri's mood swing made her uncomfortable.

Who the Hell does she think she is? Ordering me around, like I'm some kind of fuckin' maid? Bitch acts like I've got amnesia, like I don't remember everything she put me through. I lost everything, because of her. It's gonna be okay though, she'll be able to relate to that real soon.

"Yes, she will."

One of the plates slipped out of her hand. Terri watched it fall and shatter in slow motion. He'd never spoken to her in the company of others.

"Are you okay?" Ariel asked, as she hurried into the dining room. She stopped before she got to Terri because she felt the drop in temperature and sensed a presence. The hairs on the back of her neck stood up.

"It slipped out of my hand. I'm sorry." Since I got here, it seems like all I do is apologize. I'm so sick of this.

"Who's here with you?"

"What?"

"I feel a something, a dark presence. Who is it?"

"I have no idea what you're talking about."

"You're lying. This isn't the first time. I've heard you talking when you were alone in your room. Who is it?"

"I am NOT lying, sometimes I think out loud."

Leave it be, old woman.

"No, that's not it. When I came in the dining room, I felt someone else in here besides the two of us."

"You're crazy. There's no one here. It's just us, me and you."

"We'll see who the crazy one is." Ariel stormed out of the room.

Terri bent down to pick up the pieces of the broken plate.

"She feels me, she knows I'm here."

It took all of her resolve not to answer him. She concentrated hard and tried to communicate with her thoughts.

How could she?

"I don't know, nevertheless she does. Muy bien, ma petite, you did it. I heard you perfectly. Now she'll never catch us talking again."

His compliment gave her strength. She picked up the last piece of the broken dish, got the broom and swept up the rest. Ariel followed her back into the dining room and watched.

"Stop staring at me. Can't we just have a peaceful dinner?"

"Guess that would depend on if you start talking to yourself again."

"Fine, I think I'll just go eat in my room."

"Your room? Don't forget you're here because of Shevaughn's misguided heart."

That's not the only reason.

She wanted to say it aloud. She knew if she did, he wouldn't be pleased and pleasing him had now become a priority.

During the drive, Shevaughn looked out the car window. She got a little confused because she saw they weren't headed downtown to the restaurant district like she thought they'd be.

"Where are we going?"

"It's a surprise."

When Marcus pulled up in front of his apartment building, she couldn't help feeling a little disappointed.

"I thought you said you were taking me to a romantic dinner? You said something about reservations, not that we were going to your apartment. Aren't we being a little presumptuous?"

"Hey, well, I couldn't say that in front of everybody. I needed an excuse to get you out of there. Don't judge 'til after you come inside," he answered before he got out the car.

When he unlocked his front door, she saw his apartment was immaculate. There was still a hint of lemon Pledge in the air under the aroma of macaroni and cheese, collards and roast pork. Her mouth watered. It reminded of a home long lost, way back when her mother whipped up delicious Sunday dinners. Her eyes burned and she started to tear up, suddenly threatening to spoil his moment. *Not now*, she admonished herself, *not here*.

He took her hand and led her into the kitchen. Usually, he ate in the living room while watching TV, but tonight he'd set up his small kitchen table, covered it with a white tablecloth and place settings for two. He'd added roses, candles and a bottle of chilled champagne in what looked like a small beach pail filled with ice. She could see he'd gone to a lot of trouble to surprise her.

"When did you have time to do all this?"

"After we talked, I closed shop early, went shopping and got it together. How'd I do?"

"Not bad, not bad at all. I'm impressed."

"These are my Mom's recipes. I followed them as closely as I could, although I did add a dash of this or that, here and there. Come on, sit down, have a glass of champagne. It's the good stuff, Piper-Heidsieck. Dad recommended it. Dinner will be ready in a minute."

"So the whole family collaborated on this. What's your sister's contribution?"

"Damn, busted by the fuzz. She dropped off the roses," he confessed as he poured her a glass.

"I was kidding."

"I'm not, you were right. My family has read all about you and your career. When they met you, they were very impressed. They think it just might be possible you're worthy of me."

"Worthy of you? Careful, buddy, your ego's showing."

"Hey, those weren't my words, just quoting the family."

"Well, I happen to think you might be worthy of me. After all, I am the department's top homicide detective."

"I think that impresses my sister the most. Right now, she's actually considering transferring to John Jay and going for a BS in Criminal Justice."

"Dang, I did make quite an impression, didn't I?"

"Yes, on everyone in my family, including me."

"Is that your idea of sweet talk?"

The evening went well, with good food and titillating conversation. They left the table, sat on the couch and ate peach cobbler covered with butter pecan ice cream while listening to Isaac Hayes' "Greatest Hits" cassette. She hadn't been this relaxed in a long time and she wished she could prolong the moment, however when the music ended, Shevaughn gave Marcus a kiss on the cheek in an attempt to begin her good-bye. He quickly turned to face her and put all of his best efforts into communicating his need for her to stay with his kiss. She got the message, yet reluctantly extracted herself from his arms.

"Marc, baby, you really outdid yourself and I thank you, but I really have to go. You know, tomorrow's a workday."

"You called me baby."

"Um...yeah, I guess I did, slip of the tongue."

"Really? Calling me "baby" or the kiss?"

"Both," she candidly admitted.

"Is that how you're starting to think of me, as 'your baby'?"

"What happened to 'nice and slow'?"

"Turning my own words against me, huh? Touché. You want nice and slow? How's this?"

He backed her into the wall and kissed her so long and so deeply, she felt her knees buckle. *Damn.*

"Oh, I definitely have to go now," she said, as she broke free. "You have a good night."

"You could make it better."

"I could and my answer's still no."

Marcus reluctantly unlocked his door.

"Call me tomorrow?"

"Yes, 'nite, Marc"

Before he closed his front door, he said, "Hey, you never answered the question. Are you starting to think of me, as 'your Baby'?"

She gently ran her finger down his face, whispered "maybe" and left.

Terri went to bed right after dinner. She tossed and turned while she waited for him to come. When the air around her stayed warm, she tried to take her mind off him by concentrating on tomorrow. She couldn't wait to get to her new home. She didn't fall asleep until after she heard Shevaughn return home from her date. *I can hear the bitch actually humming!* Shevaughn's happiness annoyed her. She did get satisfaction with the knowledge it would be short-lived. With that thought, sleep came easy.

Chapter Seventeen

EVEN THOUGH THE day broke cold and dreary, it didn't hinder Terri's mood at all. She jumped out of bed before anyone else, anxious to get started. After showering and dressing in her sage green sweat suit and sneakers, she put her hair up in a ponytail. Today, she'd be leaving this place.

Shevaughn had beaten her to the punch and sat at the kitchen table, drinking a cup of Earl Grey tea.

"You're up early," Shevaughn noted as she buttered her toast. "Sit down and we'll plan out your day."

"I already did that last night."

"Really? So what can I help you with?"

"Not much, maybe some help getting all my things into my car. I think after that I'd like to be on my own."

"Sure you don't want me to help you unpack? I could drop by on my lunch hour."

"No, actually, you've done enough." More than enough, her mind echoed. "I'm going to get settled in and then call Dr. Callaghan to schedule my next appointment."

"Good...well then, let's grab your things and load up your car. I guess this means I won't be seeing you for a while."

"Once I get the house sold, get things in order and figure out what I'm doing with all my stuff, I'll give you a call. Maybe I can make dinner for us some night."

"Sounds like a plan, I'll look forward to it," she lied.

With the two of them loading up her car, they were finished in no time. Toni woke up and came into the living room as they removed the last of Terri's things. Her little forehead wrinkled when she realized what that meant.

"You're taking the puppies away?"

She looked so disappointed it almost broke Terri's heart. On the bright side, she knew they wouldn't be separated long.

"They'll miss you too. If it's okay with your mom, I'll bring them over so you can play with them."

"When?"

"Soon, I promise. Is that okay, Shevaughn?"

"Sure and we can visit you, see how all of you are doing."

Toni didn't think they were doing enough.

"Can we take some pitchers 'fore they leave, so I can 'member them?"

Terri went outside and while putting on their leashes, he slipped behind her and gave her that welcome chill.

"You need to leave something here in the back yard, so you can return to the house without it looking suspicious."

"Good idea."

"I know."

She took Kayla's rubber squeaky toy that looked like a hotdog and wedged it in the corner of the fence behind the large oak tree, out of everyone's sight. To make sure she'd found a good hiding place she checked it from several angles. No one would find it without a thorough search. She then leashed the dogs and brought them into the house.

Shevaughn got the Polaroid camera from on top of the dining room hutch. She took pictures of her daughter with each dog and then did a group photo with the three dogs and Toni.

"Give that to Terri, so she'll 'member me."

"I could never forget you, little one." Terri said as she crossed the room, picked Toni up and hugged her. Shevaughn snapped a picture of the two of them before Terri put her down.

Nonna and Ariel entered the living room and joined in the goodbyes. Terri watched them as they stepped back and shared a glance of relief. She could tell the old bitties were glad to see her go. *They not even try to hide it.* Still, they couldn't be as happy as she intended to be.

When Terri brought up her psychiatrist, Shevaughn saw it as a sign, a good sign. It meant that she wouldn't have to nag her about it. However, as she listened to Terri talk to Toni, a warning bell went off and her skin crawled.

She couldn't quite put her finger on it, yet every ounce of maternal instinct made her question Terri's attachment to her daughter. *Did Terri have too much emotion in her voice when she spoke to Toni?* Shevaughn watched her drive off and relief replaced concern. She'd done her good deed and now it was time to get things back to normal. She and Toni ate breakfast together and Shevaughn got ready for work.

She'd just gotten her second cup of tea and sat down behind her desk when Jared rushed in with the computer lab report.

"They've added a couple of possibles, making a total of three. Seems they all lived alone and their immediate families were either dead or lived in other states. They're still trying to track them, although it doesn't look good."

"I bet that's why he chose lonely older women. They would be an easy target and no one would miss them right away."

"Or not at all. Out of the three possibles, we only located one missing person report."

"So, we're supposed to resign ourselves with the fact this man got away with murder for years?"

"Bottom line, he's dead and that'll probably be the end of it."

"I hate loose ends."

"Everything can't be tied neatly in a bow."

He didn't get it. This would technically be her first unsolved case and whether or not it would be a blemish on her record, she knew it would be an eternal thorn in her side. *Am I losing my edge? Were all the other cases I've solved flukes? Okay, girl, now you're second-guessing yourself. You know you're good at this. Don't let those old insecurities sneak back in. Stop it.*

She'd been in more of a supervisory position this time around. Her successful years gave her the opportunity to delegate portions of the investigation to different officers. Now she wondered if it would have made a difference had she been more involved. In all honesty, she doubted that it would.

"Besides, shouldn't Suffolk County police have some responsibility?"

"No," she explained, trying to hide her frustration. "The victim died in my jurisdiction, the alleged killer lived in my jurisdiction, just because he died in Suffolk County doesn't absolve me of my accountability."

"Well, if you ask me, when he shot himself, that was justice. Hey, nobody's perfect," he said. "You're way too hard on yourself."

"You know how it is, there's always someone out there ready to criticize."

"Well, if anyone does, tell them to walk a mile in your shoes. I bet they'd change their tune."

"Thanks, man. That means a lot to me." It still didn't make her feel any better. *Come on, don't start that crap again. Don't lose your confidence. Remember, the new you is fearless.* She wished she really believed it.

Terri enjoyed the feeling of independence she got when she arrived at the duplex. After she brought all her things in and got the dogs situated in their new backyard, she drove to the closest hardware store and got the duplicate key. While there, she picked up cleaning supplies and several gallons of paint. Next, she called the Southampton real estate agent and told her to put the house back on the market. The sale would include most of her furniture since she wouldn't be moving it to the smaller home. She promised to drive out the following day to decide what pieces were staying and sign the necessary papers. Then she called Dr. Callaghan and made an appointment for Wednesday afternoon. She didn't want anyone getting suspicious.

She worked hard to get the duplex ready. She began in the second bedroom, Toni's room. She vigorously scraped off all the old ugly green vine and beige trellis wallpaper, sanded the drywall and painted the room a cool shade of lavender. Saturday, when they were coloring together, Toni told her she loved purple. Before she went to bed, she swept up all the dust. Tomorrow she would scrub the linoleum floor. She found a pencil in her purse, got the marbled black and white composition book and started the journal for Dr. Callaghan. She carefully wrote an entry for every other day until she ended with an entry for the day before. Exhausted, she went right to sleep. Less than an hour later, the cold air woke her.

"You need to make that call and return the key to its rightful place."

"I'll do it first thing in the morning after I get back from the real estate office."

She realized it felt so good to be able to talk to him without worrying someone would overhear.

"I wanted to do a little shopping anyway. I need to order her twin bed and get curtains and stuff, so I'll drop by while I'm out."

"Don't forget to get a few toys for our girl. Then we'll be ready."

She made a list of the toys she knew Toni didn't have. She hoped to find at least three, a Cabbage Patch doll, My Little Pony, a Care Bear and maybe some of their companion books. She would get and do anything to make sure of their daughter's happiness.

"I think we'll need to change her name. There should be no reference to her past."

"I hadn't thought of that. What should we call her?"

"She completes us. I think Trinity would be appropriate."

"Trinity Becker, I like it and, in your honor, how about Diamond as her middle name?"

"Perfect! Trinity Diamond Becker. You see what a great team we are? Come here and get your reward."

It never occurred to her that she'd chosen to rename Toni after two serial murderers.

The next morning Terri did as promised. She went to Southampton, toured her house with the real estate agent and signed the sales agreement. She left the real estate office and went straight to "Toys R Us" and found everything on her list. She even stopped by Dr. Callaghan's office for her hour of therapy. He seemed pleased to see the progress she'd made in her journal and for the first time the visit didn't end in a confrontation. On the way home, she drove back to Mrs. O'Brien's on the pretense of looking for Kayla's toy. During the ride, she changed the radio station to WBLS and listened to some R

& B. It made her feel closer to him. As she pulled up in front of Shevaughn's home, the rhythmic sound of a smooth sax began to play and Sade's voice crooned "Smooth Operator". Maybe it was the reference to diamonds in the lyrics, but Terri felt as if Sade was referring to Jay.

Listen, they're playing your song!

Terri took it as an omen and sat in the car until the song ended. It boosted her confidence. As she got out of the car, she felt prepared to do whatever she thought would help her accomplish her goal.

Ariel opened the door and rolled her eyes, letting Terri know she was no longer welcome there.

"Back already? You forget something?"

Terri explained about the dog's missing toy.

"It'll only take a minute," she said as she brushed past and started going through the house to the back door.

Ariel started to follow Terri out back when Mrs. O'Brien mentioned the $25,000 Pyramid would be on in a minute. She hesitated, then reconsidered and joined her buddy in front of the TV in the living room. Terri carefully dropped the key under the mat and placed it back in the faint outline, ran to the corner of the yard, retrieved the toy from its hiding place and came back inside in a flash. She knew the next time she came back it would be to collect what rightfully belonged to her.

Chapter Eighteen

AFTER WEEKS WITHOUT a single new lead, Shevaughn acknowledged having her first unsolved case. She made sure Ms. Dixon collected on the ten thousand dollar reward, although Dana's profuse appreciation didn't help lighten her mood. She attempted to ignore it and concentrate on her family, except when she found herself all alone the thought would ambush her, stealing away any joy she tried to feel. No matter how many times she told herself to get over it, she couldn't get around the sense of failure. Everyone noticed she seemed a little subdued and they all tried to let her work it out for herself. That night, after the four of them enjoyed a rather quiet dinner, Nonna and Shevaughn were silently cleaning up the kitchen when obviously Nonna decided enough was enough.

"Okay, Von, how long are you going to be miserable about the Diamond case? We miss you."

She didn't realize everyone knew she had an attitude and why.

"I'm getting better."

"Hey, promise me something."

"What?"

"That you'll never play poker, you don't bluff well. We both know you're not. You've been moping around here for days. Why don't you go see your nice young man?"

The question caught her off guard. Although it sounded like Nonna changed the subject, Shevaughn knew she really hadn't and it didn't escape her attention that Nonna referred to him as nice. She smiled as she thought of him, however when she thought of their current circumstances, the smile disappeared. She had to take the blame for their brief separation. Before this, they'd spoken to each other on a daily basis and her heart and stomach would flip every time she heard his voice. Lately, even he couldn't cheer her up. She always came up with some excuse to avoid seeing him every time he'd called to ask her out. They hadn't seen each other in nine days and the last time they'd met it ended on a sour note. He hadn't called her since. She knew he would wait until she wanted to see him, yet their separation felt like punishment.

The last time they'd been together, he'd offered a sympathetic ear. Shevaughn tried to explain to him why the case bothered her so much. The explanation didn't go well. They'd been sitting together on the couch in her living room, sipping on some Canei White and listening to Change's "Glow of Love". She loved Luther Vandross.

"It's just that, when it's all said and done, I'm still left with five Jane Does, five women we may never be able to identify. Even with the department pinning all eight murders on Diamante, we still don't know for sure. I mean, everything points to him including the fact that his fingerprints were found at the gas station, yet it doesn't conclusively prove he's responsible."

Marcus tried to interrupt her. She stopped him by placing a finger on his lips, put her glass down and continued.

"I've always loved the feeling of satisfaction I get when I see justice done. Being a part of it is a very important aspect of my life. I'm just afraid it won't happen this time. And, okay, I'll admit it has a lot to do with the fact that, to me, this is my first technically unsolved case. Don't get me wrong, I know I'm not infallible, it's just this will be a constant reminder that emphasizes the fact."

"Babe, you've got to realize, no one's ever one hundred percent all the time. You need to accept it and move on."

"You just don't get it, do you? I can't and if you don't understand, there's no point in us trying to discuss this..."

"Shevaughn, are you listening to me?"

Nonna's voice snapped her out of it and she heard the slightly metallic ring of the trimline phone in the background.

"Be right back."

Thank God, saved by the bell.

She rushed to answer it and heard his voice. Everything flipped.

"Your ears must be on fire," she said, after the customary hellos.

"You were talking about me?"

"Yes, your fan club wanted to know when we were going to see each other again."

"My sentiments exactly. Tell the ladies I appreciate their support. I thought you'd miss me by now."

"I do. You know I haven't been in the best of moods lately and I wanted to spare you."

"Look, I'm supposed to be there for you, no matter how you feel. That's what a real man does."

"And there's no denying, you are a real man."

Ariel appeared out of nowhere, stepped close and raised an eyebrow when she overheard Shevaughn's end of the conversation.

"So why do you keep him waiting?"

"Marc, I have to go. There's one too many people in on this conversation."

"On one condition, are we on for tonight?"

"Yes, I think I need to, I'll see you around eight."

"Don't sound so enthused."

"Come on, don't be like that. I'm really looking forward to it."

"So am I."

Several houses down from Mrs. O'Brien's home, Terri sat in her "nightwatch blue" 1984 Chrysler LeBaron and waited while the sun went down. Kayla lay on the backseat, sleeping peacefully. She'd just traded Eric's old Mercedes in for this almost new car because she wanted something a little more mainstream and she couldn't resist the color name. The trade-in actually put a few extra dollars in her wallet.

Each day for the past week, Terri worked tirelessly to get the duplex ready for Trinity. She made it cute-as-a-button. She even did the yard work, working on the landscape until she got it neat and tidy. She hated the outdoors, especially gardening because of her fear of bugs, yet when she looked at the finished product, she felt real pride.

She looked at everything she'd done in Trinity's room and saw perfection, right down to the completed baby blanket. She'd put the last of the finishing touches on it two nights ago and now it was large enough for the new twin bed. This morning, she surveyed the room and mentally patted herself on the back. *It turned out well.* The room looked exactly like she'd imagined it for her little princess.

Each night, she parked and secretly watched the O'Brien home. She'd been very patient, waiting for Shevaughn to leave. *Problem is the bitch never does.* The routine bored her and Terri's patience wore thin.

Tonight, all her hard work took its toll and despite her excitement, she took a catnap. She woke up suddenly when Kayla barked and realized she'd laid down across the front seat. She didn't remember putting the armrest up. Terri brought her eyes level to the bottom of the window and peeked out. Finally, she watched as Shevaughn pulled out of the driveway. *Tonight's the night!*

She waited until she saw the back lights in the house go out and then waited almost a half hour more. She wanted to make sure everyone had gone to sleep, however she didn't want to chance Shevaughn coming back early and catching her inside. She had a hard time controlling her anxiety and couldn't wait any longer.

Before leaving the car, she patted the little pocket inside the front pocket of her jeans to make sure she felt the key and when she got out she patted her back pocket where she'd put Jay's gift. He'd insisted she carried it with her, in case of an emergency.

Terri slipped the key into the back door and felt an electric jolt shoot through her body when she heard the lock click. She tiptoed through the kitchen and dining room, down the hall past Mrs. O'Brien's bedroom and walked slowly up the stairs, making sure to avoid the fourth step because she knew it creaked. When she got to the upstairs hall landing, she stopped to take a breath. *This isn't a dream.* The thought made her heart beat faster. The pounding in her ears got so loud she almost didn't hear him, except the air went cold and commanded her attention.

"Easy, ma petite, I'm with you. I want you to stop and take a deep breath. We can do this."

She did as he told her and then walked into Trinity's old room. Terri watched her sleep for a second. *Such a beautiful child.* She resembled an older version of the tiny angel in her dream. Her slightly damp hair curled into small ringlets surrounding her face. Terri gently shook her shoulder with one hand while she placed her index finger over her lips.

"Terri," Toni sat up and rubbed her eyes. "You woke me up," she whispered, showing she understood to be quiet. *She's such a good little girl.* "Where's Mommy?"

"She went out, remember? She said I could come and take you to play with the puppies 'til she gets back. Kayla's waiting for you outside in the car. I'll carry you downstairs so we don't wake up Nonna and Ariel. They're too tired to play."

"Kayla's waiting for me?" Toni smiled and reached for Terri to pick her up. "But I'm in my PJs."

"That's fine, honey, I have some play clothes for you at my house."

"Mommy says never go with strangers."

"Except I'm not a stranger, remember? I'm your Mommy's friend. I stayed at your house, right? You wanna go see my house, maybe spend the night? Kayla can sleep with you."

"Yes, I miss the puppies," she said so seriously that it tugged at Terri's heart.

"Well, then let's get a move on."

Ariel stirred in her sleep and woke with a puzzled look on her face. She knew that this old house creaked and groaned, however something else nagged at her. She got up, stuck her tired feet in her cream open-toed slides and put on her emerald green terry-cloth robe. Ariel headed to the first floor bathroom. On her way out, she stood still for a second, listening. The house was silent, yet something felt wrong. She attempted to shrug it off and started back to the little guest room next to Lorraine's. She changed her mind when the premonition wouldn't leave. Ariel always followed her instincts and they were telling her to check on the others in the house. She stood at the bottom of the steps for a moment and slowly began the climb.

Halfway up, the stair creaked and she felt the air grow colder. She pulled the lapels of her robe tighter around her neck to ward off the icy discomfort. She stopped outside Toni's door and thought she heard muffled voices coming from inside. Ariel pressed her ear against the door and strained to hear what was being said when suddenly it stopped.

"Shhh… she knows we're here."

His voice, inside her head, instantly calmed her.

"What, who?"

"Somehow, the little old bitch can feel me."

Terri knew he meant Ariel. She also knew nothing or no one would stop her from getting her due.

"Listen to me, do exactly as I say. We still have the element of surprise in our favor. First, get Trinity to get back into the bed, way under the covers. Then go and wait behind the door. Make sure you have what I gave you ready. She'll peek in and when she does, I want you to reach around the door and quickly slit her throat. You have to cut deep so she won't have time to scream. You two are almost the same height. It should be easy."

"You want me to kill her?"

"You want the child to complete our family, don't you? Sometimes unpleasant things need to be done in order to get what you want. And what do you want, more than anything?"

"I want the three of us together."

"Then do what you must. Hurry up."

She went back to the bed and whispered as she cupped her mouth and spoke directly into the child's ear.

"I'm gonna go see if your Nonna or Aunt Ariel are up, just to make sure it's okay for us to go now. Get back under the covers and I'll come back for you in a little bit, promise."

"Yes," Toni whispered back. "Ask first, so you don't get in trouble later. That's what Mommy always says."

The mention of Shevaughn fueled her resentment and made her more determined to pull this off. She made sure the covers were over Trinity's head to block the girl's view as she tucked her in. Then she removed the straight razor from her back pocket and opened it. Terri stood behind the bedroom door and waited.

Ariel pushed the slightly open door a few inches, her hand brushing up against the cold wood. When she felt the cold draft of air coming from the room, her inner alarm went off.

It's here.

The hair on the back of her neck stood straight up. She felt the evil presence and it terrified her. Something grabbed her from behind, causing the cold to become even more intense. What first felt like frostbite crept down from the point of contact and radiated to her heart. It skipped a beat and then fluttered.

The pressure in her chest increased and her heartbeat become more irregular, yet stronger. She felt nauseous and light-headed. Something turned her around. Ariel placed her hand over her heart and even though she was freezing, the pain in her chest seemed so intense that she broke out in a sweat. *God help me, this is real!*

She closed her eyes tight and tried to make it all go away. Instead, she felt crushed by a feeling of impending doom. Ariel found it hard to control the added panic. She recognized the beginning of another heart attack and tried to call out. Cold fingers wrapped around her throat. At first, she thought strangulation, but instead the touch became softer, almost loving. She waited for the fingers to tighten, waited for the hand to slowly squeeze what little life she had left out of her, waited for her heart to stop. Instead, they gently trailed down from her throat and cupped her breast. That's when she knew the presence was male. He pulled her to him and pressed his large body against her, his cold rigidity against her thigh. His muscular body seemed to envelope her. He stood so close and felt so cold. It took every bit of courage she could gather to open her eyes and look up into his face. In front of her stood one of the most handsome Black men she'd ever seen.   And his eyes, his strangely beautiful blue-green eyes...

Although terrified, she recognized him from his picture in the paper. Terror ignited within her. It exploded when he began to speak inside her head.

"You didn't think I'd let you stop her, did you? You're no match for me, you pathetic little witch. You're just like all my other benefactors. I bet, considering your condition, fucking you to death will be like a walk in the park ...for me. And for you, I do believe it's the best way to go."

"Who are you?" she managed to whisper as they slid down the door onto the carpeted floor. She thought she heard soft laughter.

"Don't play coy with me, ma petite. I know you recognized me. You know exactly who I am, Ariel. I'm the man of your dreams."

♥♦

When Terri heard the soft thud of Ariel's body hitting the floor, she couldn't believe her luck. The old bittie just gave up and died without her having to put a hand on her! She closed the razor and put it back in her pocket and walked around to the front of the door. Ariel's small body lay crumbled on the floor, sprawled in a somehow obscene pose. Her knees were drawn up and her legs spread wide apart. It almost looked like death had interrupted her while she'd been making love and for a second, Terri rocked with envy until she realized if he did have sex with Ariel, he'd done it for her, for them.

"I knew you'd understand. That's why we're meant to be together. Now hurry, hide the body, get the girl and get out of here before we get caught."

Terri grabbed Ariel's arms and slowly, silently dragged her into Shevaughn's room. It was harder and took longer than she thought it would. She now truly understood the meaning of "dead weight". Besides, she didn't have any choice. She couldn't make a sound. She didn't know how she would handle Mrs. O'Brien if she woke up and found Terri inside her home.

As she placed Ariel's body out of sight, on the far side of the bed in front of the night table, he came up behind her and grabbed her around the waist, pressing himself against her, hard and throbbing with the promise of things to come. For a moment, she closed her eyes and rested against him. He gave her strength.

"You see? I can help you with so many things, just like I helped get the old woman out of your way. I guess she really felt me in the end, so to speak, which saved you from having to use my razor. Look how neat and tidy. It's a shame we have to get

out of here so quickly. I would have so enjoyed making love to
you on Shevaughn's bed. It would have been the ultimate
disrespect. Guess I'll have to wait until we're home. Then you
can really thank me, cherié."

"You know I will."

"I'm counting on it and you, ma petite."

Once back in the room, she calmly picked up their
child. Toni rubbed her eyes and stretched.

"We can go now?"

"Yes, little one. Remember, quiet as a mouse."

"Quiet as a mouse," Toni echoed, putting her
forefinger to her lips. Terri didn't think she could love her
any more than she did at that very moment. And now
they were going home.

She slowly and carefully went down the stairs. With
her arms full, it made it difficult for her to miss the
squeaky step on the way down, yet somehow she
managed. Once they were out of the back door, she
locked it and dropped the key back into her pocket.
Elated, she held Trinity close, her little head snuggled in
Terri's cleavage. It felt so warm and so right. Shifting the
child's weight, Terri ran to her car as fast as her legs could
carry them.

When Kayla saw Toni, she quickly rolled over on her
back.

"She wants me to rub her tummy," Toni giggled and
jumped into the back seat, eager to fulfill Kayla's wishes.

"Put on your seatbelt and we'll go to my house," Terri
said as she got behind the wheel. Thanks to him, it turned

out much easier than she imagined it would be and she couldn't have been happier. Finally, she'd caught a break.

Marcus planned the whole evening with the sole purpose of elevating Shevaughn's mood. They dined on a fancy seafood dinner at Chowder's, complete with an excellent Riesling. Next, although he didn't usually go for this kind of movie, he suggested they go see "The Color Purple". When she burst into tears near the end of the movie, he thought all of his efforts were for nothing. Then she explained how much she loved it and thanked him for taking her to one of the most moving films she'd ever seen. It seemed her crying brought her some kind of relief. *Women… I'll never get it.*

On the drive back to her car, which they'd left in the restaurant parking lot, he did get that her mood seemed softer and warmer, which meant he'd done his job. Hopefully, that meant she'd agree to come home with him. He reached for her hand.

"The evening doesn't have to be over. Why don't we swing by my place?"

He'd put all her needs first and Shevaughn felt totally relaxed for the first time in weeks. He'd remembered when she told him how much she loved lobster and that she didn't get it often. She also knew "The Color Purple" wouldn't be on the top of his must-see list. He liked action, more of a "Rocky IV" kind of guy. Because he'd made her his priority once again and she felt both blessed and loved, Shevaughn wanted to accept his invitation, except once again, she had work in the morning.

"I can't, Marc. I need to get home. It's late."

"Okay, so we can get together this weekend. You go home and get some sleep. I'll give you a call tomorrow."

He'd put the icing on the cake by understanding and not pressuring her. As he pulled to a stop next to her car, she leaned over and kissed him. The intensity guaranteed they'd be together soon.

"I'll ring twice to let you know I got home safe."

"You do that. You wouldn't want me up all night worrying, would you?"

"No, when you're up all night, I should be there."

She drove home, went inside, closed the door, leaned against it and smiled to herself. Mr. Williams is definitely a keeper. She could hear Nonna's soft snore in the quiet house as she walked upstairs to her room. Before going in, she stopped at her daughter's door and decided to peek in on her. The little nightlight gave her just enough light to see the bed. At first, she thought she saw Toni sleeping on the bottom end of the mattress. She came closer and realized it wasn't her daughter. It turned out to be a jumbled up sheet and blanket. Shevaughn's heart stopped as she flicked on the light switch, flooding the room with light. Suddenly, she felt a heavy feeling in the pit of her stomach, along with nausea and dizziness. The bed was empty! She quickly looked around in the closet and then ran to the bathroom. They were empty, too. Before running downstairs, she had the vague hope that maybe Toni had snuck into her bed. Shevaughn crossed the hall, turned on her bedroom light and quickly glanced into her room. Her bed was still neatly made...and empty.

As she ran back down the stairs and headed into Ariel's room, she tasted the acidic bile that lodged itself at the base of her throat. In the hall, she squeezed her eyes shut and a prayer started screaming in her head. *Let her be with Ariel, please God, let her be there.* When she turned on the light, she saw that although it looked like Ariel had just gotten up, her bed was empty too!

Shevaughn burst into Nonna's room without knocking.

"Is Toni with you?" she questioned, flicking on the light switch. She heard her voice tremble and go up in pitch and the sound of her own fear intensified.

Nonna sat up, instantly awake.

"No, we put her to bed right after you left. What do you mean she's not there?"

"Ariel's not in her bed either."

As if planned, they both yelled for Toni and Ariel in unison and waited for a reply. The house stayed as quiet as when she first arrived home. Only now, the silence had an ominous quality. It closed in on her and sucked all the air out of the room. She couldn't breathe. Shevaughn flashbacked to that night long ago in a ghost town of a restaurant, the last time she shouted his name with the same feeling of trepidation. Trembling, she dialed "911" and reported Toni and Ariel missing. Then she called Jared and Captain Campbell. While they waited for someone to arrive, Shevaughn found she couldn't keep still, so she went to her room to look for Toni's fingerprint identification kit. She kept in the metal lockbox that contained all their important papers.

Going around to the other side of the bed, Shevaughn stopped when she saw the drag tracks in the carpet. They ended at Ariel's feet. Even though she looked like she might be sleeping, before she touched her face, Shevaughn knew they'd lost her. Screaming for Nonna, she tried to find a pulse. She had a moment of hope when she realized Ariel still felt warm. Then she checked her neck, lightly touching the carotid artery and the inside of her wrist. She couldn't find a pulse. The sense of loss overwhelmed Shevaughn. How could this have happened? How could she have lost them both in the same night? She sank to the floor next to her good friend and placed Ariel's head in her lap. She cried out and rocked her friend until Nonna came upstairs to find them huddled together.

The shock registered on Nonna's face and she placed her hand over her mouth to keep from screaming. She ran to them, got down on her knees and joined Shevaughn in mourning the loss of their good friend. When they were both emotionally exhausted, they worked together and lifted Ariel to Shevaughn's bed and covered her up by pulling the left side of the blanket over her lifeless body.

"I've already notified the police. I've got to call Dr. Spencer. He needs to examine her," she said softly, patting Nonna's hand.

Shevaughn found the identification kit she'd filled out just last year and lovingly touched the picture of her daughter. She remembered how excited Toni had been to have her fingerprints taken. "Like TV, Mommy". Funny, at the time, she'd never thought she would have to use it.

After making the call to Dr. Spencer from the bedside phone, Shevaughn calmly told Nonna she'd be back and returned to Toni's bedroom. The truth hit her hard and knocked the wind out of her. She stumbled and collapsed on her daughter's bed. Her stomach cramped. She grabbed the sheet and buried her face in it. She could still smell the scent of Ivory soap. She didn't want to think it...*but what if...what if she never saw Toni again, what if she was...NO, stop it.* She refused to let that thought creep in. *Just because it's your line of work doesn't mean everything ends in murder.* After losing Tony, she didn't think she could stand to go through it again. How would she exist without her? She prayed that God and Tony were looking over her daughter, keeping her safe. She cried into the Black Raggedy Ann until she couldn't cry anymore, then put the doll down and tried to think. She knew Ariel's death and Toni's kidnapping were connected and she knew they both were connected to Terri.

Running back to her room, Shevaughn saw Ariel lying there, alone on the bed.

"Nonna?"

Her voice sounded louder than she intended.

"I'm downstairs getting dressed and I'll put on a pot of tea," Nonna answered.

Like tea will help now. Shevaughn wanted to scream. She knew her attitude had nothing to do with Nonna. Putting her anger towards something constructive, she searched the little wicker basket on her dresser for Dr. Callaghan's numbers. He'd given her both his office and home numbers when she'd told him her intention to have Terri stay at her home. She found it and dialed him immediately. He answered on the fourth ring, his voice heavy with sleep.

"What's wrong? Do you know it's after midnight?"

"I know what time it is, Dr. Callaghan. Look, I just found my good friend dead and my daughter, Toni, is missing. She's only three, so you'll pardon me if I don't really give a damn about the time." She took a deep breath and asked, "Have you seen Terri this week?"

"You said your friend's dead. What happened? You don't think Terri killed her?"

"I don't know. There's no obvious cause of death. That still doesn't mean she's not responsible for it."

"You suspect Terri took your daughter?"

"Do you think she's capable of kidnapping?"

"I didn't think so. She has been fixated on crocheting a baby blanket for over a year and would never tell me why. Once she finished it, I never saw it again. I didn't give it much thought, especially since Mrs. Becker seemed to have made quite a breakthrough after leaving your home. She even began writing in the journal that I wanted her to start weeks ago."

"I'm thinking her breakthrough may have hinged on her plans of kidnapping my daughter. She fooled us all. Why didn't you mention any of that when I asked you what you thought about her staying with us?"

"It just didn't seem relevant at the time."

"So crocheting a baby blanket isn't relevant when we both knew part of her problem stemmed from her infertility?"

No sense in arguing with him, we both should have suspected.

"I'm sorry, doctor. Hindsight's always twenty-twenty. She didn't happen to give you her new address, did she?"

"I understand you have every reason to be upset. I just didn't see it playing out like this. No, she didn't. In fact, she led me to believe she'd returned to Southampton. So I take it she can't be reached at her old number?"

"I haven't tried it, would you mind doing that for me? I don't know what I would do if she answered. If you speak to her or come across anything, call me immediately. I'm going to check with the phone company. Maybe they can give me her new listing and we can track her down from there. I'll call you later."

"Please do. If it's any consolation, I don't think she would hurt her."

Shevaughn's tolerance snapped.

"You didn't think she would steal her either. I can't take that risk. You told me not to worry about bringing her into my home and now my daughter's life could be in jeopardy, so you'll pardon me if I don't give a damn about what you think."

She hung up, called the precinct and instructed them to try and locate Terri Becker's new phone number and address.

She went downstairs and explained her theory to Nonna. It didn't surprise her to find her dressed and ready to help.

"I need to find the newspaper from two weeks ago Sunday with the apartment ads we looked at. It may be quicker to get her address that way. I'm calling Charlie to see if he can help. I just can't sit here and wait for the precinct to call me back. I have to do something."

She didn't care who she woke up. With each passing moment, she grew more worried and desperate to find her child.

♥♦

Terri had never felt this good before. She brought Trinity in and showed her around her new home. She saved her room for last, like the icing on the cake.

"Do you like it?"

"Oh, yes, purple's my favorite color. Are all these mine?" Toni asked as she ran to the bed and selected the Cabbage Patch doll from the collection of dolls and stuffed animals. "I always wanted one. Mommy said not 'til Christmas."

She hated to hear Trinity call another woman mommy. She wondered how long it would take before the child acknowledged Terri as her real mother.

"She said I could give her to you." *Like I need her permission.* "So, yes, she's yours now. Hey, do you want Kayla to come and sleep with you?"

The dog ran into the bedroom as if on cue.

"How 'bout we get up early tomorrow morning and go to the zoo? Would you like that?"

"Yes, I'd like that a lot. I love aminals. Can I call you Auntie Terri?"

The question came out of the blue and took Terri by surprise. A wave of love hit her so hard she almost lost her balance.

"Of course you can, chérie" she said and gave her a small kiss on the nose. She couldn't have imagined life better than this and she could wait because that would come in time. One day soon, Trinity would call her Mommy and then they'd both forget about Shevaughn. She tucked her beautiful child in and patted the bed, beckoning Kayla to join her. She did and Trinity put her arm around the dog. The two of them made such a delightful picture. It could have been on a Christmas card. Terri turned on the nightlight, turned off the lamp and went to her bedroom. She hoped he would be there, waiting for her.

Before Shevaughn could get to the phone, it and the doorbell rang simultaneously. Nonna went to the door and opened it. Jared burst in as Shevaughn answered the phone.

"Thought you said you were gonna call me? I got worried."

When she heard his voice, she broke down again and told him everything. He didn't let her finish.

"I'll be right there."

"Why did I invite her into my home? I should have known better. Everyone warned me, but I didn't listen. I thought she needed my help. I thought it was the right thing to do."

"You didn't know, Von, you couldn't have known."

"I'm going to see if I can find her. Why didn't I ask for her address before she left? God, I just wanted her gone. I needed my life back. Now if I don't find Toni, it'll never be normal again. I'm sorry, I can't...I've got to go."

"I'm on my way, even if it's only to keep you ladies' company."

"Thanks, Marc, I'll try to keep it together until you get here." She rubbed her forehead in response to a headache that began throbbing behind her eyes. "Bye."

"Von, you've gotta stay strong and have faith that you'll get your daughter back. I don't think that woman would hurt her." Marcus tried to reassure her.

"I know that." Shevaughn tried not to snap at him. She knew he was trying to give her hope. "We didn't think she'd steal Toni either and I'm telling you, somehow she's responsible for Ariel's death."

As soon as she said it, she realized she brought all of this on herself by inviting that woman into their home. She felt like such a fool. Why had she been so stubborn? Everyone warned her against it. Why hadn't she listened? What kind of cop couldn't even protect her own? She hung up, even more despondent.

"Don't do it," Nonna advised after overhearing the end of the phone conversation.

"Don't do what?"

"Blame yourself."

"Who else should I blame?"

"We'll find her, "Jared interjected.

"We found her father," she miserably reminded them.

Dr. Spencer, followed by Captains Bowen and Campbell, rushed in next with several officers, some in uniform and some not. One of them bugged the phone, in case someone called to ask for ransom, while others dusted for fingerprints. *Terri's fingerprints are all over the house, so how could that help?* She held her tongue and gave the I.D. kit and Polaroid of Terri and Toni to one of them. Shevaughn watched all the activity through veiled eyes, unable to concentrate on anything except the loss of her daughter. She knew Terri kidnapped her. *Why were they all wasting time?*

Dr. Spencer gave Ariel a quick examination. His preliminary conclusion confirmed what Shevaughn already suspected.

"There are no ligature marks, defense wounds or physical evidence to suggest suffocation. There would have been the presence of petechial hemorrhaging in the eyes and traces on her eyelids and face."

"Come on, Doctor, English, please?"

Everything worked on her last nerve and she'd had enough. She was scared and running out of patience. That made her rude.

"Petechiae are tiny purple or red spots on the eyes and skin that are caused by small hemorrhages under the skin, created by strangulation or suffocation. I'm going to have to get her back to the lab to examine her fully. However, my preliminary diagnosis is she died of a massive heart attack. I'll know more after the autopsy."

"No, no autopsy," Nonna announced as she returned to Shevaughn's bedroom. "We knew about her weak heart, you just said so yourself, Doctor. We also know she'd just suffered a heart attack and stayed here to recuperate after her hospital stay. She only wanted an autopsy if the circumstances of her death were suspicious. Ariel was adamant when we talked about it and I want her wishes to be respected. You'd be surprised how often death becomes the topic of conversation when you reach our age. No autopsy."

Shevaughn saw how upset Nonna was getting and told Dr. Spencer not to argue. His diagnosis didn't absolve Terri. Someone had dragged Ariel's body into her room to keep it hidden and no one could convince her otherwise.

Suddenly snapshots of happier times flashed through her head and all of them included her daughter or Ariel. She couldn't remember life before either of them. Feeling flush, Shevaughn went to the hall linen closet to get a washcloth. When she saw the pale aqua Care Bear appliqué, she burst into tears again. She quickly held it under the cold water and then up to her face. It didn't help her enough.

Nonna went back downstairs to her room, satisfied they would do as she wished. When the doorbell rang, she opened the front door. It was Charlie. He bustled in with an arm full of classifieds. Shevaughn came downstairs, solemnly greeted him and lead him to the kitchen table. The edition she needed sat on the top of the pile. She spread the paper out on the table and tried to remember which apartments she'd looked at, except her mind wouldn't cooperate. All the ads looked alike. Nonna came, sat across from her, took her hands and spoke to her softly.

"This is important. You know, if Ariel were here, she'd tell you to try to relax, erase everything from your mind and go back to that Sunday when you were first looking for an apartment for Terri. Remember the criteria you thought would be good for her and recreate the moment."

"I feel like I'm losing my mind," Shevaughn said and rested her forehead on her arms. "I don't know if I can do this, I can't think."

"Yes, you can, you must. Remember and circle the ads as you did that day."

She raised her head, unfolded the paper and concentrated on it. She began to circle the ads that seemed to stand out. When she finished, she counted the six ads she'd circled.

"We only went to four places. We mapped out the route to save time and she settled on the fourth apartment. I think I know where she is. Thank you, Nonna."

She hugged Nonna so tightly she thought she might hurt her, yet it took more strength to let her go.

"No, Von, you did it all on your own."

Shevaughn ran to Jared and grabbed his arm.

"Come on, I've got a lead."

Chapter Nineteen

BEFORE THEY REACHED the door, Captain Bowen stepped in front of it, blocking their departure. Despite her protests, he insisted they don't start the search before daybreak.

"First, you two are crazy if you think we're gonna let you do this alone. Shevaughn, you know we can't let you run out of here half-cocked. You shouldn't even be in on this. It's your daughter, for Christ's sake. Look, it's already almost three a.m. All the local newspapers have agreed to post their picture in their morning edition. The department will have flyers made and distributed immediately. We'll get the search teams together at dawn. I promise they'll search each apartment and the surrounding neighborhoods, for at least a mile radius. I know you want to find her tonight, but you need to get some sleep, even if it's only a couple of hours."

"Sleep, you think I can sleep? I have to go get her. My baby needs me." *Calm down, you're just proving their point.*

"Dr. Spencer wants you to take this," Bowen said as he placed a couple of pills in her palm. She threw them across the room.

"I'm supposed to take a nap? Now? Are you out of your fuckin' mind?"

Marcus heard her and rushed to her side. He gently led her back to the table.

"Come on, honey, sit down."

"Marc, that nut has my baby. There's nothing you can say that will get her back to me any sooner. We don't know what she's going through. She's probably scared to death."

"I don't think so. She knows Terri and you know Terri cares for her."

Shevaughn remembered the warning bell. Why had she chosen to ignore it? Talk about hindsight being twenty-twenty. She knew that Terri thought she loved her daughter.

"Take the sedative, Von, rest for a while. When you wake up, we'll join the search party and find Toni. And she'll be fine, I know she will."

"You don't know. No one does."

Her eyes started burning and she knew another breakdown was imminent. She didn't want to crumble in front of everyone.

"Give me the damn pills."

Chapter Twenty

THE NEXT MORNING began with a hazy blue gray sky that matched Shevaughn's mood. A cold breeze cut through her as she stood on the precinct steps and addressed the crowd. She implored them to help her find her daughter. She looked across the sea of faces in the parking lot and felt everyone's love. She recognized many of them. Everyone who'd been in her home last night came to help, well, all except Nonna. She'd stayed home to get ready to visit the funeral home. She insisted on handling Ariel's funeral arrangements alone. The other volunteers were her fellow police officers and people from the families she'd touched during her career. She saw a representative from almost every case she'd investigated in her last four years as a homicide detective. Right now, she couldn't remember most of their names, yet she thanked God for each and every one of them. A wave of gratitude tussled with a feeling of desperation and threatened her outward demeanor. *Keep it together, girl.* It took all she had to remain strong and calm. She helped organize the search parties and designated each to an address she'd circled in the classifieds the night before. Her party included both Captains, Jared, Marcus and a few others including the Goldbergs. The three of them came to her and Mr. Goldberg spoke while his wife and daughter nodded in agreement.

"You brought our daughter's murderer to justice. How could we not help?" Mrs. Goldberg handed Shevaughn a tissue when she could no longer control her tears. She knew they understood the devastation caused by the loss of a child.

She pulled herself together and gave her group directions to the apartment Terri seemed the most interested in. She hoped they would quickly find her daughter and bring her home. When they arrived, she saw the apartment was still vacant. *Did that crazy bitch pull one over on me?* Before she panicked, she took a moment and thought about Terri's situation. She realized that out of all the places they'd seen during their short apartment hunt, the two-bedroom duplex would fit her needs a lot better, especially if she'd been contemplating stealing Toni. With everyone keeping a close eye on her, how could she sneak out of the apartment and head to the duplex? She decided to make Jared her confidant.

"I think I know where she is. We need to get to 119th Avenue and 220th Street right now. Please clear it with them. I need a search warrant, so I can go into the premises," she said, nodding towards the Captains. After a short explanation, Bowen and Campbell decided they'd finish canvassing the neighborhood surrounding the apartment with the rest of the group and follow her after they checked this location off the list. Campbell didn't try to stop her, although he did stipulate he wanted Jared to accompany her.

Another policewoman ran up with the warrant. She informed them the phone company finally located an address and number. The details corresponded with their intended destination. They were on the right track.

Marcus insisted on going along.

"I want to be there when you get your daughter back."

At first, words failed her and she couldn't express her gratitude. Shaken, she turned to Jared.

"Would you mind driving?" she asked him as she handed him the keys. She couldn't hide the fact that her hands were trembling.

"I think I'd prefer it," Jared answered. "Let's go."

When Terri woke up, making a ransom call was the last thing on her mind. She didn't have any intention of returning Trinity for any amount of money. They were a family now. The only thing better would have been to wake up with Jay next to her. Last night, she'd waited for him for what seemed like hours. She'd finally gone to sleep disappointed and alone. His not being there bothered her. She convinced herself he'd be back and then she'd thank him for everything they'd accomplished.

She got up and showered, taking her time, all the while waiting for him to join her.   A little disappointed when he didn't, Terri shrugged it off and went into motherhood mode. She laid out Trinity's clothes for their trip to the Bronx Zoo. The jeans and chenille cowl neck sweater appeared almost identical to Terri's outfit for the day, except for the color difference. Trinity's lavender sweater almost matched the color of her room. Terri's sweater was gray, a marbled tweed that reminded her of him.

The corduroy jacket she'd bought last week came in handy since there'd been a drop in the temperature last night and she didn't want her little one to be cold. They were going to have their first day together and she wanted it to be one Trinity would always remember.

Terri went into her room and woke her precious child with promises of puppies and the zoo after breakfast. The sweet girl responded cheerfully, which put Terri in an even better mood, except his absence still nagged at her. For a moment, she wondered if, now that she possessed their child, he thought she didn't need him any longer. That couldn't be further from the truth.

"I know that. I need you, too."

She shuddered when she heard his familiar whisper behind her right ear as she helped Trinity put on her jacket. The sound of his voice filled her heart with delight. The three of them were going to have a wonderful day.

When they pulled up to the duplex, Shevaughn saw the improvements that had been done on the property in such a short time.

"Marcus, would you take these flyers, talk to the folks that live across the street and see if anyone recognizes either of them. Post them wherever you can. Take the staple gun."

"Where are you going?"

"Jared and I are going inside to see if there are any signs of Toni."

Speaking to the neighbors in the surrounding homes, Marcus kept hearing that the new tenant didn't know the meaning of neighborly, yet they liked what she'd done to the duplex's exterior. When shown the flyer with the picture of the two of them, some of them recognized the woman. No one remembered seeing the little girl.

Shevaughn walked directly to the front door of the duplex. Even though she knew technically she should wait on another warrant specifically for this address, she couldn't. She knocked and shouted, "Portsborough Police, open up." When no one answered, Jared proceeded to kick the door in. With their Smith and Wesson .38s drawn, they walked around the apartment, only to find it empty. She could still smell the fresh paint and realized Terri's renovations included the inside of the house as well. She hoped Terri paid as much attention to her daughter as she did to her new home.

Jared followed right behind her into the duplex. He didn't want Shevaughn to have to handle any confrontation alone. No matter what, he still cared. They walked into the small bedroom at the back of the house.

"This is Toni's room," Shevaughn said softly as she went toward the twin bed, pulled back the obviously handmade blanket and lightly touched the crumpled sheet. She looked so miserable he wanted to touch her, to console her, but he didn't know how she would react, so he just stood there, helpless.

She swore she could still feel her daughter's warmth lingering there. She picked up the PJs and held then to her face. The Ivory soap aroma she loved surprised her. Getting up and going to the closet, she found several new little girl outfits with the tags still hanging on them.

"She set all of this up for her, even down to buying the same brand of soap that we use. The whole time she stayed with us, she planned to kidnap Toni. Jared, please, we need to see if she left a hint as to where they were headed. Help me look for anything she may have written on. You never know."

She went to the kitchen while Jared headed toward Terri's bedroom across the hall. While he rifled through the night table, Shevaughn went straight to a pad and pencil on the counter under the wall phone. Although it looked blank, she took the pencil and lightly shaded the faint imprint left by a prior message. It revealed the "Bronx Zoo" and a number.

"I think I found something. How fast can we get to the Bronx Zoo?"

"With sirens and flashing lights, maybe twenty minutes to a half hour."

"Then we better get a move on."

As they hurried and jumped into the car, Marcus ran up.

"Hey, you weren't gonna leave me, were you?" he asked as he hopped into the back seat.

"No, and buckle up. We need to get to the Bronx Zoo."

Jared drove the majority of the way with lights flashing and siren blaring. Once they reached Southern Boulevard, Shevaughn insisted he shut them both off. She didn't want anything to alert Terri of their arrival, so they pulled into the zoo parking lot in silence. Marcus volunteered to be the lookout and stay at the exit, just in case the two of them got past Shevaughn and Jared since he could identify them both.

"I've got this covered. You two go and find Toni."

Flashing their badges at the admission gate, they entered the zoo and began their search.

There weren't many visitors at the zoo. Terri and Trinity had gotten there at ten when the gates opened. She assumed the weather kept a lot of families away. It was almost as if the zoo had been reserved for their private use.

First, they went to the new "Jungle World" exhibit that opened last spring. Terri held Trinity's hand and led her through the exhibit, pointing out all the different animals. Designed to mimic the animals' natural habitat, you couldn't see the separation between them and the spectators. It created an experience as close to a real jungle as Terri could have imagined. Next, they went to the Children's Zoo. Trinity 'oohed' and 'aahed' at the baby animals and got excited when Terri allowed her to participate in feeding some of them.

By the time they left the Children's Zoo, the day warmed up. The clouds evaporated and the sun peeked out of the clouds. The weather seemed almost too perfect. As the two of them happily made their way to the World of Birds exhibit, Terri froze when she thought she caught a quick glimpse of a familiar face on the other side of the exhibit less than one hundred feet away. *This can't be happening. How the hell did she find us?* She knew the only reason the bitch could be there was to ruin their day and their future. She would do everything in her power to make sure that didn't happen. She knew she would have to make sure Trinity didn't see her. Terri no longer thought of Shevaughn as Trinity's mother, she just happened to be an obstacle that could take away everything they'd worked so hard to accomplish.

"You know what, I'm starved. Come on, little one. Let's go get a hot dog."

"I don't want no hot dog. I ain't hungry. You said we were gonna see the pretty birds next."

"Now you listen to me, Trinity, I won't have a disobedient child. Let's go," she commanded, yanking her arm so hard Toni cried out in pain.

"Oww, you're hurting me and my name is Toni."

Both Shevaughn and Jared heard her cry. It confirmed they were close and her stomach turned over in apprehension. She waved to Jared indicating he should circle left as she went to the right. He began to walk away from her and pulled out his gun.

"No," she said, grabbing his arm. "Put that away. We don't want to spook her. We have to keep Toni safe and we don't know what she's capable of."

After he re-holstered his gun, they slowly circled around the World of Birds exhibit, stopping at any hint of movement they saw. Rounding opposite corners in unison, suddenly they were standing with Terri between them with Shevaughn in front and Jared behind. She clutched Toni in front of her and glanced cautiously back and forth between the two of them.

"Mommy, she hurt me," Toni yelled and tried to break free. Terri held on tightly and refused to let go.

"No," Terri screamed, "you can't have her. We need her," she said as she picked Toni up, holding her even closer.

"Calm down, Terri, you're scaring her."

"You can't take her. She belongs with us."

We, us, who the hell did she mean?

"Let me go. I want my mommy."

Toni twisted back and forth against her captor's chest, her small upturned hands beckoning for Shevaughn.

"Toni, listen to Mommy. I want you to stay still and be very quiet. Everything's gonna be okay."

She watched as her daughter stopped squirming and settled down and turned her attention back to Terri.

When she looked into Terri's eyes, Shevaughn saw hate and anger and a hint of something else, something Shevaughn never saw before, something Terri kept well hidden. It resembled the feral look of the totally insane.

"You said she belongs to us, Terri? Who are you talking about," Shevaughn asked as she stepped in a little closer. Something told her the answer would frighten her even more, yet the need to save her daughter blocked out every other emotion that ran through her body.

"Don't come any closer. You need to stay away from us."

Shevaughn took a step back.

"Terri, please, put her down. You're scaring her."

"She doesn't belong to you. She's ours."

"Ours? Did someone help you steal her? Hold on, I know you're not referring to Mr. Diamante, are you? You know he's dead. We were there, remember? You saw him commit suicide."

"No, don't say that, you better stop saying that. Tell her to stop saying that."

Terri spoke to someone only she could see.

Shevaughn saw her talking to a third person. She knew she needed to get her daughter away from this crazy woman as soon as possible. Even Terri's psychiatrist didn't know the depths of her insanity. She kept her talking, kept her mind occupied. Maybe one of them would get a chance to slip in, grab Toni and get her to safety.

"What did you do to Ariel? She's dead, you know."

"I didn't kill her."

"I didn't accuse you."

Toni wiggled.

"Be still, Trinity," Terri said with an obvious edge to her voice.

"Who's Trinity?" Shevaughn inquired.

"Our daughter, Trinity's our daughter. We're a family now."

"No, you're mistaken. That's Toni, that's my daughter."

She had to stop herself from saying "you crazy bitch." She knew it wouldn't help to antagonize Terri in this situation.

"Nooooooo," Terri shouted.

The guttural scream gave Shevaughn chills and she trembled in the afternoon sun.

"You need to let her come to me."

"No, I don't. Do I, Jay? Tell her what you did. Tell her, I didn't have anything to do with the Knight woman's death. I just brought Trinity home."

Terri pleaded into the empty space to her left. Now Shevaughn couldn't be sure Terri wouldn't hurt her daughter and it terrified her...it terrified her a lot.

Chapter Twenty-One

AFTER WAITING AT the entrance for almost an hour, Marcus reconsidered his decision to stay out front. As he stood there, shifting his weight from one foot to the other, he got the undeniable feeling that Shevaughn needed his help. Although he'd promised to stay put and watch the exit, he paid the ten-dollar admission and entered the zoo. He slowly walked around the exhibits searching for a familiar face and wondered if he'd made the wrong decision yet again. He hadn't been to the Bronx Zoo since childhood and didn't remember it being so huge. Now he realized the odds of him finding any of them were pretty slim. The sense that she needed him kept him looking despite the ever-present sinking feeling that his actions were in vain. His love for Shevaughn fueled his determination. She and Toni were becoming his family and as a man he felt an obligation to take care of them and keep them safe. He wouldn't give up.

The heat made Marcus take off his army camouflage jacket and he slung it over his right shoulder. This caused him to inadvertently glance in the same direction. A tall, Black man caught his attention. He stopped to make sure and yes, *thank God*, it was Jared.

Marcus broke into a run and then quickly stopped. Maybe it would be best to approach with caution and check out the circumstances before he barged into the midst of what might be a dangerous situation. He spotted an ice cream concession stand that would provide a little cover as he took a moment and checked out the situation before he proceeded.

Focusing on Jared, he expanded his line of vision to his left and saw Terri and Toni. He took a deep breath of relief. They'd found her and she looked okay. Then his eyes landed on Shevaughn and her body language told him everything. She was tense. Her hands were slightly extended, palms down. It looked like an attempt to calm Terri down. They weren't out of the woods yet.

He left the concession stand and began to walk slowly towards them with the intention of positioning himself directly behind Terri so she wouldn't see his approach. He stopped less than two feet away and started to make a grab for Shevaughn's little girl. Terri must have heard something or maybe her instincts were just that sharp because she turned her head and caught him like a deer in headlights. The look in her eyes caused him to hesitate, just for a second. That gave her enough time to back away from him and search for an avenue of escape. He sprung into action, trying to grab her arms from behind. Terri let go of one of Toni's arms, dangling the child, turned and lashed out, scratching Marcus deep enough to draw blood.

A young couple with a child in a stroller stopped when they heard the commotion and came closer to investigate. To them it looked like a couple of Black guys were getting ready to pounce on a poor defenseless woman and child. The man started to intercede and stepped forward.

"Hey, what's going on here?"

"This is police business. Don't interfere." Shevaughn shouted and pulled out her badge. "Back off and stay out of it." She held the badge at arm's length to make sure they saw it and understood.

The couple stepped backed, although their curiosity got the best of them and they continued to watch the scene unfold. Then the woman whispered something to her husband. Obviously, she'd seen the morning paper and she relayed the story to him. He took a small step back and gave his wife an incredulous look.

Suddenly everything seemed to accelerate. Jared saw Terri's attention shift from Marcus to Shevaughn and dived at her blind side. She screamed and scurried to hold onto Toni as the two men tackled her. The four of them fell to the asphalt, but Terri still refused let go. Running towards her daughter, Shevaughn heard a small 'pop' and although Terri's body partially smothered the sound, it sounded to her like something broke. Toni immediately let out a yelp of pain and Shevaughn knew she'd been right. She watched as Toni struggled to twist her way out from under her captor, her little face a combination of pain and determination.

Shevaughn ran to her daughter's side and before even she saw it coming, she let loose a right cross that sent Terri sprawling. Marcus ran over and tried to grab her arm, but she shook him off and turned her attention back to Terri.

"You stole her, you crazy bitch. After everything I did for you, you take my daughter? Are you out of your mind? You'd have to be, to steal the child of a cop. And what did you do to Ariel? What did you do, Terri?"

Screaming, Shevaughn placed her hand on her weapon and got right in Terri's face. She saw her flinch and hesitated, realizing she had everyone's attention. They all were watching and waiting to see what she'd do next. The wide-eyed look of surprise on her daughter's face stopped her. *She shouldn't see me like this.* Shevaughn realized she needed to get herself under control and stepped back. Marcus came to her, put his arms around her and softly reassured her by whispering, "She's okay, Von, we've got her now. Toni's safe."

Shevaughn knelt and gingerly scooped her daughter up into her arms. She seemed unaffected by everything that happened in the last fourteen hours and immediately started complaining.

"Mommy, stop, you're squeezin' too tight," she said, as she tried to wiggle away. The movement caused Toni pain and Shevaughn saw her grimace. Her right hand looked a little swollen, starting at her wrist. Gently kissing her, Shevaughn stood up and took her left hand. They turned to watch Jared, his knee in Terri's back, as he put her in handcuffs. Once they were secure, he pulled her up and patted her down. Terri turned and looked at her with an expression that resembled a cornered animal. Shevaughn, Marcus and Toni huddled together as the two adults assessed her injuries.

"I think her wrist might be broken."

"Let's get her to the emergency room."

"They can look at your face," Shevaughn said.

"It's just a scratch. I've done worse shaving."

"Did Auntie Terri hurt you too?" Toni asked as she gingerly touched his face.

"It's just a scratch, Munchkin. We'll have a doctor take a look at it after he checks your wrist."

"Kiss it better, Mommy," Toni instructed and Shevaughn gently obliged.

"You three go on to the hospital. I'll wait here for backup and catch up with you later," Jared volunteered.

When he'd looked up after cuffing Mrs. Becker, he'd caught a glimpse of his future. He would be forever watching, waiting. He couldn't deny it any longer. The three of them were becoming a family right before his eyes. He decided to stop fooling himself. *Accept it and move on, man.* At that very moment, he pledged to finally let go. The first step was staying behind.

Chapter Twenty-Two

ON THE RIDE to the hospital, Shevaughn put in a call to Captain Campbell.

"Yep, Captain, she's safe, I have her. You can call off the search. We're on our way to the emergency room. I think her wrist might be broken. Would you please thank everyone who joined the search for me? Jared's bringing Terri Becker in. As soon as we leave Memorial and get Toni home, I'll be in. What? Sure, hold on."

She gave the phone to Toni, making sure she took it with her left hand.

"Captain Campbell wants to talk to you."

Toni mimicked her mother's conversation.

"Yes, Cap'um, I'm okay. We were at the zoo. I saw the baby animals. And then Auntie Terri hurt me. Mommy punched her in the face and Unka Dred put the police bracelets on her. Now we're gonna go to the 'mergency room. I still didn't see no birds though. Huh? Okay, bye."

Marcus and Shevaughn laughed as Toni handed her the phone. Shevaughn hung up without talking to Campbell again. She didn't want to give him a chance to reprimand her for striking Terri. She'd deal with that later.

"She has priorities," Shevaughn told Marcus with a smile.

"Piraties? Like Peter Pan?"

The laughter felt so good.

"Marc and I will take you to see the birds another day."

"Promise?"

"Cross our hearts," Marcus answered.

The doctor confirmed Toni's greenstick wrist fracture. He gave her a small dose of Tylenol and put on a mini-cast. Then he cleaned and bandaged Marcus' scratch.

On the ride home, Shevaughn told her about the custom of having people sign her cast. Toni started planning.

"I want Nonna and Auntie Real to write on it first."

Oh, God, how am I going to tell her?

"Baby, Aunt Ariel won't be there when we get home. She's with God now, in Heaven."

"Like my daddy and Bubbles?"

Toni's pet goldfish, Bubbles, went belly up last May. Shevaughn saw her daughter was beginning to understand the meaning of death. Although she wanted to keep her as innocent as she could for as long as possible, some things couldn't be avoided. She couldn't shield her from the truth.

"So she's never coming back?"

"Well, God loves her so much He wants her to live with Him."

"I'll never see her again?"

"I'm afraid not, Munchkin," Marcus answered.

"S'not fair. God can have anyone. Why'd He want my Auntie Real?"

"He needed her to be one of his angels."

Shevaughn looked at Marcus, grateful for his explanation. She saw her daughter's tears and hated the helpless feeling it gave her. These were the things a mother wanted to shield her child from. Taking a tissue from her purse, she wiped her face and gave her a gentle hug.

"I'm gonna miss her so much," Toni announced, too serious for her years.

"So will I, little one, so will I."

It should have been a joyous occasion when Shevaughn, Toni and Marcus returned from the hospital to Nonna's, except Ariel's death hung in the air and subdued them all. Marcus excused himself early.

"Mom opened the Nook for me this morning. I really need to get back, tell her everything's okay and relieve her. I'll call you after I close."

He gave Toni and Nonna a peck on the cheek. Shevaughn's kiss lasted a little longer.

"Thanks for helping me get her back."

"Munchkin's having a hard time of it. I wish I could do something to make her feel better," Marcus said as he gave Shevaughn a comforting hug.

"We're all better just having her home."

"You know I'd do anything for you two, don't you?"

"Yes...I do now."

"If I can help with the arrangements or anything, just let me know."

"Nonna and I can take care of it. Thanks for the offer. You go on, we'll talk later."

When Shevaughn got back from seeing him out, she found Nonna sitting at the kitchen table, cradling her granddaughter in her arms and softly crying. Shevaughn knelt down beside them and they cried over her safe return and the loss of their dear friend. Then Nonna got up, made Toni a peanut butter and banana sandwich and poured her a small glass of milk. The children's Tylenol the doctor gave Toni before he set her wrist kicked in, so Shevaughn put her down for a nap and told Nonna she needed to stop by the precinct. She wanted to ask some questions only Terri could answer.

Chapter Twenty-Three

WHEN SHEVAUGHN ARRIVED at the precinct, the police psychiatrist went over his notes with her. He'd spent the last hour talking to Terri. Listening to his notations and conclusion, Shevaughn sat speechless for a minute and then felt the need to verify what she'd just heard.

"So, all right now, let me get this straight. What you're telling me is she believes she's having a relationship with a dead man? That he's returned to her as some kind of, what do they call it...incubus? That the two of them were having consensual sex in my home?"

"That's it, in a nutshell."

"Interesting word choice, Dr. Jordan, nutshell, I'd say it's a little too appropriate."

"She also believes he's the one responsible for Mrs. Knight's death."

"Oh, come on, she's blaming that on him, too?"

"Even though the coroner listed her death as cardiac arrest, Mrs. Becker swears Diamante did her in."

"I need to talk to her."

"Help yourself."

She walked into the small interrogation room where Terri sat with her head down, handcuffed to her chair. She saw the malice on her face when she looked up.

"Okay, Terri, you wanna tell me what happened?"

"Why? You won't believe me."

"Try me."

"You won't understand. I didn't either, so I spent the last hour thinking about it. You have to know I didn't do this by myself. We did it together because we love each other. Now everything is ruined and it'll never be right. He wanted this for me. He wanted this as much as I did."

"You're referring to the late Mr. Diamante."

"Yes, Jay stayed with me every step of the way. He found me somehow and knew all about our connection. I bet you he knew about Eric too. That day, the day you showed up at my house, he'd just told me some BS story and begged me to believe in his innocence, but I couldn't. He got angry and wanted to hurt me 'cause I didn't believe him, just like you don't believe me now. You really don't have a clue. Do you know the last thing he said to me before he pulled the trigger? Did you know he died with your name on his lips, with you on his mind? Now why would he do that? Think the devil made him do it?" Terri chuckled, not giving a damn if it made her sound crazy. The jury already reached that verdict.

So he'd known about me? As impossible as it seemed, there seemed to be a ring of truth to it, that is, unless Terri imagined it all. And for some odd reason Shevaughn didn't think so, but she knew she couldn't rely on this woman's version of the story.

"What happened next?"

"He first came to me when you invited me to stay with you", Terri lied. "He coaxed me, helped me, told me I should make it my business to get into your home."

"And why is that?"

"To get our daughter. Somehow, he knew I wanted a child. I'm not sure how he knew, it's not like we ever talked about it. The very first time we made love, I dreamt about a beautiful caramel-colored baby, our baby. He came to me in your house and every time he touched me, I gladly gave in. What we did together when we made love, well, let's just say it was hot. You know, Mrs. Knight overheard us once. That's why we learned to communicate without words, like we could read each other's minds. She could feel him too. That's how he killed her."

"How?"

"Well, if she could feel him he could have strangled her or knowing him, maybe he fucked her to death. I don't know and I don't really care. It had to be done."

"You knew about her heart condition, that's why we were looking after her. She'd just gotten out of the hospital. It wouldn't have been too hard for you to scare her to death."

"No...I didn't do it, she didn't even see me, I swear. I hid behind the door. If he hadn't killed her, he told me I'd have to cut her throat. I had his razor and I would have done it too. She died before I needed to."

"You have his razor? Where is it?"

"It's at home, in the bathroom under the sink. It's not like I kept it hidden."

Shevaughn wished she'd been aware Terri knew where he'd kept his razor a long time ago, before Mrs. Elliott's family had her cremated. She wondered if they could have matched the wound to the weapon. Now they would never know.

"And you had to kidnap my daughter because...?"

She'd never heard a weirder story. Shevaughn knew Terri really believed she'd gotten kidnapping instructions from a dead man. Without a doubt, it was definitely time for the rubber room. Her thoughts were interrupted when Terri continued.

"We needed her to complete our family. We even named her together."

"Trinity."

"Yes, Trinity."

Terri got a dreamy look in her eyes.

"We planned it perfectly, our little duplex love nest. Did you see all the work I put into it?"

He didn't help you with that? Shevaughn wanted to ask, but she held her tongue. Antagonizing Terri wouldn't do either of them any good. At first, she wanted Terri punished for all the harm she'd caused her family, yet deep inside Shevaughn had to admit she felt sorry for her.

"Yes, you did a great job fixing it up."

"They're not going to let me go back there, are they?"

"No, Dr. Callaghan will be here shortly. He's going to take you back to Blackstone."

Terri tried to jump up from her chair. The handcuffs restrained her.

"I don't want to go back," she snarled.

"You really don't have any say in the matter."

Looney Tune.

"And I suppose you think that's best?"

"Yes, Terri, I do."

She sat down and lowered her head, defeated.

"So I'm back where I started?"

No lady, you've dug your crazy ass into a deeper hole, especially with the additional pending criminal charges and your ghost story. Funny, when this all first went down, she'd wanted to beat the shit out of Terri for putting her daughter in jeopardy, for killing Ariel, for scaring the hell out of everybody and now after hearing her twisted story, she felt more pity than anger. Shevaughn kept her feelings to herself and simply answered, "Yes."

"Can I ask a favor?"

A favor? Now she wants a favor? This crazy heifer has balls. What the hell else could she want? She already tried to steal my first-born.

"Please see that my dogs are taken care of, you know, see that Baron and Khan are put in good homes. I know you can't keep them all, but could you at least keep Kayla for Trin...Toni? She really loves that dog."

This fool is too much, now she's worrying about those damn dogs. Do her a favor. Is she outta her freakin' mind? Scratch that. At least taking Kayla would help keep Toni occupied and maybe she wouldn't miss Ariel as much. She does love that dog.

"I can't believe I'm saying this. I'll see what I can do. Anything else?"

"No, that's it."

"I have to tell you there were moments when I could have killed you with my bare hands. Now all I feel is sorry for you. I know you need help, just don't look for it to come from me. I don't want you to ever contact anyone in my family again, you got that? Otherwise, I promise you, I won't be responsible."

"I want you out of my life just as badly as you want me out of yours. You're just unhappy memories for me."

Ain't this a bitch, now she's dismissing me?

"The feeling is more than mutual. Goodbye Terri."

On the ride home, she heard an oldie, but goodie on the radio. A Ben E. King song came on that sent a cold chill up Shevaughn's spine. After hearing Terri's confession this afternoon the words now held a whole new meaning and she knew she'd never enjoy "Supernatural Thing" again.

Chapter Twenty-Four

SHEVAUGHN MADE GOOD on her promise to see the dogs were taken care of. Khan and Baron went to the North Shore Animal League and she brought Kayla home. When Toni saw Kayla, the look on her face showed more fear than happiness and she backed up as the dog walked towards her. She looked around as if expecting someone else and ran to hide behind Nonna.

"What's wrong? I thought you'd be happy to see her."

"Is *she* with her?"

"No, honey, Terri is far away and I promise she'll never hurt you again. You're safe here with me and Nonna. I just thought you'd like having Kayla with you to keep you company."

"I do, I love her..."

"You never have to worry about Terri again, promise."

"And I can keep her?" she whispered, looking at the dog.

"Yes, she's yours."

"I'll take good care of her. Come on Kayla, you can stay in my room." Kayla ran over to Toni. She bent down to pet her and the little dog jumped up to gently lick her daughter's face. She giggled and the two of them ran off to her room.

"Just something else for us to take care of, but I'm glad you decided to keep her."

"So am I."

With Toni home safe and Terri back in Blackstone, everything should have gotten back to normal. Then the media found out about Mrs. Becker's involvement in the Robinson kidnapping and her odd story of being aided by the dead murderer. TV and newspapers kept calling, asking for interviews. Shevaughn refused to talk to them, let alone give them permission to do a story on her family, so they interviewed everyone remotely connected with the case; Campbell, Jared, Dr. Callaghan, Dr. Jordan and even Dana Dixon.

Someone connected to the case made the front page of the Portsborough Journal for five days straight, an accomplishment Captain Campbell regarded as the best public relations money couldn't buy. Everyone noticed his extremely good mood and jokes started circulating around the precinct about his "PR glow".

The police department showed up at the funeral in full force, showing their support for their fellow policewoman and in recognition of the help Ariel gave the department with her psychic gift. They even gave her a twenty-one gun salute, an honor usually only given to a fallen officer. Shevaughn appreciated their attendance, yet it did nothing to heal the ache in her heart. She knew Ariel wouldn't have been impressed with all the grandeur. She'd always been way too laid back for that.

After Ariel's funeral, Nonna, Shevaughn, Jared and Marcus returned to the O'Brien home. Kennedy let them in. She'd volunteered to stay home with Toni during the service. People stopped by, exchanged condolences and Ariel stories. Shevaughn and Nonna stayed busy, weaving in and out of the crowd, making sure everyone ate. Some were standing with food and drinks in their hands or sitting on folding chairs, trying to keep their plates perched precariously on their laps. Everyone looked slightly uncomfortable.

Everyone, that is, except his sister. Marcus noticed her sneaking glances at Jared, who seemed totally oblivious. He snuck up behind her and whispered.

"It's not polite to drool at a funeral."

"I'm not," Kennedy countered, however the small smirk on her face told it all. "Is he seeing anyone?"

"I don't think so, just take it easy. You don't want to scare him off."

"Oh, I think it'll take a lot more than me to scare Detective Benjamin."

Her brother knew her too well. From the moment she saw him, the term "sexual chocolate" popped into her head. Tall, dark and smooth, she wondered what it would be like to have him melting in her mouth. She'd actually been licking her lips when her brother caught her. She decided she wanted this to be the start of something hot. *Besides, he deserves me.*

Later that month, when Marcus told Shevaughn he thought his sister had a crush on Jared, they began planning how to get the two of them together.

Chapter Twenty-Five

TERRI GREW TIRED of trying to catch a glimpse of the side yard from the small corner window. She pulled the thin cotton belt of her pale blue seersucker robe tighter, crossed the small room and stretched out as much as she could on her tiny cot. She placed her hands behind her head and stared at the ceiling. Life sure hadn't turned out the way she'd hoped. Although she'd been there for almost six weeks, Jay's face, complete in every detail, flashed across her mind and the intensity of her lust shocked her. *Must be time for my medication.*

She realized things weren't really any different now. The world kept going merrily on its way and she lay here, stuck in this hellhole. The only time she experienced any freedom was twice a day for an hour when they all went out to the yard to exercise. She couldn't even enjoy that since she could always feel the eyes of the attendants drilling a hole in her mind, watching her, trying to read her thoughts. She stayed on her guard, always careful not to let them know that they were always planning a way out. She found it hard to believe that she'd ended up institutionalized again and for what? What crime had they really committed?

"Just a simple day trip to the zoo, ma petite. If you ask me, I think everyone just overreacted."

She totally agreed. The punishment didn't fit the crime. That's why they needed to find a way out of there. They had to make things right.

Nurse Cooper came in and gave her two small pills in a paper cup, fussing all the while. Her sheer size intimidated Terri. She resembled Refrigerator Perry except with makeup and titties. After Terri's relapse, Nurse Cooper tended to be a little easier on her. Some of the "guests" could tell you a story of how she subdued a raving 6'5" ex-bodybuilder. He believed anyone would poison him if they got the chance and proceeded to attack whoever stood in his line of vision. Alone, it took her all of two minutes to get him under control!

"Girl, I thought you'd be ready to go to the dining hall. Supper's in twenty minutes. You better git a move on, hear me?"

Terri swallowed one pill and held the other under her tongue. She'd become a pro at slowly weaning herself off her medication. *Need to have a clear head if I'm ever going to get out of here.*

The nurse fussed with her water pitcher and poured her a glass. The second she saw she wasn't being watched, Terri spit out the bitter, slightly dissolved pill and palmed it, carefully placing it into her robe pocket. She would hide it with the rest of them in her special hiding place as soon as she got the chance. She'd begun hoarding them again the very first day she'd returned since they'd found and confiscated her first stash when they'd searched her home after booking her for kidnapping.

Terri shuffled behind Nurse Cooper, following her to the cafeteria and meekly sat down and ate her dry processed turkey and cheese sandwich, mixed vegetables, Jell-O and chamomile tea. She closed her eyes and remembered the gourmet meals Jay used to prepare. Twice, she slowed down to keep from gagging. She knew she had to eat it all because she needed to keep up her strength. She also wanted to appear as cooperative as possible. Their freedom depended on it. She'd convinced them before and she could make it happen again. *We won't be in here forever.*

"You expect me to stay here with you?"

She heard the laughter in his voice and for a moment it paralyzed her with fear.

"What do you mean? You said you'd never leave me?"

"Well, I thought we'd be a family of three in a charming little duplex. Even though the housing didn't quite live up to my standards, I'd make that sacrifice for you. You do remember I killed myself to avoid being institutionalized and now you think I'm going to stay in this nut house with you?"

This can't be happening. The thought of never talking, seeing or touching him again put her in total panic.

"No, you can't go, you can't leave me alone. Please, you promised."

"I don't have a choice. I tried to, for you, but we both know this can't continue."

"I can't stay here alone."

"Then you know what you must do."

Epilogue

SHEVAUGHN REALIZED THE old saying "time heals all wounds" was only partially true. Although she saw a positive change in her loved ones in the next few months, Nonna turned out to be the one setback. Ever since they'd lost Ariel, her social life seemed to mainly consist of wakes and funerals and she convinced herself she didn't have much time left. She began spending more and more time at church, participating in every religious function she could attend. Marcus said she was campaigning for heaven.

She also saw when Jared finally noticed Kennedy noticing him. She'd hoped he'd be flattered by the young woman's attention. She and Marcus tried to include them in every family get-together. They even invited him to their Bid Whist parties. Kennedy waited on him hand and foot and flirted with him every chance she got. A couple of weeks later, he finally got up enough nerve to ask her out. They'd been inseparable ever since. Shevaughn recognized the look of adoration that came into Kennedy's eyes whenever she glanced his way. Then one day, when she saw him return the look, she knew he'd finally outgrown his crush. Things finally got better between the two of them, to the point they started double dating. Now, Shevaughn and Marcus considered themselves the "older couple" and both enjoyed the responsibility. It felt good to be a role model. They wanted to set a good example.

That's why the four of them were in Atlantic City on New Year's Eve. They'd spent a long weekend seeing the New Year in and everyone enjoyed gambling and partying together. So much so, that Marcus let Jared in on his surprise, after swearing him to secrecy.

After dinner, they did a little gambling and then took a walk on the Boardwalk. When the clock struck twelve as the New Year arrived, the fireworks went off. Everyone started kissing or shouting. Marcus grabbed the lapels of Shevaughn's coat, pulled her to him and whispered in her ear, "Von, I love you and want you in my life forever. Will you marry me?"

♥♦

At first, with all the noise, she thought she hadn't heard him right. Her eyes grew wide as she watched him fall to one knee in front of her and open the small, hinged black velvet box. He wanted her to be his wife! The smile on his face confirmed it. Her heart began to race and she couldn't catch her breath. She began to cry and this time she didn't care who saw her tears.

On Friday, April 18, 1986, Shevaughn Jeanette Robinson became Mrs. Marcus Williams. They planned a simple ceremony in her home with all of the Williams family, Captains Bowen and Campbell, Jared, Nonna and Toni in attendance. Toni and Shevaughn wore identical mocha dresses with pink trim since Marcus insisted he should marry both of his favorite ladies. Even Kayla wore a matching tutu with a pink bow in her hair.

Captain Bowen stood in for her father and proudly walked her down the aisle. Shevaughn wondered if Tony and Ariel were with her as she walked towards the handsome man in the mocha suit, chocolate shirt and pink tie. The man she wanted to spend the rest of her life with. At the end of the ceremony, Marcus shocked her with his rendition of "Pretty Lady" by the Whispers. She couldn't remember ever telling him they were one of her favorite groups and he'd kept his beautiful baritone voice a secret. *All that and he can sing too!* Every time she thought she couldn't love him more, he surprised her.

They held the reception in the Queens Botanical Gardens on that beautiful spring day. Marcus wanted Toni to join them for their first dance. Then everyone got on the dance floor and they all had a blast. When the dancing and dining ended, they played "Bid Whist" until the sun went down, forcing them inside.

Jared didn't even flinch at the sound of Shevaughn's 'I do'. He looked at his lady, who, in this man's opinion, made a stunning maid of honor. She must have felt him looking at her because at that moment her eyes found his and she gave him a demure smile. He smiled back and marveled at how God blessed him with this fine-looking young lady who appeared to be head over heels in love with him. It took him a long time to get over his feelings for Shevaughn and now he couldn't be happier. By the end of the day, he thought about the possibility that just maybe, someday soon, he too might be ready to jump the broom.

♥♦

"Well, Mrs. Williams, now that you've made an honest man of me, I'd say it's time for us to celebrate. There's something I've always wanted to do..."

He took her by the hand and began leading her to the door of the cruise ship's honeymoon cabin when he stopped and turned. Marcus looked into her eyes and smiled.

"I hope you packed your handcuffs..."

She didn't remember much of her honeymoon night, except the smell, taste and touch of him and every time she thought about it, a different moment of hot, frequent sex flashed through her mind, giving her body a sexual tremor. She gladly gave in to him whenever he wanted.

On the first night of formal dining on their honeymoon cruise, they went to their table dressed to the nines. Shevaughn wore an empire-waist, dark chocolate sleeveless chiffon knee length gown. The color matched her skin so well it gave the illusion of air brushed nudity. She saw the look of appreciation on his face when she stepped out of the bathroom after applying her makeup. The feeling was mutual. He looked quite dapper in his olive three-piece suit.

At dinner, when Marcus found out he could have two appetizers and two entrees, you would have thought he'd hit the jackpot. Shevaughn watched him enjoy his meal with the same slow appreciation that he'd shown while enjoying her. They were so in tune that watching the way he occasionally licked his lips made her tingle. She knew that sexual tension like this couldn't possibly last forever, but they were off to a damn good start and she was going to try and hold on to this feeling for as long as possible. Shevaughn felt so alive and so loved, she found it hard to believe. Once she actually pinched herself to make sure it wasn't all a dream.

Although the staff made it difficult to get news of the outside world in Blackstone, Terri tried her best to keep tabs on Shevaughn. Months ago she'd found an article about her impending wedding in a newspaper she'd dug out of the administrator's wastebasket. At first it made her angry, until he came to her one final time and told her she should join him. *So what if today was Marcus and Shevaughn's wedding day?* Tomorrow would be hers.

On Shevaughn's honeymoon night, after lights out, Terri turned on her bathroom light, went to the corner of her room and for the last time, quietly pulled the vinyl molding away from the bottom of the wall. She carefully located all the medication she'd been stashing since her return to Blackstone. She took them into the bathroom and slowly started to count each pill. She hadn't realized she'd accumulated so many, obviously she'd lost track. She quit when she hit fifty and estimated she had at least double that amount. She swallowed several pills at a time as she cupped her hands under the faucet to catch the water she needed to get them all down. She repeated the process until she'd taken every single one of them.

Terri got back into her cot, pulled the sheet and scratchy blanket up under her chin and waited. She lay there and wondered how her life had come to this.

Without him, loneliness was her only companion. She needed him and knew what she had to do so they could be together again. Ready, she closed her eyes and patiently waited to join him. Suddenly, she was hit with a series of severe muscle spasms, so severe they prevented her from losing consciousness. She feared the noise of the rattling bed would alert the night nurse. After what seemed like forever, they suddenly stopped and she quietly slipped into a coma.

A little later that night, she drifted into her own version of reality. Jay stood in the doorway of their duplex, waiting to greet her. She ran to him as he held out his arms and brought her close.

"I'm glad you're finally here, ma petite. I've waited so long," he whispered.

This time, when his breath softly caressed the top of her ear, it felt warm.

Ace of Hearts

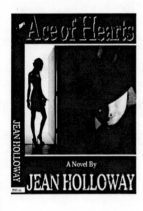

Something sinister is going on...
And Love has nothing to do with it.
First, he seduces them...
Then he kills them...
What he does next is unspeakable.

NY Detective Shevaughn Robinson gets her first big case, investigating an especially gruesome murder case, which emerges into serial murders.

The story evolves as she follows murder after murder trying to solve the case, not realizing the murderer is a man who not only becomes obsessed with death, but also obsessed with her.

Title: Ace of Hearts
Author: Jean Holloway
ISBN: 978-0-9824475-9-8
Price: $15.95

To learn more about Jean Holloway visit: www.deckofcardz.com.

LaVergne, TN USA
07 September 2010
196118LV00001B/1/P